LO

The Emerald Flame

WARRIOR PRINCESS BOOK THREE

The Emerald Flame

— WARRIOR PRINCESS BOOK THREE —

Frewin Jones

HARPER TEEN

An Imprint of HarperCollinsPublishers

HarperTeen is an imprint of HarperCollins Publishers.

www.harperteen.com

Library of Congress Cataloging-in-Publication Data
Jones, Frewin.
   The emerald flame / Frewin Jones. — 1st ed.
   p. cm. — (Warrior princess ; 3)
   Summary: Branwen has accepted the role of Chosen One,
and now, with a growing army including her half-owl, half-
human friend Blodwedd and the dashing yet maddening
Iwan, she must overcome terrifying odds if she is to succeed
in saving Wales from the Saxon invaders.
   ISBN 978-0-06-087149-9 (trade bdg.)
   [1. Princesses—Fiction. 2. War—Fiction. 3. Magic—
Fiction. 4. Saxons—Fiction. 5. Wales—History—To
1063—Fiction.] I. Title.
PZ7.J71Em 2010   2010004604
[Fic]—dc22   CIP
                                                  AC

Typography by Ray Shappell
10 11 12 13 14   LP/RRDB   10 9 8 7 6 5 4 3 2 1
❖
First Edition

For Amanda Fleming and Tracy Rossi

1

A PROFOUND DARKNESS had fallen among the close-packed oaks, and it felt to Branwen ap Griffith as though she and her small band of riders were wading through a flood tide of shadows, thick as black water.

They were climbing the forested flanks of a great hunchbacked mountain in the deep dark of a starless night. Heavy clouds blotted out the sky. The going was hard as the five horses picked their way slowly through the rising trees.

Branwen leaned forward, her thoughts racing; a fire burned so brightly in her mind that she felt she would never need sleep again. Between the new moon and the old, her life had changed beyond all recognition.

My brother killed—my dear, gallant Geraint— slaughtered by Saxon raiders. And before the ashes of his funeral pyre were cold, I was sent from my home to escape from danger. And all the while I was thinking I might never see my parents again. Over the mountains they sent me, to the safety of the cantref of Prince Llew ap Gelert. Safety? Ha! A poor refuge that turned out to be. And what was to happen to me after that? A long journey south to marry that loathsome boy Hywel, although I met him only once, almost ten years ago. Well, at least my destiny spared me that ending.

It would have been a miserable fate for a girl who had spent her first fifteen years riding the hills of her homeland, free as an eagle, untamed as the landscape that she loved.

But Branwen never went south. Rhiannon of the Spring saw to that. One of the Old Gods—the Shining Ones—Rhiannon told Branwen of the path that lay ahead.

"You are Destiny's Sword. The Bright Blade! The Emerald Flame of your people!"

Branwen sighed now to think of the way she had fought against that destiny. It was only when Rhiannon had warned her that Garth Milain, her beloved home, was in danger that Branwen had acted.

Although I rode hard and arrived in the garth in time to warn my mother and father, I was still too late to save them from all harm. The Saxons were thrown back, but Father died in the battle. And if that wasn't hard enough to bear, I had to leave my home and my mother that same night to follow this pitiless destiny again.

Rhiannon's words rang in her ears.

"All of Brython will be your home, and you will gather to you a band of warriors who shall keep the enemy at bay for many long years."

And what a strange group of wanderers they were!

Riding directly behind her was the shrewd and crafty-tongued Iwan ap Madoc. She had first encountered Iwan at the court of Prince Llew. He had annoyed her and fascinated her in equal amounts in that first meeting—and he still did.

Ahead of her, only half visible in the darkness, Branwen could make out the shapes of Blodwedd and Rhodri, riding tandem on one horse. Even if there were enough horses to go around, Branwen suspected Blodwedd would wish to ride with Rhodri.

She shook her head. Theirs was a strange affinity— the half-Saxon runaway and the half-human owl-girl. *Half* human? Blodwedd was nothing more than an owl wrapped in a human shape . . . save for her eyes. They were huge and golden and had no whites whatsoever. No one looking into those eerie eyes would have any doubts that Blodwedd was not human.

Govannon of the Wood, another Shining One, had sent Blodwedd. Govannon, the huge man-god of ancient times, with his sad green eyes and the twelve-point antlers that soared majestically from his temples.

Branwen had detested and mistrusted the owl-girl at the start, but Blodwedd had proven herself faithful and true.

Iwan's voice made her turn.

"Are you managing to keep awake, Branwen?" he asked. "I'm told a spur of hawthorn in the britches is a fine way to stay alert on a long ride."

She looked back at him sitting upright in the saddle, his light-brown hair falling over his lean, compelling face. His eyes met hers and he gave her a crooked smile.

"I'll be fine, thank you," she said. "This is not such a night that I will have trouble with drowsing."

"No." His eyes were bright and wakeful. "I imagine not."

She gazed back beyond him to where the rest of her band rode, two to a horse. They were four young woman of Gwylan Canu—fiery Dera riding with lithe little Linette, and flame-haired Banon riding with heavyset Aberfa, who had dark, brooding eyes.

In the dying embers of the day just passed, this wayfaring band had won a great victory. The Saxon warlord Herewulf Ironfist had sought to conquer the seagirt citadel of Gwylan Canu, guardian outpost of the coastal road that led into the very heartland of Powys.

But speed and stealth had not been the only weapons in Ironfist's arsenal. He had deep and dreadful treachery to help him. Prince Llew ap Gelert—the richest and most powerful of the nobles of Powys, second only to King Cynon himself—had turned traitor!

Branwen still did not know the reason for this terrible betrayal. It was almost beyond belief that a

4

lord of Powys would side with the ancient enemies of Brython. For two hundred years the people of Brython had battled wave after wave of Saxon incursions, and they had always thrown the butchering invaders back. Why, then, did Prince Llew go against his homeland? As a result, never had Powys been closer to defeat than in the battle they had just fought. If not for supernatural aid this night, all would have been lost.

Govannon himself had joined in the battle, beating down upon the Saxons with an army of birds and beasts, even awakening the trees of the forests to help sweep them into the sea.

And upon a rocky promontory, Branwen had done her part—fighting furiously with Ironfist himself. Almost bested by him, she had been saved at the last moment by the beak and claws of her faithful companion Fain the falcon, who had flown into Ironfist's face and sent him plunging over the cliff and into the raging sea.

Then had come the momentous meeting with Govannon. He had towered above her, wild and dangerous and yet strangely benevolent, and told her what she needed to do next—what new effort her great destiny required of her. He had pointed the way up the mountains. *"Thither wends your path, Warrior-Child, up into the cold peaks, into the high places of the land. You must seek Merion of the Stones."*

Faithful, kindhearted Rhodri had insisted on coming with her, of course. And Blodwedd, too. But it had been Iwan's insistence on journeying alongside her that had filled Branwen with a heady mix of joy and confusion.

"Don't you remember what I said to you when you bound me and escaped with the half Saxon?" he had asked, his eyes shining.

"You said you thought I would have an interesting life. You said you wished you could have shared it with me."

"And now I shall. If you will have me as a companion."

She had no control over her destiny. It was harsh and relentless, and people had died on the way.

But these people shan't die. I won't let that happen. I am Branwen ap Griffith. The Emerald Flame of my People. I will keep them safe from harm.

But the responsibility weighed heavily on her. What perils was she leading them into on these high mountains?

She knew virtually nothing of Merion of the Stones. In a mystic glade that had been shown to her in a vision, she had seen a devotee dressed as Merion—bent-backed, stumbling, clutching a stick, masked as an ugly, wrinkled old woman.

But Branwen had learned not to trust appearances. The forms that the Shining Ones took when they interacted with humans were not their true ones. What would Merion want of her? So far the requirements of the Old Gods had all been for the good of Brython. Surely the most vital task now was to unmask the traitor Prince Llew ap Gelert, and to bring him down before he could do any more harm.

To that end, riders had already been sent from

Gwylan Canu, racing pell-mell down the long road to Pengwern—to the court of King Cynon—with urgent warnings from Iwan's trustworthy father.

Hopefully, that would be enough to thwart Prince Llew's grim ambitions. But even with Llew's duplicity laid bare, there was still a great Saxon army on the border of Powys, poised to strike at Branwen's homeland.

And here Branwen was—a thousand lifetimes away from the world she had once known—treading again the veiled path of her destiny . . . riding through the impenetrable night with seven souls in her care.

"Ware!" It was Blodwedd's scratchy voice, its low pitch at odds with her small, slender body. An owl's voice in a human throat.

Branwen snapped out of her thoughts, alert in an instant. "What is it?"

Blodwedd had by far the keenest eyesight of them all. That was why she had taken the lead through the forest once the night had grown too dark even for Fain's sharp eyes. The falcon was at rest now, perched upon Branwen's shoulder, his claws gripping her chain-mail shirt.

"I am not sure," called Blodwedd.

Branwen urged Stalwyn on with a touch of her heels to his flanks. She came up alongside Rhodri and Blodwedd. The owl-girl's golden eyes shone in her pale, round face.

"I smell something not of the forest," Blodwedd

said, arching her back, lifting her head to sniff, her long thin hands resting on Rhodri's broad shoulders, the nails white and curved.

Branwen heard a metallic slither. Dera ap Dagonet, daughter of a captain of Gwylan Canu, had drawn her sword.

"No beast shall come on us unawares," she growled, peering into the fathomless dark that lurked under the trees.

"It is no beast," said Blodwedd. "It is worse than beast."

Her head snapped around toward a noise beyond Branwen's hearing and she let out a feral hiss.

Branwen drew her own sword. There were shapes in the forest. Large, fast-moving shapes, blacker than the night.

Moments later, with a rush and a rumble of hooves, a band of armed men came bursting into view, their swords glowing a dull gray, iron helmets on their heads, and their faces hidden behind iron war-masks.

2

THE ATTACKERS CAME crashing into Branwen's band, horses neighing and kicking, shields raised, swords slashing. In the forest gloom and in the utter chaos of the assault, Branwen could not make out how many horsemen had fallen upon them. *Five at least*, she thought, *maybe more*.

She saw a blade slice down torward Iwan. He managed to draw his own sword and deflect the full blow—but the flat of the blade still struck Iwan savagely on the side of the head. The last Branwen saw of him was as he tumbled from the saddle.

A scream of alarm came involuntarily from her throat. "Iwan! No!"

She was given no more time to fear for him. The largest of the attacking horsemen came for her, his face hidden behind a ferocious war-mask, his sword raised high.

The attacker's horse butted up against hers, forcing it to stumble sideways so that she struggled to keep in the saddle. Fain rose from her shoulder, wings spreading, screeching raucously. Fighting for balance, Branwen managed to bring her shield up high, the top edge angled outward to fend off her attacker's blow.

His sword struck her shield like a thunderbolt, and had she not been holding it at an angle, the hungry iron would have split it in two. As it was, the force of the blow numbed her arm and shoulder and sent her rocking back in the saddle.

She had never fought on horseback before. She was used to feeling solid ground under her feet to be able to maneuver—step forward, step back, circle the enemy, come at him from the side. She felt awkward and vulnerable in the saddle—and like an easy target in the darkness of the forest.

The man's sword arm rose again, this time swinging in a low arc, clearly intending to slip the blade in under the curve of her shield and strike at her belly. The natural defensive move would be to smash down on the encroaching blade with her shield, driving its tempered edge into Stalwyn's neck.

No!

Instead, she threw herself forward, lunging half out of the saddle, beating her shield hard into the attacker's chest, her own sword jabbing for his neck.

She felt the hilt of his sword strike against her side, hurting her, taking the breath out of her—but her sudden move forward had caused his blade to sweep past her, gouging the empty air where she *had* been only a moment before.

She followed up, using her shield as a ram, pressing in on him with all her weight. She felt him slip sideways from his horse as she pushed him. But even as he was falling, his sword arm hooked around her waist and she was dragged down with him.

For a few moments she was too winded, dizzy, and hurt by the heavy fall to do anything other than gasp and flounder in the forest bracken, menaced on every side by the pounding hooves of the frightened horses, dimly able to hear the shouts of the battle around her. Then she realized she was on top of her attacker, lying across his chest. One good thrust of her sword and it would be over. But she was not given the chance. He heaved up under her, throwing her off in a tangle of arms and legs. Branwen only just had the presence of mind to keep hold of her sword and shield as she came smashing to the ground, tasting earth and blood in her open mouth. The horses backed away, neighing and whinnying.

She turned onto her back, her thoughts scattered. The gloom of the night-shrouded forest swam in front of her eyes and it seemed that the earth beneath her rocked and pitched like a tormented sea. Then a deeper darkness loomed over her—a black pillar topped by a grimacing metal face.

A sword came scything down. She twisted away and the blade bit deep into the forest floor. She kicked out, catching her attacker's knee, making him roar with pain and stagger backward. A moment later, Fain was in his face, pecking and clawing, his gray wings whirring.

But the iron mask protected the man from the falcon's attack, and soon it was Fain who had to withdraw, speeding upward and away from the man's whirling blade.

Ignoring the pain that jangled in every part of her body, Branwen sprang up, moving in on the man cautiously, balancing on the balls of her feet, her shield up to her eyes, her sword arm bent back, ready to unleash a killing blow.

There was no time to take in the mayhem that was erupting around her in the deep shadows, no time to organize and encourage her embattled followers. But she quickly scanned the scene around her, catching a momentary glimpse of the fighting taking place among the trees.

So far as Branwen could tell, there were four other men involved in the confused skirmish. One was large and broad-shouldered. Banon and Aberfa were on foot, attacking him on horseback while he rained ringing blows down on their shields. Rhodri and Blodwedd were also unhorsed—Rhodri lying on the ground with Blodwedd standing over him and holding off another mounted swordsman with a length of broken branch. A little farther off, the fighting between Dera and Linette and the third man was partly obscured by trees and branches, and Branwen could not see who was getting the upper hand.

There was something odd about the last horseman—he was small and slight. Even in the gloom that much was obvious. No more than a boy! And he was holding back from the fighting. His helmet had been knocked off and he looked terrified as he tried to control his bucking and rearing steed. And he was unarmed.

Why would a band of warriors bring a weaponless child with them?

Who were these horsemen? Where did they come from? Branwen's first thought had been that they must be a band of Saxon raiders, but they did not seem to be wearing Saxon war-gear; and behind the iron masks, she saw no trace of the telltale Saxon beards.

But even if they were men of Powys, that was no reason for her to feel at ease. Prince Llew had declared her a traitor and an outlaw when she had freed Rhodri from confinement in the prince's fortress of Doeth Palas. If these were Prince Llew's men, they would show no mercy. If not killed, she would be bound hand and foot and dragged back to the prince's citadel on the coast. A swift trial and a bloody death was all that awaited her in that place.

But the thought that these might be Prince Llew's warriors made her look more closely at her opponent. He had positioned himself to mirror her pose: balanced well on feet spread to the same width as his shoulders. His knees bent, muscles flexed. His shield up to his hidden eyes, his sword arm bent over his back, ready to unleash murder.

She circled to the left, and he moved his feet easily, turning so that his shield was always between her and him. She feinted a move in on his right, and he danced lithely backward, then shifted his footing and came leaping in from the side.

His sword sliced down at her unprotected right shoulder, and she only just skipped back in time to avoid serious injury. She sprang aside, bringing her sword down and into his neck. His shield caught the blow, and for a moment her sword was snagged where she had split the rim.

He drove in on her, their shields clashing—and now for the first time she saw his eyes through the slits in the metal mask.

She pushed him off, wresting her sword free and dancing backward, gasping for breath.

There was gray hair visible under his helmet, and there was something familiar about the way he moved.

An old man, then—but a serpent-quick old man who gave her not one moment to regroup as he came for her, blow after blow beating on her shield. She fell back, stumbling, her heels catching on roots and creeping undergrowth.

At last her opponent spoke. "Surrender to me, Branwen ap Griffith!" he demanded, his voice deep and graveled. "I would not have you die here by my hand!"

"Gavan!" The suspicion had already dawned, but the sound of the old warrior's voice confirmed it.

It was Gavan ap Huw, a battle-hardened old warrior of Powys—and the man who had taught her the basics of sword fighting in the innocent times before she had earned Prince Llew's enmity.

"I will not be taken back to Doeth Palas!" shouted Branwen. "I am not the traitor here! Look to your own lord if you seek treachery against the land of Brython!" Her voice rose to a howl. "Look to Prince Llew!"

Gavan stood before her, sword arm raised but no longer attacking.

"What do you mean by that, Branwen?" he growled.

Branwen's whole body was trembling from the power of his blows. A few more moments and her shield would have been riven in two and she would have been defenseless before him.

"Call off your men!" she gasped. "Let us talk! I have things to tell you, Gavan—things that will change all!"

3

GAVAN'S VOICE WAS like the bellowing of a bull in the night. "Boys of Doeth Palas!" he roared. "Hold back! Hold back, I say!" He pulled off his helmet, revealing his weather-beaten face. A long white scar ran down the left side of his jaw, a trophy won at the battle of Meigen, where he had been standard-bearer to the king. "Bryn! Padrig! Andras! Lower your weapons!"

Branwen knew those names. They were lads of the prince's court in Doeth Palas—boys she had seen often in her brief stay in that place. So, that accounted for three of Gavan's followers. But who was the fourth: the small, frightened boy riding a horse too tall for him?

To learn that, the fighting must first of all be halted.

Branwen ran forward, her sword and shield down. "Dera—Aberfa! All of you!" she called. "Stop! *No more!*"

The clash of sword on sword and of iron on wooden shield ceased. Branwen's people backed off from the horsemen. Blodwedd's eyes burned with a deadly fire as she threw down the branch she had been wielding. She stooped and helped Rhodri to his feet. He had a raw graze across his forehead and seemed woozy but otherwise unhurt as he leaned on the owl-girl's shoulder.

"Is anyone injured?" Branwen called. "Where is Iwan?"

"I am here, barbarian princess" came an unsteady voice. Iwan lifted himself on one elbow from a bed of ferns. "My head is buzzing like a nest of wasps; but it is still attached to my shoulders, so I should not complain." He groaned as he tried to rise. "At least I shall not if someone lends a hand."

Linette ran forward and Iwan was soon on his feet, his arm across her slender shoulders.

"Women, for the most part," rumbled Gavan's voice as he stared around at Branwen's followers. He frowned. "Dera ap Dagonet—you at least I know. I saw you last at your father's side in Doeth Palas. I believe you to be loyal and true, child; what is your part in this venture?"

Dera stepped forward, her head held high. "I follow Branwen ap Griffith," she declared, looking keenly into Gavan's eyes. "And if you are still in service to the traitorous prince of Bras Mynydd, then I tell you to your face that you do wrong, Gavan ap Huw!"

"Is it so?" said Gavan. "That's twice I've heard Prince Llew named traitor. I'd know the meaning behind your words, Dera ap Dagonet."

"Prince Llew has betrayed us to the Saxons," said Branwen. "He works now for the downfall of Powys."

Gavan looked sharply at her, then his eyes moved beyond her and narrowed in revulsion and distrust as he gazed at Blodwedd. "I cannot take the word of one who has allied herself with demons," he muttered. He stared again at Branwen. "You are no longer your mother's daughter, of that I am most certain. The Old Gods have tainted and ruined you, girl."

"That may well be the case," Iwan said wryly, limping forward with his arm still across Linette's shoulders. "But I am no follower of the Old Gods, Gavan ap Huw!" His eyebrow rose quizzically. "Will you take my word for it that the prince has betrayed us?"

"This is all lies!" shouted Bryn, the big bullying boy from Doeth Palas. He had challenged Branwen to a fight with quarterstaffs and had hated it when she had proved less of an easy conquest than he had assumed. As he called out, he pulled off his helmet, revealing his pale, freckled face and mop of unruly red hair. "The prince is no traitor, nor ever would be!" He glared at Gavan. "Why are we wasting our breath on these liars?"

Aberfa sprang at him, her face savage. Before he could defend himself, she pulled him from the saddle and threw him to the ground, where he lay, sprawled. Others on both sides started forward, hands moving to sword hilts, faces uneasy.

Bryn stared up at Aberfa in shock and alarm as she planted her foot on his chest and aimed the point of her sword at his throat.

"Liars, is it?" she shouted. "You'd not call us so if you'd seen the Captain of Doeth Palas bend his knee to Herewulf Ironfist! You'd not say so if you'd seen the Saxon dogs carousing in the Great Hall of Gwylan Canu!"

Banon moved forward and caught her arm. "Peace, Aberfa!" she said. "Let it not be we who break this truce."

Aberfa glowered at her. Then she nodded and lifted her foot from Bryn's chest. But she kept the sword point at his throat.

"Aberfa—do not harm him!" called Branwen. "If faith in the faithless is worthy of death, then which of us shall escape the slaughterhouse?" She turned to Gavan, her heart aching that this man whom she so admired could place no trust in her. "Whose tale will you believe, Gavan ap Huw?" she asked. "If not mine, then whose?"

"I may believe Iwan, the son of Madoc ap Rhain, lord of Gwylan Canu," said Gavan. "But I will need

19

more proofs than hearsay ere I give credence to his words."

"Then let's put up our weapons and perhaps build a fire to warm us on this bleak mountainside," said Iwan. "We have food enough to share, if you have ears for our sorry tale."

Gavan nodded. "So shall it be." He sheathed his sword. "Bryn, you fool!" he called gruffly. "Get to your feet, boy. Would you shame us all, lying on your back in the dirt with a maiden's sword in your face?"

It was a strange, tense gathering under the spreading oak branches in the dying reaches of the night. A fire had been built, and its flames threw a ghoulish light over the trees as well as ruddied the faces and clothes of the two uneasy bands. They sat and watched each other warily across the fire while Iwan spoke of the events that had unfolded at Gwylan Canu over the past day and night.

Food and drink had been shared out between the two groups, and Rhodri had made up some herbal salves for the minor injuries inflicted in the skirmish. Fortunately no one had been seriously hurt, and the worst abrasion was to Iwan's head, although he made light of it. The horses were close by, tethered loosely and able to graze. Fain watched Gavan suspiciously from a low branch above Branwen's head as though ready at the first hint of aggression from the grizzled old warrior to launch himself down with a stabbing beak and rending claws.

Branwen looked at the newcomers. With their grim, iron-faced helmets removed, they were suddenly just a bunch of lads from Prince Llew's citadel: sullen-faced Bryn with his huge muscles and his swaggering ways; skinny Andras with his gangly limbs and his startled-chicken face; and Padrig ap Gethin, a boy with jet-black hair and a thin mustache hidden by a great, craggy nose. Not exactly a cadre of weathered warriors for such a man as Gavan ap Huw to ride with.

And there was still the puzzle of the fourth lad. Branwen guessed he was no more than seven or eight years old, his hair tawny, his face showing an expression she recognized: the downcast eyes and flinching demeanor of someone used to dodging blows. A servant, she guessed, but not a Saxon captive by his looks. A boy of Brython, then—one recently rescued from some Saxon household.

"And believe what you will of the Shining Ones," Iwan was saying, his eyes fixed on Gavan. "But I tell you I was there; and I saw the great Green Man of the ancient woods—and dreadful and unknowable as he may be, he was our friend at that moment; and without him a Saxon army would now be squatting in Gwylan Canu, plotting the conquest of Brython."

A long, suspenseful silence followed while Gavan stared into the flames as though he hoped the leaping tongues would reveal something to help him make up his mind. Padrig and Andras were looking at each other with puzzled, worried faces. Bryn's stubborn features were unreadable.

It was Blodwedd's voice that broke the crackling silence.

"If you wish for further proofs, I can give them to you," she growled, eyeing Gavan with open hostility. She lifted her hands, her white fingers spread like raking claws. "I can show you things, man of war—things you will not doubt. Proofs of perfidy indeed."

Gavan's lip curled, and he shrank away from her. "Do not seek to touch me, demon," he said. "For I will smite you to the bone if you try to work your sorceries on me!"

"What use will the spilling of blood serve?" asked Rhodri, reaching to draw back Blodwedd's hands and cradle them in his. "Have we not already seen blood enough to last us a lifetime?"

Branwen peered into Gavan's closed face, dismayed at the thought of having to fight again but frustrated at the delay this strange encounter was causing. Upon the mountain peak, Merion of the Stones was waiting—and Branwen knew from experience that the tasks set her by the Shining Ones did not allow for procrastination.

"Speak your mind, Gavan ap Huw!" she said. "What choice do you make? To let us go on our way unmolested or to try and take me back to your master's cruel justice?"

"You'll wade to the hips in your own blood ere that happens!" warned Dera.

Gavan looked slowly from face to face of Branwen's followers, seeing defiance and grim determination in every one. He turned at last to Branwen.

"You misunderstand my purpose here if you believe I have come onto the mountain to take you back to the prince," he said slowly. "I have no desire to return to Doeth Palas; I have a mission in the east. A mission that will brook no delay."

"It's the boy, isn't it?" Rhodri said, nodding toward the scared-looking lad. "I know the look of a boy who has been in servitude to the Saxons, and I know a runaway when I see one."

Branwen glanced at her friend—so she had been right in her guess! The boy *was* an escaped prisoner of the Saxons.

Gavan looked at Rhodri with a new respect. "A shrewd man you are," he said. "It *is* news from the east brought to me by the boy Dillon that has hastened me from Doeth Palas." He turned to Branwen. "Forgive my slow response, Branwen of the Old Gods," he said. "I am a man of action, not thought; but your tale of the prince's perfidy chimes all too well with an encounter I had with him before I departed his court." He paused, his face grim, as though the words were bitter in his throat.

"When Iwan came to Prince Llew with his tale of

a Saxon army approaching Gwylan Canu, it seemed strange to me that the prince should choose to send out fifty horsemen," he said. "Were that citadel taken by an enemy, all of Brython would be in danger." He shook his head. "If an army were marching on Gwylan Canu, fifty men could not hold them back—and the prince had not called for a muster of footmen or armed riders to follow on after Captain Angor's troop. Yet if the prince believed Iwan's tale to be false, then why send so many? A brace of swift riders would be enough to gauge the situation and report back."

"So," said Branwen. "Fifty was too few—or too many. Yes, I understand. We thought the same . . . until we learned the truth."

"I went to the prince with my thoughts," Gavan continued. "But he became angry and dismissed me with my questions unanswered." Gavan's jaw set. "So I left him; but it rankled with me, although I had no inkling of the reason behind his decision." His hand balled to a white fist; rage was building in him. "But were he indeed in league with Herewulf Ironfist, then the sending of Captain Angor and his fifty riders had a good purpose."

"Exactly," said Iwan. "To delude my father into allowing them to enter Gwylan Canu at their ease and then to hand over the citadel to Ironfist upon his arrival. And the plan would have worked if not for the loose lips of one of Angor's men." He looked at Branwen, his eyes shining. "And if not for this princess of the eastern cantrefs, whose allies you despise, all would still have been lost."

"Aye," growled Gavan. "She has served the land well; but the Old Gods have their own purposes, I deem, and the lives of those who are caught up in their webs are of little value to them."

"I do not think that is true," said Branwen.

"It is not," added Blodwedd. "All life is sacred to the Elder Powers—I wish the same could be said of you humans!"

"But do I understand you correctly, Gavan ap Huw?" asked Iwan. "Do you now believe that the prince has betrayed us?"

There was a heavy silence. Branwen saw that the eyes of Gavan's three lads were riveted on the old warrior's face. "I do," he said at last. "It grieves me to the heart—but I can see no other answer to the riddle of his actions." He clenched his fists and shook them at the blind sky. "Traitor most foul!" he shouted. "Had I known of this when I stood at his side, a knife to the heart would have been his reward!"

Branwen saw Bryn and Andras and Padrig staring at Gavan in consternation. There were tears in Padrig's eyes.

Gavan surged to his feet. "Bryn! Fetch my horse! I must return and unmask the prince's villainy!" His hand clamped onto his sword hilt. "I have not lived the life of a warrior these three score years and five only to see Brython fall to such base corruption!"

The three boys also scrambled to their feet.

Branwen got up. "You will ride to your certain death if you head westward, Gavan ap Huw," she said urgently. "The prince cannot be taken by one man alone."

"Riders have been sent to Pengwern," Iwan reminded him. "King Cynon will raise an army against Bras Mynydd."

"Do not go back, lord," said Andras. "They are right—you will be killed before you can come nigh the prince."

"And what of your daughter if you die such a useless death?" added Padrig. "Would you have her spend the rest of her life in captivity?" He looked appealingly at the old warrior. "Remember your mission in the east, my lord. Remember Alwyn."

Branwen looked sharply at Gavan.

Alwyn! Gavan had spoken to her once of his stolen daughter.

Brython had been at open war and Gavan in service to the king when his wife had been killed and his young daughter carried away into captivity. By the time Gavan could be released from the king's side, the girl's trail had long gone cold. For a year and a day the doughty warrior had moved in stealth through the dangerous Saxon lands to the east, but of his daughter there was no hint or rumor. It was as though the wild Saxon kingdoms had swallowed her up.

At last he had admitted defeat, and he had turned back to his homeland and taken service with Prince Llew ap Gelert, tasked with training the young for the war that had no end.

That was the tale that Gavan had told her—but now it seemed that unexpected news of his daughter had come out of the east.

"What did the boy tell you?" Branwen asked, sitting again. "Is Alwyn alive, then?"

As he was reminded of his daughter, Gavan's face became even more careworn. "Aye, it seems she is, if the boy Dillon is not mistaken." He also sat down, looking toward the small lad. "Tell your tale again, boy. Stand, and speak it with a brave heart; you've nothing to fear here."

Trembling and with an anxious gaze, the boy got unsteadily to his feet. All eyes were upon him; but as he spoke, he looked only at Gavan, as though gaining courage from the old man's face.

"I don't remember when I was captured," he began, his voice shaking a little. "I lived on a farm in the northeastern marshes of Teg Eingel." Branwen knew where he meant: Teg Eingel was the cantref directly to the north of her own homeland. "The Saxons came. They looted and burned our home . . ." Dillon paused, swallowing.

"An all too familiar tale," muttered Linette.

"I was carried away as a prisoner," Dillon continued. "I think everyone else was killed. Leastways, I never saw any of my family again. I was taken to a great town on a wide river."

"Name the town, boy," Gavan said gently.

"It was called Chester," said Dillon. "And the river was the Dee."

These were names Branwen knew. The old town of Chester was in Saxon Mercia, no more than a day's ride from the eastern border of Cyffin Tir.

"I was taught enough Saxon words to be able to serve my masters," Dillon said. "Many moons passed in servitude—two or three summers, I think—and by then I had given up hope of ever being rescued. Then word came that an encampment of soldiers had been set up outside the town and that servants were needed there. I was sent to serve the soldiers."

"I know the camp well," said Rhodri. "I was also brought there as a servant, and would be there still had I not done as Dillon here did and escaped when opportunity presented itself."

Dillon looked at Rhodri in amazement, although there was no sign that he recognized him from the camp. "Every day more men poured into the camp," the boy continued. "Brought together by a great warrior of the Saxon kingdoms, a man named Horsa Herewulf Ironfist, Thain of Winwaed."

"My old master!" murmured Rhodri.

"Yes, we know him," said Iwan. "Branwen saw him plunge to his death, thank the Three Saints!"

A bleak smile touched Dillon's lips. "I'm glad he

is dead," he said. "He was a bad man—but his son is worse still!" He shivered as though at some dreadful memory. "Redwuld Grammod he is called."

"Redwuld the fierce," added Rhodri. "Redwuld the cruel. I know of that creature, although he did not live with Ironfist when I was with him. He lived at the court of King Oswald and had been there from early childhood. I never saw the man, but I heard tales of his bad temper and his viciousness."

"Then you must have made your escape before he returned to be with his father," said Dillon. "He is a very wicked man! I was set to work in Thain Ironfist's Great Hall, and Redwuld Grammod was my master. There were many servants in that horrible place . . . but one woman stood out from the others. Redwuld had brought her with him from the north. Very beautiful she was, with flowing chestnut hair and big eyes like a doe; and Redwuld treated her as a favorite. Leastways, I never saw her beaten as the rest of us were. She told me once that her name was Alwyn and that her father was a great warrior of Powys—one of the greatest warriors ever in the whole history of the Four Kingdoms. Lord Gavan ap Huw, hero of the battle of Rhos."

"And you escaped and sought out the great warrior?" asked Rhodri.

"I did," said Dillon, a proud light igniting in his eyes for a moment. "I was serving at a feast, and I broke a favorite drinking goblet of Redwuld

Grammod's. He ordered that I should be whipped before the whole household the next morning. I have seen such beatings. People die of them. So I waited until the dead of night, and then I crept quietly away under the noses of the guards."

"He arrived in Doeth Palas the same day you cut the half Saxon captive loose," Gavan told Branwen, glancing at Rhodri. "In the aftermath of your actions, I had little time to spend on a runaway out of the east, but eventually I gave an ear to Dillon's tale. I have no doubt that the woman he met was my Alwyn—closer than I could have ever imagined, and under the thumb of our greatest foe!"

"And Prince Llew gave his permission for you to seek her out?" Branwen asked in surprise. Gavan had told her that the last time he had asked permission to go in search of his daughter he had been told he could not be spared. And surely the Saxon threat was as great now as it had been then.

"He gave his permission willingly," said Gavan. "And at the time I thought it strange that he did not refuse my request; but I see now that he was glad to have me out of his court with my unwanted questions." His brows knitted. "I believe now that I may have been the only man in the prince's court who did not know what he was planning. Angor was certainly deep in his counsels, and many others, too."

"He knew you could not be corrupted, I'd say," commented Iwan. "But at some point, as his plans grew to fruition, I think you would have been quietly done away with. Angor would relish such a duty!"

"I doubt it not," said Gavan. "But we shall see who will gain the upper hand when next I see that villain, the fires of Annwn take him!"

"The prince would not allow Lord Gavan to take any soldiers on his hunt into Mercia," said Andras. "But he said he could pick three lads of the court." Pride showed on his thin face. "He chose us to travel with him."

"Aye," said Gavan. "The best of a poor bunch, but trustworthy and stouthearted. And the lad Dillon asked to come with us."

"That was bravely done," said Rhodri, looking admiringly at the boy. "I'd have thought twice before returning to Ironfist's lair!"

"He'll not be put in danger," said Gavan. "But he knows the layout of the camp, and he will help us get in and out undetected."

"I'm glad for you, Gavan ap Huw," said Branwen. "I know how your heart aches for your daughter. I hope you are successful."

Gavan looked silently at her for a while, the firelight flickering in his eyes. Branwen got the impression he was turning thoughts over in his head, weighing her before speaking again.

"And so all tales are told," he said at last, looking into the eastern sky, where the glowing gray of dawn came creeping through the branches. "A new day has come." He got up and walked around the fire toward Branwen. Crouching in front of her, he rested his hands on her shoulders.

"I have a boon to ask of you, Branwen," he said solemnly. "Do this thing for me and be your mother's daughter once more!"

She looked warily into his rugged face. "What thing?"

"Turn from the Old Gods while you still can," he said, his fingers biting into her shoulders. "I do not believe you are truly lost yet, Branwen; but if you do not repudiate them, they will devour you, body, spirit, and soul. Go back to your home, Branwen—go back to your mother. Be the child that the Lady Alis needs! Be Prince Griffith's daughter! That is your true destiny! That is where you belong."

Branwen gazed into the old warrior's time-riven face, and she saw fear in his eyes—fear for her—fear that the Shining Ones would destroy her.

A small voice whispered within her mind.

He's right. Why not go home? Haven't you done enough?

But she had heard that voice too often to listen to it now.

B RANWEN SHRUGGED OFF the urgent pressure of Gavan's hands and stood up. She looked at the others—her followers. All eyes were on her. But what were they thinking? Did they hope that she would turn away from the Old Gods? Would they rather she led them off this mountain and down to the burned-out hulk of Garth Milain, there to build new defenses against the Saxons?

"We each have our own path to tread," Branwen said, her voice thick and slow as she rejected Gavan's plea. "Go into the east, Gavan ap Huw; seek for your daughter and bring her safe home!" She walked toward the tethered horses. "I have a different way to go."

"You are a fool, Branwen," Gavan said, getting to his feet. But there was more sorrow than reproach in his voice. "This destiny will hurl you into your grave!"

She paused. "Maybe so," she said. "But the destiny is mine alone." She turned and stared up at the looming mountain. "I do not know what awaits me up there." She looked at her small band. "You agreed to follow me in the white heat of victory. Perhaps this chill dawn has brought wiser thoughts to you." She gazed from face to face. "I freely release any of you who would rather go with Gavan."

"Not dawn nor dusk nor deepest night will weaken my resolve to stay at your side," said Dera. Her eyes gleamed. "To the death, Branwen!" she cried. "I shall follow you to the death!"

Branwen saw the same determination in the faces of the others.

Iwan spread his hands. "You're wasting your time if you're looking to be rid of us, barbarian princess," he said. "We are hooked to you like burrs of teasel in a woolen cloak." His eyes flashed. "And they are not easily removed!"

"Then all is said and done," growled Gavan. "I wish you well, Branwen of the Old Ones. I doubt we shall meet again." He turned away from her and strode toward the horses. "Come, lads—we've a long road ahead of us," he called back. "Let's leave these folk to their doom."

"We have not warned them of the coming of Skur!" piped Dillon, looking at Gavan in consternation. "They should be warned!"

"Who is Skur?" asked Linette, kneeling in front of the small boy, smiling and taking his hands.

"A dreadful man!" said Dillon, looking into her face with wide, anxious eyes. "A great warrior from the Northlands!"

"A phantom to scare children!" said Bryn. "I've heard his tale; it's nothing!"

"That's not what they were saying in Thain Herewulf's Great Hall!" Dillon shouted, frowning at Bryn. "They believe he is real! And they say that he is coming. They say that when he arrives, the father of all battles will begin!"

Iwan looked questioningly at Gavan. "He sounds a formidable fellow," he said. "Skur? I have not heard his name before."

"Neither have I," said Gavan. "But if Dillon understood the rumors right, then he is a Viking from across the North Sea."

"I *have* heard the name," said Rhodri. "It means *storm* in the Norse language. The Saxons certainly believe in Skur Bloodax, although I was never able to decide whether he was a real man or a legend."

"What do you know about him?" asked Branwen.

"Very little," said Rhodri. "No one I ever heard speaking of him had ever seen the man nor known anyone who had, but his deeds were the stuff of fireside sagas. Some tales had him a giant: seven feet tall with shoulders as wide as a bull. But others spoke of him as being slender and lithe as a feather, and able to kill as quick and silent as the wind. And they said he had eyes like flames and that he drank the blood of his victims."

"That's right!" cried Dillon. "But some stories said he was invisible and that he suffocated his victims in their sleep by squatting upon their chests and that when they were dead he would rip out their hearts and eat them."

Rhodri smiled grimly. "I had not heard that tale," he said. "But the stories of Skur Bloodax are as wild and as varied as imagination allows. Some say he is a bear or a werewolf or even a demigod who can turn himself into smoke. But whatever his true appearance, all agreed that he is a deadly foe and that he is protected by the Norse god Ragnar."

Dillon's face was pale. "Ragnar is a terrible god," he said. "He gave Skur a huge ax—double headed and decorated with an engraving of a raven in flight."

Rhodri nodded. "Whatever his appearance, he is said always to be accompanied by a raven—a foul and evil bird named Mumir."

"I cannot believe this man exists," said Iwan. "And what if he does? Why should we fear him? Even the greatest warrior can be brought down by a well-aimed arrow."

"I know of the cursed spirit that is named Ragnar," said Blodwedd, and Branwen was surprised to hear horror in her voice. "My lord Govannon has spoken of him; he is a vile and poisonous hellion, much beloved in the barbarous and brutal Northlands. If this man Skur is under Ragnar's protection, he must indeed be a formidable champion." She looked at Iwan. "And what use are arrows when Mumir the raven can pluck them from the very air before they come nigh their target?"

Iwan's eyes narrowed uneasily.

"All this talk is without purpose," said Branwen. "He may be real, or he may not. He may be coming, or he may not! And if he is protected by some grim half god of the Northmen, so what is that to us? We have our own protectors! I don't fear him or Ragnar!"

Gavan frowned at her. "I wish you *did* fear such devils," he said. "But I will waste no more time." He turned away. "You have chosen, and I am done with you. Come, lads."

Dillon pulled away from Linette and joined the other three boys as they ran toward their horses. They were quickly mounted and ready to leave, and Branwen could see from their faces that they were glad to be getting away from these lunatic followers of the Old Gods.

Gavan avoided her eyes as he rode past her into the dawn. A chill came into Branwen's heart as he led the boys away through the trees. The old warrior had offered her one last chance of saving herself, and she had rejected it. What a poor, blind fool he must think her!

"The mountain wears a less gloomy face in the light of a new day," said Rhodri. "I think the old man is wrong, Branwen. I don't think the Shining Ones have anything to gain by your death—quite the reverse, in my opinion."

"In *your* opinion, indeed?" Iwan said with the

flicker of a smile on his lips. "And what weight do we give to that, Master Runaway? Was there much time for deep musings on the nature of the Old Gods while you were scraping out the cook pots of your Saxon overlords?"

Blodwedd glared at him, but Branwen was glad that Rhodri didn't allow himself to be provoked by Iwan's casual taunting. "My name is Rhodri, not *Runaway*" was all he said. "It's of little consequence I know, but you might try to remember it if you are able."

Iwan laughed, and turned to kick earth over the dwindling fire.

Branwen stared up at the bleak humps and crags that lifted above the ragged line of the forest. The rising sun had burnished the lifeless rocks so that the mountain glowed like beaten bronze.

Rhodri was right—it did look less threatening now; but Branwen could not clear her mind of the memory of the dancer she had seen dressed as Merion: the crooked old hag with the wispy hair and the ugly face.

Rhiannon had been beautiful and strange and full of riddles; Govannon, ancient and mighty and dreadful.

But what was Merion of the Stones, what did she want of Branwen, and what power did she hold?

Only a hard morning's ride would answer those questions.

5

B ANON STOOD ON a lofty and narrow peak of bare
rock, staring up at the jagged and furrowed face
of the mountain. Branwen's band had come above the
last few straggling trees, and for some time they had
been moving slowly and tortuously through a tumbled landscape of barren boulders and loose scree
and impossible crags.

"Take care up there!" Branwen called up to her.
"What do you see?"

"Rock!" Banon called down to where the rest of
the band was gathered. "Rock and sky, but little else;
and nothing to guide us farther!"

They had followed what pathways there were
on the mountain, sometimes retracing their steps
when some impossible bluff reared in front of them.
Sometimes dismounting as they traversed slopes of

loose shale. Always seeking a way to the upper reaches, but so often thwarted that Branwen began to suspect that the mountain disapproved of their presence and was actively trying to discourage them and to drive them down again.

As the morning bled away, they found themselves moving through a narrow defile, a crack in the rind of the old mountain that led them steadily upward but that was so deep, they lost all sense of where they were. Branwen sent Fain to scout for them, but he was gone so long that she grew impatient.

She called for a halt, intending to climb to the highest point and see what progress they were making; but flame-haired Banon beat her to it, leaping from the saddle and quickly climbing the rock face with her long, gangly arms and legs.

"If there is danger of falling to the death, better me than you!" she called back in response to Branwen's cries of protest.

Banon made the ascent without mishap and stood high above the others, her long red hair blowing in the wind, shielding her freckled face from the glare of sunlight with one long hand as she scoured the mountainside.

"Do you see a cave?" Blodwedd called up to her.

"I see many cracks and crevices," Banon replied. "How am I to tell one from the other?"

"What does Merion's cave look like?" Rhodri asked Blodwedd.

"I do not know," said Blodwedd.

Branwen frowned at her. "Your lord Govannon sent you as our guide, Blodwedd," she said impatiently. "Guide us!"

"I am not a child of the stones," Blodwedd retorted. "Merion does not speak to me. I am sorry."

Iwan clicked his tongue. "Well now, here's a fine thing," he said under his breath. "A curious destiny it is that plays hide-and-seek with its minions." He glanced at Branwen. "Perhaps you should have asked for more specific directions when the Green Man sent you up the mountain."

Branwen combed her fingers fretfully through her hair. "Why is she hidden from me?" she wondered aloud. "How am I to do what the Shining Ones ask if they will not reveal themselves?"

"Can you see where this vale leads?" Dera called up to Banon. "Is there a clear way ahead?"

"Wait," Banon called back, "I cannot see from here. I will . . ." Her voice rose to an alarmed cry, and suddenly she disappeared from view.

"Banon!" Aberfa howled, scrambling down from her horse and clawing her way up the rock. "Banon!"

"She's fallen! She's fallen!" called Dera.

Branwen leaped for the rock, instinct driving her faster than thought, panic lending her the speed to go scurrying up the rock face. She should never have allowed Banon to go up there in her place. She was their leader—it was her job to keep them safe!

41

She quickly overtook the heavier-set Aberfa, finding toeholds to support her weight while she groped with her fingers for higher purchase. She could hear voices from below as she climbed. Others were following.

She had a horrible vision of reaching the top and staring down to see Banon's mangled body lying at the foot of a deep precipice.

My fault! All my fault!

It was a few frantic moments before Branwen pulled herself onto the narrow summit of the rock. "Banon?"

"Branwen?" It was Banon's voice, from blessedly close by.

With a gasp of relief, Branwen moved across the narrow, uneven crest of the rock. She saw white fingers gripping the stone. She knelt and snatched at Banon's wrists. "I've got you!"

Leaning forward, Branwen blanched at the fall that swam beneath her. The mountain dropped away as though cut through with an ax. Had Banon not somehow managed to cling to the rock, she would certainly have plunged to her death.

"I have you!" Branwen cried again, straightening her back, tensing her muscles, opening her shoulders to pull with all her might.

For a few moments Banon's weight was too much for her; but Branwen bit down hard in concentration, her mouth filling with a sour, rusty taste, her muscles straining as she knelt on the ledge and hauled.

Banon's face appeared over the rim, alarmed and relieved. Aberfa's thick-muscled arms reached down past Branwen's shoulders. The large hands gripped Banon's arms and pulled, and a few moments later, Banon was sprawling on the rock, her chest heaving, her fingers digging into Branwen's arms like iron nails.

"I told you to take care!" said Branwen.

"I took *great* care," gasped Banon, relaxing her hold and getting shakily to her knees. "The rock shook and threw me off! I heard the mountain laugh as I fell!" She looked round eyed at Branwen and Aberfa, her voice trembling. "It tried to kill me, I swear!"

"That cannot be," said Aberfa, lifting Banon bodily to her feet. "We would have felt it. There was no movement. No laughter. You lost your footing is all."

"I did not!" Banon insisted. "We should go back. This mountain wants none of us! It will kill us if we seek to go higher."

Branwen looked into her face. "You heard laughter, you say?"

Banon nodded. "Like . . . the laughter of an old woman . . . but cruel and hard and without joy." She looked into Branwen's face, her eyes confused. "You heard *nothing*?"

"I heard it" came a sepulchral voice behind them. "I heard the laughter of the stones."

Branwen stood up. "Blodwedd?"

She cautiously circled the owl-girl. Blodwedd's face was drained of color, her eyes huge, her lips parted to show her sharp white teeth. Branwen looked into Blodwedd's face, but the owl-girl's glazed eyes were fixed on a single point among the high rocks.

"She relishes the taste of fresh-killed falcon," Blodwedd intoned in a flat, expressionless voice. "But she would rather dine on human flesh. Her laughter freezes the marrow in my bones. She calls for you to go to her, Warrior Child—alone and weaponless." Blodwedd's arm shot out, her finger pointing. "She is there! She waits for you, and she hungers. . . ."

Branwen took hold of the owl-girl's narrow shoulders and shook her. "Blodwedd!" she shouted into her face. "Stop this now! Come back to me!"

Quite suddenly Blodwedd's body relaxed, and she almost collapsed into Branwen's arms. There was still fear in her face as she stared into Branwen's eyes, but her own amber eyes were clear again.

"She is terrible, Branwen," Blodwedd groaned. "Do not go to her. She will kill you. Fain is already dead—I see his blood-wet feathers sticking to her lips. She will devour you also. By Govannon's grace, do not seek her out!"

Fain dead? No—it cannot be true! I will not believe it. Blodwedd must be mistaken!

"Why would Govannon send me to a creature that would do such a thing?" Branwen gasped, trembling to see fearless Blodwedd so shaken.

"I do not know," moaned Blodwedd. "I only know what I feel: Merion is deadly—she is famished—she will kill you."

Branwen turned to stare up the mountain. "Show me where she lives," she said.

"I'll not guide you thither, upon my life!" said Blodwedd.

"I don't ask you to," said Branwen. "Point to the place."

"I'll accompany you," growled Aberfa. "Merion will need a wide gape indeed to swallow me!"

"I won't let you go alone," added Banon.

Branwen shook her head. She stepped to the edge of the rock just as Rhodri and Iwan reached the top and joined them.

"Is Banon safe?" Iwan panted.

"She is," Branwen said. "Go back down, all of you. Blodwedd has shown me where Merion's cave is. I'll seek out the mountain crone and return as soon as I can."

Rhodri scrambled to his feet in front of her. "We should all go," he said. "There's safety in numbers."

"No. She is too dangerous."

"Then all the more reason to approach her together," added Iwan.

Branwen stared at him. "Do you truly believe that if Merion of the Shining Ones desires my death, you would be able to protect me from her?"

"I don't know," said Iwan. "But I would try."

Branwen felt a cool hand on her arm. It was Blodwedd. "The fear I feel for the Stone Hag is beyond all reason," she said. "But if you must go, then I will attend you. I should die of shame otherwise."

"Good," Branwen said. "Thank you." She turned back to the others. "Blodwedd will go with me to the cave mouth. I need for the rest of you to keep a safe distance." She saw the doubt and dismay in their faces. "I am not afraid of Merion," she said. "I do not believe she will kill me." She put her hand to the hilt of her sword. "I am the Sword of Destiny! The chosen warrior of the Shining Ones! Govannon would not have sent me up here to my death."

Her heart was less steady than she showed, but if the Mountain Crone was as bad as Blodwedd feared, Branwen was not prepared to lead the others to their doom.

"Are you sure?" asked Rhodri.

"I am."

"Then I'll go down and tell Dera and Linette," he said. He looked anxiously into her face and then turned and held Blodwedd's eyes. "Be safe—both of you. Come back to us as soon as you can."

Branwen saw indecision and concern in Iwan's face. Despite what she had said, he still wanted to go with her.

"You can share my journey, Iwan," she said. "But the destiny is mine alone."

He frowned. "All the same . . ."

"I won't put you in danger!" she said earnestly, staring deep into his eyes.

You of all people!

Curious. Why should she think *that*?

"If Merion harms you, I'll dig her out of her mountain hole and beat her to death with my bare hands!" Iwan said gruffly. "You tell her that!"

Branwen almost laughed at the gallant absurdity of Iwan's threat. "I shall," she said. "She will be most impressed, I don't doubt." She turned to Blodwedd. "Let's get this over with," she said. "Lead me to Merion of the Stones."

Blodwedd jumped lightly from boulder to boulder, her arms out for balance, her fingers spread like wing feathers.

Branwen followed more slowly, clambering cautiously over the heaped rocks that formed a precarious stairway to the sinister cave mouth.

It loomed above them, a ragged black hole gouged into the face of the mountainside, shaped so that it looked to Branwen like a human mouth twisted and wrenched open and fixed in a scream of uttermost agony.

Branwen tried not to think of what was waiting for her in the darkness. If Merion really had killed Fain, that would be heartache enough for her without adding to it with the phantoms of her imagination.

As she climbed, she remembered with a keen bite

of grief the first time she had laid eyes on Fain, a gray sickle shape against the sun, swooping down from the sky above Garth Milain with his bright eyes and his challenging call.

Rhiannon's messenger, a strange, brave creature that she had at first feared and then grown to love and to rely upon.

And if Merion would kill one such as he, what hope do I have?

Blodwedd crouched on a boulder, her head twisted over her shoulder, her eyes cavernous and brimming with golden light. "Do you not feel the chill, Branwen?" she said, her voice low, as though she feared to be overheard.

Branwen nodded; even though the sun was now high and the climb was making her sweat, she was aware of the coldness that came creeping down the mountainside.

"I don't need you to go any farther," Branwen said. "Wait here for me."

Blodwedd stared down at her. "If it were any other thing that awaited you, I would accompany you, even if my death were assured," she said.

"Yes. I know you would."

Blodwedd reached out a thin hand. "Be wary, Warrior Princess," she murmured. "Do not let the Stone Hag be your death."

Branwen took her hand for a moment. "I'm not afraid."

48

The huge eyes reflected the sunlight. "You *are* afraid, Branwen," the owl-girl whispered. "And you will be more so ere you face her. One last word. Do not take your sword into the cave. Do not forget that the iron of which your sword is forged was hacked from the hills; Merion may choose to slaughter you with your own blade if you carry into her cavern a reminder of that desecration."

Branwen frowned. "What desecration?"

"You humans burrow into her very bones, Branwen," said Blodwedd. "Seeking for your metals and your precious jewels. You suck out her marrow and leave her bereft and aching. The closer I come to her, the more deeply I feel her anger and misery and pain." She shook her head. "If Merion has become cruel and vengeful, it is not without reason."

"But I've come here to help. . . ."

"Indeed. But an injured bear will lash out at anyone who ventures near, and there's little purpose in protesting your goodwill from within its belly!"

Branwen drew her sword and handed it to the owl-girl. Now the only things left on her belt were her leather slingshot and the trinkets that she carried with her to remind her of home: the small golden key given to her by her father, the pouch of white crystals from Geraint, and the comb that was all she had of her mother.

"Keep the sword for me, then," she said to

Blodwedd. "I'll go unarmed to my doom!"

"Destiny, Branwen, not doom."

"We shall see."

As cold as the air had been on her climb up to Merion's cave, it seemed far, far more bitter now that Branwen stood under the gaping lintel of the agonized mouth. It came from the black cave, rolling out over her, chilling her to the core, making the fine down on her arms and legs prickle uncomfortably, causing the hair on her scalp to crawl. Breathing in, she felt ice in her chest, as though sharp frozen crystals were piercing her lungs.

She turned, seeing Blodwedd's tawny head among the rocks below.

She felt vulnerable without her sword—she felt naked.

But there was more. She felt the kiss of death in this place. And she felt a brooding malevolence so intense that it made her head reel.

"Merion of the Stones!" she called into the gaping darkness. "I have come as I was told to! My name is Branwen ap Griffith—do you know me?" But the frozen air blasted her words back into her throat, and there was no reply from within.

Taking one last glance at the living and breathing world of light and warmth, Branwen stepped into the gloom.

Her eyes gradually adjusted to the dimness, and

she found herself in a long tunnel. Brittle things snapped and cracked under her feet. Dry twigs? Bracken? She paused, staring down at the uneven ground. The tunnel floor was strewn with bones. She shivered. Mostly animal bones, she guessed, by the size of them. There was also a scattering of skulls: some no bigger than her thumb—rodent skulls with pointed teeth—and others huge and strangely noble even in such a setting—the tan-brown skulls of deer and boar and wolves.

But there were human bones, too. An arm bone had fractured under one of her feet, the groping hand still attached to it by stretched and dried sinews. Close by she saw the broken lattice of a human rib cage. A half-crushed human skull, its jaw grotesquely askew, gaped at her with empty eye sockets.

Terror took Branwen in its grip and she drew back, pressing herself against the cold stone wall. In the hateful darkness she could hear the blood pounding in her ears; she could feel her thumping heart bruising against the cage of her chest. Her legs were weak under her. She wanted to be sick, wanted to double up and crawl away on hands and knees, like some wounded animal.

She will kill me. How could I have thought otherwise? Oh, my poor dead father! How did it come to this? Geraint—I'm coming; I'll be with you soon. Mother—I'm so sorry. . . . I did my best. . . . I'm such a fool. Rhodri, dearest friend . . . and Iwan . . . oh, Iwan . . . I wish . . .

oh, I wish there had been the time to know you better. . . .

A strange sound echoed along the tunnel. A raw, harsh, scraping sound like stones grinding one against another. But it was more than that; it sounded almost as though the ancient stones were laughing. Yes! It was clearer now; within that dreadful sound Branwen could hear the joyless laughter of the closed throat and of the cavernous stomach.

But appalling as the inhuman laugher was, at least it shook Branwen out of her despair.

"I am sent by Govannon of the Wood," she shouted. "What do you want of me?"

The horrible laughter gurgled again, setting her teeth on edge, tearing at the inner walls of her skull. And then there was a groan—a deep, reverberating, desolate sound that all but stopped her heart.

"Speak to me!" Branwen shouted.

To me! To me! To me! came the echo of her voice.

"I will not go away!"

Go away! Go away! Go away!

"No! I will see you!"

See you! See you! See you!

Branwen walked forward over the grisly remains, trying not to notice the bones breaking under her step. A deeper darkness formed in the distance—the exit from the tunnel, a hole into nothingness.

As she drew closer, she felt an uncomfortable tingling in her fingers, as though her jangled nerves were warning her of peril.

She stepped into the darkness, horribly aware of a

lurking presence that watched her and waited for her.

"What do you want of me?" she asked, her voice frail and weak in her own ears.

She heard a sharp sound: stone clicking against stone. A feeble light ignited at the far end of the cavern. Branwen narrowed her eyes, and she saw it was the flame of a yellow candle set on the skull of some large animal. Behind it Branwen could make out a humped shape, like a black boulder, against the cavern wall. But it was not a boulder; the shape exuded malice and sleepless vigilance. Branwen fancied she saw eyes—points of flickering yellowish light—staring out from near the top of the shape.

The cavern walls were daubed with crude black images, ugly shapes that might have been dredged from some horrible nightmare—not human, not animal, and yet somehow alive and aware and dreadful. And there were forms on the ground, brought to life as the candle flame writhed. Small, almost human bundles, like dead babies made from sticks and brown skins, their deformed bodies stuffed with dry moss and fungus, their faces taut and featureless save for great, hollow, staring eyes.

Horrified, Branwen struggled against an urge to flee.

She managed a hoarse whisper. "Did you kill Fain?"

The guttural laughter sounded again, and the dark shape leaned forward so its face came into the light.

It was an ancient face, scored and pitted and as desiccated as weather-worn stone. It was ugly in a way but also beyond any human idea of ugliness, with its beetling brow, its hollow cheeks and its hidden eyes. Its nose was a rough, hooked splinter, its mouth a thin crack. Hair hung about it like filthy cobwebs. It was a face as old as time, and in the black pools of the eyes lurked a yellow loathing.

Branwen sucked in a sharp breath as the narrow crack of the mouth gaped suddenly wide. A dark shape burst out from between the taut lips, flying into Branwen's face in a shrieking mass of gashing claws and battering wings.

6

"*CAW! CAW! CAW!*"

At the last moment the bird skewed off to one side, one wing slapping Branwen's cheek as she ducked to avoid being struck.

"Fain!"

The terrified falcon circled the cavern, screeching in its wild flight, its wings striking against the stone, its shadow cavorting over the walls.

Branwen lifted her arm, relieved that he was alive but hating to see her friend in such distress. "Come! Come to me!"

The falcon darted through the darkling air, and at last it came onto her wrist; and she winced as the talons dug into her flesh.

"Don't fear, Fain," Branwen murmured, ignoring the pain. "You are safe from harm." The bird sat shivering, its head tucked deep in its neck feathers, its beady eyes on Merion.

"Safe from harm?" Merion's voice was like a winter wind blown across an ocean of ice. "Think you so, Warrior Child?"

"I do," Branwen said, forcing her voice not to betray her dread.

"Why so, Warrior Child?"

"Because if you wished me dead, I would not be standing here before you."

The head nodded. "A wise fool you are."

"Why a fool?"

"Only a fool would meddle in the affairs of the Shining Ones."

"Meddle?" This was absurd! "I do not *meddle* with you. I have done everything I can to keep away! It's you—you and Rhiannon and Govannon—who have brought me to this!"

"Is that so?" came the cold, parched voice. "Then why do you wear the stones? Why do you bear the key? These are the tokens of one who offers herself willingly." There was that cruel laughter again. "Or is it that you do not know their purpose?"

"I don't know what you mean," Branwen said, a spark of anger igniting among her fear. "I am half dead of riddles and conundrums. I was told to come here. I came. What do you want of me?"

"I want to relieve my hunger and slake my thirst," croaked the voice. "What do I want of you, Warrior Child? Why, I want to gnaw the scalp from your head and wear your long dark hair around my neck to ward off the winter chills. I want to eat your face, child: lips, cheeks, and chin. I want to feel your eyeballs burst between my teeth. I want to chew on your tongue and suck the soft meats from your bloody and raw-boned skull."

Branwen stared at the old hag in horror. Was this it, then? Had Blodwedd been right? Had she come here to face nothing but a dreadful death?

The humped shape rose from behind the candle flame and came slowly forward, one clawed hand clutching the handle of a misshapen stick. Merion of the Stones looked very much as Branwen had imagined. A hag, stooped and humpbacked, clad in shapeless ragged gray robes, tottering on feeble feet. But it was a shock to Branwen to see how Merion, bent and withered as she was, towered over her as she shuffled closer, her gray head almost scraping the stone roof of the cavern.

Branwen's hand moved to her hip—reaching for the hilt of her sword. But it wasn't there; she had left it in Blodwedd's keeping! But the sword was not Branwen's only weapon. With adder-quick fingers she slipped her leather slingshot from her belt and then ducked down and scooped up a small stone from the ground. Watching Merion as she approached, Branwen fitted the stone into the folded slingshot.

"Come no closer!" she warned. "Or I shall put out your eye!"

Merion chuckled in her throat.

Branwen swung the slingshot twice and loosed the stone. She had little hope of doing Merion any harm, but she was determined to try to defend herself against the terrible old hag.

The stone flew as swift as a bolt toward Merion's huge and hideous head. Yet the old crone did not even flinch; and at the last moment the stone changed trajectory, veering off and cracking against the wall, breaking up and spitting sparks.

"Think you that *stone* will work against me, Warrior Child?" Merion said. "Why, the very ground beneath your feet will come alive to aid me!"

Branwen tried to back away from the approaching monstrosity; but before she could move more than a single step, cracks opened under her feet and lips of rock snagged around her ankles, holding her fast.

She struggled, trying to get her feet loose, but the stone only bit harder against her ankles until she had to cry out with the pain. Merion loomed over her, the lipless mouth opening like a grave. Branwen's gorge rose as she looked up into the sunken eyes, seeing nothing but the flicker of a macabre yellow light under the heavy brows. She had at first thought that gleam to be reflected candlelight, but now she understood that the malignancy burned from deep within the hoary Mountain Hag.

Fain's wings fluttered uneasily as Branwen fought in vain to free herself.

"Kill me then and be done with it!" Branwen shouted.

A hand snaked out, and a cold grip clamped viciously on Branwen's upper arm. The huge face loomed closer.

"I have such power as you have never seen." Merion's breath was like ice on Branwen's face. "I am the earth shaker, the rift opener—the devourer. My mouth is wide, my belly insatiable. I can drink an ocean dry. I can eat forest and field and moor. You are but a sweet passing morsel to me, Warrior Child. I shall rip you open like a ripe plum, and I shall gorge on you!"

Branwen struggled to pull free; but the fingers were locked agonizingly on her arm, and already a numbness was creeping down to her hand. Fain spread wide gray wings and took to the air, cawing loudly.

The words of a song sung to her by a bard in the Great Hall of Doeth Palas came into her mind:

> *Merion of the Stones*
> *Mountain crone, cave dweller, oracle, and*
>   *deceiver . . .*

Deceiver?

Branwen stopped struggling, trying desperately to clear her mind, to see beyond the pain and the fear and the yellow flames in the hidden eyes.

"Why do they call you deceiver?" Branwen shouted. But she thought she knew. "This is not real! This is untrue! Get away from me! I was not brought here to be your supper!" Already the pain was lessening in her arm, the grip loosening, the cold breath no longer blasting in her face.

She staggered as the jaws of rock pulled away from her ankles. The huge, loathsome shape was gone. The yellow candlelight flickered. Merion crouched against the wall, small and shrunken and watching with an amused and curiously satisfied expression on her misshapen, unlovely face.

"You will do," Merion croaked, beating her stick on the hard ground. "You will do very well. It was a good choice She made." She cackled for a few moments, her mouth hanging open to reveal brown peg-teeth and a tongue like cracked leather.

"You were testing me?" Branwen cried, striding forward angrily. "Haven't I proven myself enough for you by now?" She paused as something the hag had said rang in her mind. "What do you mean, 'It was a good choice *She* made'? Do you speak of Rhiannon?"

"No, Warrior Child, it was not she who chose you. Do you not know that by now? We are Guardians—we make no such choices."

"Then who?" Fain came to Branwen, perching on her shoulder, gripping tight, and keeping close to her head.

"*Who* is of no consequence to you at this time,

Warrior Child" came Merion's grinding voice. "*How* is more to the purpose. *How* you are to serve me."

"Rhiannon warned me of a great canker in the land," said Branwen. "Now I know the true meaning behind her words. Llew ap Gelert must be destroyed. And you are to tell me how."

"That is not your task, Warrior Child," growled the ancient crone, stamping again with her gnarled stick. "Riddle me this: Who is it that soothes the blistering mountain when the summer sun beats down so fierce? Whose hand cools the brow of the lofty crag when the air rises in a shimmering haze and the buzzards hang motionless above the valley?"

Branwen stared at her, baffled by her questions, not even sure whether she was meant to answer.

"Who brings news from distant places when all the world is frozen? Who speaks in the gullies and ghylls? Whose voice echoes through the caverns?"

There was silence.

It became obvious that Merion was waiting for a response. Branwen thought through the odd questions. "Is it the wind?" she asked. A sudden understanding hit her. "The north wind! You mean Caradoc of the North Wind!"

The crone laughed again, slapping her knee and cracking her stick on the floor. "Did I not say a wise fool? Yes, Warrior Child, I speak of my brother the wind—my lost brother Caradoc." A bony finger pointed across the candlelight. "This is the task I lay upon you, Warrior Child—to seek for the place where the Saxons have caged my lovely brother . . . my droll and diverting brother . . . my dancing clown, my shape-shifting brother. . . ." Her voice lowered to an incoherent muttering, as if she had forgotten Branwen was there.

"Is Caradoc a prisoner of the Saxons?" Branwen asked incredulously.

The hag's head had thrust forward, the wattles of her neck shaking like hanks of rope. "He is!" she cried. "They trapped him in their foul webs, the dirty priesthood of the Saxons. Ten times ten years ago he fell to their wiles and was borne away." Her voice rose to a wail. "My brother! My beautiful, bonny brother! I ache to hear your voice again! But you shall be restored to me. You shall be set free! The child has come to me at last—the child with the golden key!"

Branwen was astonished. She stared at the crone in utter bewilderment and disbelief. Of all the ends she had feared on this mountain—of all the tasks she had contemplated—to be asked to rescue one of the Shining Ones was so far beyond expectation that she was dumbfounded.

Merion peered into her face. "You will travel east, Warrior Child," she said as though oblivious to Branwen's consternation. "You will seek out Caradoc's prison and you will bring it to me, for only under my eye will it be safe for you to use the key and release him." There was a pause, then the stick cracked down hard on the ground. "Warrior Child? Are you struck witless? Do you understand your task?"

Branwen started at the shout. "That's no task for me," she said. "My destiny is to save Brython from the Saxons, to defeat the traitor Llew, to raise an army against the invaders. That is what Rhiannon told me." She shook her head. "If Caradoc of the North Wind cannot save himself, what hope do I have?"

Merion's voice became impatient. "My brother is held by spells and incantations that have no power over you, Warrior Child," she said. "And why do you bear the golden key if you are not to be the instrument of his release?"

"What key?" demanded Branwen. "I have no key. What is this key of which you speak?"

The hag lifted her arm and jerkily pointed the stick toward Branwen's waist. "The golden key!" she growled. "I see it there, hanging from your belt! Do you think me blind, child?"

Branwen stared down at the few precious possessions that hung from the leather belt: a poke with flint and tinder in it, a haircomb that her mother had given her. A leather pouch that held six pieces of white crystal that Geraint had found on the mountain and given to her as a keepsake. And a small golden key gifted to her by her father on the tenth anniversary of her birth.

Branwen fingered the small key.

"You're wrong," she said, closing her fist around the key as though wanting to protect it from Merion's cold gaze. "This has nothing to do with the Old Gods; my father found it in the ruins of a Roman temple when he was but a youth. He gave it to me as a birthday present."

Merion's crowing laughter rang around the cavern. "And who do you suppose guided your father's footsteps to that desolate place, and who revealed to him at that moment the golden glint among the wreck and the ruin?" She cackled. "And who put it into his heart years later to pass the key on to his daughter?" The yellow eyes sparked like igniting flame. "Do you not perceive the truth yet, Warrior Child? There have been no loose threads in the pattern of your life; all that has happened to you is but part of the same great design." The stick hammered again. "The key will open Caradoc's prison—of that truth have no doubt, Warrior Child. All that you bear has its own purpose, its own part to play. Think you the white stones came to you by chance?"

"The stones?" Branwen clutched involuntarily at the leather pouch. "Geraint's crystals, you mean?"

"Found by your brother, given to you," said the Crone. "A thread in the tapestry."

Branwen gaped at her. "Have you been haunting my family's steps from before I was born?" she exclaimed. "Has there been no moment of my life free of your wiles and your ruses and intrigues?"

Merion shook her head. "You do not *listen*, Warrior Child," she rebuked her. "It is not *we* who chose you; it is not *we* who wove the tapestry of your fate. It is *She*! Hers is the guiding hand—Hers the whispered word, Hers the womb from which all life springs, Hers the arms that embrace the past and the present and the future. Hers the burden of love for all of creation."

As Merion spoke, Branwen felt a strange and overwhelming sensation. It was indescribable, inexplicable; but for a fleeting moment it was as though the vast, unknowable power that held the world in balance had turned from its unending task and focused its attention on her. For that splintered fraction of time, Branwen felt its presence bearing down on her, as strong as the heat and light of the noonday sun.

Then, in an instant, the sensation was gone. Branwen understood now that it would be pointless to seek from Merion of the Stones further knowledge of this great She. Such wonders would only be revealed in their own time and in their own way.

Branwen wiped her sleeve across her forehead, feeling feverish. There was a gaping feeling of emptiness under her ribs and a cold sweat on her skin.

"What must I do?" she asked Merion, wanting now only to get out of this bleak and chilling cavern and to see blue sky overhead and to be with her companions again.

"Come here to me," said Merion. "Show me the white stones."

Trembling, but not from fear, Branwen loosened the leather pouch from her belt as she stepped forward. She untied the neck and tipped the six crystals into her palm, then came around the yellow candle and stood in front of Merion, offering out her hand with all the determined trepidation of someone reaching into a fire to pull a friend to safety.

The Mountain Crone leaned forward. Her cold breath eddied around Branwen's fingers. The crystals glittered and shone as though frosted with ice; and deep in the heart of each of them, Branwen saw a tiny rainbow coiling.

She had seen those beguiling flecks of colored light before—they came when the crystals were held up to sunlight and tilted in exactly the right way. But never before had the rainbows revealed themselves in such darkness.

Merion lifted an arm and passed her wrinkled old hand over the stones, muttering to herself words that Branwen could not make out.

"There, 'tis done," said the Stone Hag. "Keep them safe, Warrior Child. I have breathed part of my own powers into them. I am diminished by this loss, and I will not be whole again till you return from your mission and need them no more."

Branwen gazed at the translucent crystals. "What have you done to them?"

"They have now in them the power to allow you to pass unnoticed among your enemies," said Merion.

"Use them wisely, Warrior Child. They will not make you invisible, but they will cause the eyes and the attention of ill-wishers to pass you by."

"Is the power only for me?"

"Nay, any of your followers who hold in their hand one of the stones will be protected by their powers," said Merion. "And one other virtue they have: they will allow the bearer to understand foreign speech."

"I'll be able to know what the Saxons are saying, even in their own language?"

"You will," said Merion. "But the stones will not allow you to speak their tongue, only to understand it." The yellow points in her hidden eyes flashed. "Know the limits of their powers, Warrior Child."

"And will they help me to find where Caradoc is imprisoned?" Branwen asked.

"Nay, they have not the power for that," said Merion. "You will need wit and perseverance to find where my brother is being held. But certain signs I can give you—pointers to help you on your road. The prison of Caradoc of the North Wind lies under the hand of the one-eyed warrior."

Branwen nodded, closing her hand around the crystals. "The one-eyed warrior. Yes. I understand."

"Seek the one-eyed warrior in the land of Mercia. You will recognize him; he is known to you."

Branwen frowned. "I don't know any warriors with one eye," she said. "I'm sure I don't."

"You will know him well enough when you see

him," Merion insisted. "Do not doubt it."

"And how will I know the prison?" asked Branwen. Her first thought was that Caradoc must be held in some strong fortress—in a stone room with a door of thick oak. But if that was true, then surely its lock would be a great iron device—certainly not a lock that could be opened with the small golden key her father had given her.

"You shall know the prison by this sign," said the crone, passing her hands in front of Branwen's face. A haze hung in the air like breath on a frosty morning, and there was a moving silhouette in the haze, like something seen through thick mist.

Branwen lowered her eyebrows, squinting as she tried to focus on the shape. It was an animal, padding silently through the gray haze, its back long, its head lowered as though on the scent. Its fur was short, gray like the mist; and it had tufts of hair on its pointed ears. Large paws it had and a blunt face and a short, thick tail.

"It's a cat!" Branwen murmured, recognizing the smooth, predatory glide of the stocky body. "A big cat."

"Aye, a lynx," said Merion, lifting her hands again and dispersing the mist. "Where you see the lynx, there will you find Caradoc's prison. But do not seek to use the key. Bear the prison back to me as swiftly as you can. If you free him and I am not at hand, he will kill you and all who are with you. Caradoc is a deadly force, and his anger will be great after being held so long against his will."

"But what *is* the prison?" Branwen asked. In her mind she saw Caradoc as a full-grown man—so what kind of cage was it that could hold him?

"I do not know," Merion said. "But remember this: we are not as you see us, Warrior Child. Divested of my human form, my true spirit is as vast as the sky. But its essence is also so small that it could be held between the cupped palms of your two hands." The crone stared at her. "And now you have all the knowledge that I can give you," she said. "Be gone from here and do not return but that you have Caradoc of the North Wind with you."

And as Merion spoke these words, Branwen was hit by a blast of bitter, biting wind. Half blinding her, it sent her staggering backward, out of the cave and into the tunnel, Fain fluttering above her head. Turning her back to the icy gale, Branwen ran over the carpet of bones, her hair snapping and her clothes cracking as she threw herself gratefully toward the bright light of the cave mouth.

7

THE SUN HAD passed behind the mountain, and the shadows of afternoon were long among the summer-warm rocks as Branwen gathered her followers and told them all that had happened in the cave of Merion of the Stones.

Blodwedd crouched on a high boulder at her back, knees splayed, shoulders hunched, and head low—more frog than owl at that moment. She had already heard the tale, and she was more relieved that Branwen had survived the ordeal than she was astonished by the nature of the task that the Mountain Crone had set her.

But it quickly became clear to Branwen that not all her followers were so at ease with Merion's enterprise.

"Are the Shining Ones not all powerful?" asked Dera. "How is it laid upon us to help *them*? I thought it would be the other way around."

"So it has been up to now," said Rhodri, looking uneasily at Branwen. "Are you sure Merion can be trusted?"

"Hist!" breathed Blodwedd, her eyes flickering. "Among the stones such things should not be voiced. Every pebble is an ear to *her*. Every cleft a whispering mouth!"

"And is that not enough to give us pause?" murmured Iwan. "That we should fear to voice our doubts lest the Mountain Hag rolls boulders down the mountain to help us on our way?"

Branwen looked at him. "I understand your fears," she said. "But the question I would have you answer is this: do you trust *me*?"

"Of course," Iwan replied. "Why else would I be here?"

Their gazes locked for a few moments. Branwen felt a curious fluttering in her chest as she stared into Iwan's unblinking eyes. She looked away and turned to the others. She saw confused and uncertain faces—especially among the four girls of Gwylan Canu.

"Listen, all of you," she said, her voice firm and resolute. "I have been given a duty to perform, and I *will* go into the east as Merion of the Stones asked, and I *will* seek out the prison of Caradoc of the North Wind. That is the path of my destiny. I have no other choice."

She saw Dera peering astutely into her face. "But *we* do have a choice, you mean," she said after a few moments. "I see. Once again you'd be rid of us, Branwen."

"Yes," Branwen said. "Yes, I would. I would be rid of any who have doubts or distrust in their hearts. Dera, and you others—Aberfa and Banon and Linette—you joined with me to fight the Saxons and to see Llew ap Gelert brought down. My quest in the east is not of that business. You owe me nothing."

"Nothing but our lives," said Linette. "Where would we be now, Branwen, if not for you?"

"Trammeled like beasts in the pits of Gwylan Canu we would be," added Banon. "Awaiting the pleasures of our Saxon captors—death or servitude, or worse abominations!"

"It wasn't I who saved you when the Saxon ships appeared," said Branwen. "It was Govannon of the Shining Ones."

"All the more reason for keeping faith with you, Branwen ap Griffith," growled Aberfa. "I am not considered wise or quick-witted, but it seems to me that if we cannot trust the Old Gods after they gave us their help at Gwylan Canu, then we may as well throw ourselves from the heights and put a swift end to our torments." She looked up at Branwen from under her deep brows. "If the Shining Ones lead us false, then Brython is doomed and all its people with it."

"A good point well made," said Iwan. He gave a casual shrug. "But I need no convincing. I'll follow the barbarian princess all the way to the court of the Saxon king Oswald if she desires it of me." He cocked an eye at Rhodri. "What's your word on the matter, Master Runaway?"

"Where the stinging nettle grows, the dock leaf is also found," said Rhodri. "The one to inflict pain, the other to offer relief. While you ride with her, I'll certainly not part from Branwen's side. Nor shall I leave her when you become bored and wander off in search of new diversions."

Branwen frowned. Nettles and dock leaves. Yes, there was something in that, although the effect that Iwan had on her went much deeper than the smarting of irritant needles in her skin.

"New diversions, is it?" Iwan laughed, staring pointedly at Blodwedd. "Well, a fine animal can be diversion enough, I've found; and my gallant Gwennol Dhu soothes my heart when human companionship palls." His eyebrow raised in a taunting challenge. "But I'd not bed down in the stable with her, no matter how her eyes glowed."

Rhodri's hands balled into fists. "What do you mean by that?" he said with suppressed anger. "Speak plainly, Iwan ap Madoc."

Iwan gave Rhodri a nonchalant look. "The runaway's so angry, he's spitting feathers!" He laughed. "How has it come about that his mouth is full of feathers, I wonder?"

Rhodri got to his feet. Iwan's hand snaked to his sword hilt. The tension was like a fire in the air.

With a single bound, Blodwedd was off the rock and standing between the two young men, her eyes burning into Iwan's face, her teeth bared. The other girls watched anxiously from the sidelines.

Branwen was among them in a moment, catching hold of Blodwedd's arm to prevent her from throwing herself at Iwan.

"Stop this!" Branwen shouted. "Rhodri—do you know no better than to rise to Iwan's bait? And Iwan—keep your taunts to yourself. Do we not have enemies enough that you must amuse yourself by such antics?"

"'Twas but a merry quip to lighten the mood," Iwan said, spreading his hands.

"Then it should have been funny," said Dera, her face stern. "And yet it was not! You always had a sharp tongue, Iwan. Sheath it now!"

Iwan bowed to her. "At your request, my lady," he said, unperturbed. He looked at Rhodri. "Forgive me if I angered you," he said. "As the scorpion said to the frog: it is in my nature."

"Then beware your nature," said Blodwedd, "lest it lead you to an untimely end."

"Enough of this," said Branwen. "We have no time for such foolishness!" She looked into the sky, still bright but showing the signs of the oncoming evening. "If you are all resolved to go with me, then let's ride down into the forest and find some shelter and a spring of water. It's a long time since we slept. We will camp in the forest tonight and ride eastward at dawn."

It was a little before sunrise when Branwen awoke, sweating and shivering and brimming with bad dreams. A bird sang a dancing tune in the distance, full of hope and joy. Voices were whispering in the aromatic darkness under the oak trees. Branwen leaned up on one elbow. Two slender figures were creeping away from the encampment and were quickly lost among the trees. She sat up, pulling sleep-tangled hair off her face. Rhodri was close by, also sitting up, watching the darkness into which the two shapes had vanished.

Seeing her eyes on him he smiled. She noticed that Blodwedd was not at his side, although she had been there when they had gone to sleep, curled up like a cat with his arm slung across her shoulders.

The humped shapes of the others were scattered in the small clearing. In the quiet, Branwen could hear slow, heavy breathing. Aberfa was snoring. The unsaddled horses stood together, their reins looped around branches to stop them from straying. There was no sign of Fain, but Branwen assumed he had found himself a perch somewhere close by.

Rhodri came crawling over to Branwen and sat huddled at her side.

"Blodwedd and Banon have gone hunting for some breakfast," he whispered to her. "Blodwedd said she could smell woodcocks. We should feast well before we depart—if you think we have the time to build a fire and roast a few small birds."

Branwen frowned. "Blodwedd doesn't mind killing birds to eat?" she asked.

"She's not squeamish where food is concerned," said Rhodri.

Branwen looked away, biting down on the thoughts that filled her mind.

I do not understand your feelings for her, Rhodri; but if the owl-girl gives you joy, then so be it. Who am I to judge the right and the wrong of it?

"What is it?" he asked softly. "What's on your mind?"

She turned and looked into his eyes. "Things were simpler when it was just the two of us," she whispered. "The more people . . . the more chance there is of conflict, it seems to me."

"That's always true," said Rhodri. "And also the more hope of fellowship and amity, not to mention the strength that we gain from our companions. And where we're going, we'll need their fighting strength, Branwen." He gave her a crooked smile. "I have the gift of healing, and I'm strong enough if you want a tree felled or a field plowed; but we're heading into unfriendly territory, and swords will be needed unless the luck of the pooka travels with us."

She looked sideways at him. "You wouldn't wish for maybe one less sword, though?"

"Iwan is a loudmouth and a mischief maker," Rhodri said without rancor, understanding immediately whom Branwen meant. "But I've suffered worse abuse than any he can throw at me, and he has fighting skills that we cannot afford to lose."

"I don't know why he needs to challenge people the way he does," Branwen murmured. "He has no need to be so quarrelsome and arrogant."

"You heard what he said yesterday; it is his nature to behave like that."

"No, I don't think it is," Branwen said under her breath. "I think in his heart he is quite different. He angers me so much at times. And yet . . . every now and then . . ." She paused, suddenly aware that she was about to speak aloud things that she had not even voiced clearly in her own mind.

"Every now and then . . . ?" Rhodri prompted.

She shrugged. "I don't know," she muttered. "I don't know what I was going to say." She stretched and yawned. "It's almost dawn," she said briskly. "Let's make up a fire to welcome back our two hunters. We do all deserve a good meal before we ride headlong into a forest of Saxon swords."

She stood up and glanced around at the sleepers under their cloaks.

One face was turned toward her. One pair of eyes was open.

Iwan was watching her; and for a fleeting moment in the darkness she saw on his face an expression that both thrilled and alarmed her with its raw intensity.

But then his shoulder hunched, and he tucked his head down into his cloak again.

8

"**B**RANWEN, I FEEL a great sadness in you. Does the burden of leadership weigh heavy?"

Blodwedd's voice brought Branwen up out of a deep reverie. They were riding together on Stalwyn in order to give Rhodri's horse some respite from carrying two riders. Iwan was now doubling with Linette for the same reason, while the rest of them paused and changed every now and then to relieve the other horses.

They had left the mountains and the forests behind, and they were now passing through the rough and tumble of Cyffin Tir—the cantref of Branwen's dead father and widowed mother, the land of her home.

The sun was high in a sky marbled with white cloud. A warm breeze ruffled the heather and set the grasses hissing. All about them were raw, bony hills and steep-sided valleys sparkling with swift white streams. Birds sliced the sky like arrowheads. Insects darted and droned.

All so familiar to Branwen. And yet . . .

"I was thinking of my mother," Branwen replied, her voice soft and melancholy. She looked into the south. Somewhere, hidden in the folds of the untamable landscape, lay the solitary hill of Garth Milain, with the burned shards of the citadel of Lord Griffith and Lady Alis upon its crown.

Gazing into the distance, Branwen almost believed she could smell the acrid smoke drifting in the air, although she knew it must be only in her imagination. The charred timbers were long cold now; and under her warrior-mother's formidable will, it was even possible that reconstruction had already begun.

"And thinking of your mother makes you sad?" asked Blodwedd.

Branwen paused, not sure how to answer this. "Thinking of her gives me strength," she said at last. "Not knowing when I shall see her again makes me very sad."

"You would be with her if you could?" asked Blodwedd.

"Of course I would. I think of her and of my poor dead father and of my brother, Geraint, all the time." A catch came into her throat as images of her shattered family swam into her mind. She lowered her voice so that it was no more than a whisper. "I will tell you this, Blodwedd, for your ears alone. If not for the fact that I am given no time to dwell on what I have lost—no time to grieve for my slain father and brother, no time to mourn my stolen life—I believe I would have lost my wits by now; truly I do."

Branwen found herself wondering why she had confided such a private thing to the owl-girl—a thing she would have hesitated to say aloud even to trustworthy Rhodri. It surprised her how much their relationship had changed. Perhaps it was because Blodwedd was part of the destiny that was driving her ever onward. Perhaps because Blodwedd would not judge her in human terms. Or perhaps because Blodwedd had also been torn from her former life by forces beyond her control. And in the owl-girl's case, that was a severance that would never be healed. In order to bring the aid of Govannon of the wood to Branwen in the battle of Gwylan Canu, Blodwedd had sacrificed her true shape and given up forever the twilight world she had always known.

"Do not tell Rhodri of these things," Branwen murmured. "I know he has seen me weak and indecisive, but he now needs me to be strong and resolute—as do all of the people who follow me. What faith would they have in our cause if I hesitate and falter?"

"I need it also." Blodwedd sighed. "For if you fall, what purpose do *I* have in this twilight life?"

"I won't fall!" This was spoken for reassurance, not out of conceit.

The approaching clop of hooves and jangle of harnesses made Branwen turn her head. Iwan was closing in on her, Linette's slender, pale arms twined around his waist, her light brown hair shining in the sun, and her eyes bright. The thought flickered across Branwen's mind that she did not need to cling quite so tightly to him, nor take such pleasure in the intimacy of riding tandem with him. But then he *was* the heir to Gwylan Canu—quite a catch for any maiden.

"Are we close to the border now, Branwen?" Iwan asked.

"Hmmm?" Distracted for a moment: Linette was slender and pretty—what young man would not wish to have her arms wrapped around him?

"Have we reached Mercia yet?" Iwan said. "You know these lands better than any of us. Do we need to be stealthier now?"

"We are close," said Branwen, dragging her thoughts back to the moment. She pointed ahead. "See that ridge of high land? That is where Cyffin Tir ends and the great plain of Saxon Mercia begins. But we should be safe from prying eyes for a while—and Fain is on the wing. He will spy out danger before it comes upon us."

"But Mercia is a vast land, from what I have heard," said Linette. "Did Merion give you no token to help you in your search?"

"None save that Caradoc is captive of a one-eyed man, and that his prison will be marked by a lynx," said Branwen.

The others had caught up with them by now: Dera and Rhodri riding solo, Aberfa and Banon mounted together close behind.

"Did you not tell us that Caradoc's jailer was a one-eyed *warrior*?" Dera asked. "A man that you would know on sight?"

"So Merion told me," said Branwen. "But I don't see how that can be."

"Could he be someone you met in battle?" asked Banon.

"I've encountered many Saxons at sword point," said Branwen. "But none that I'd remember. They all look alike to me: savage, pale-eyed brutes with bristling beards and foul breath."

"And yet Merion said he was a warrior," said Rhodri. "And when they are not on the march, the Saxon army is encamped outside the town of Chester. Might he be there?"

"How would I know that?" Branwen retorted, frustrated for a moment that she was unable to answer these questions.

"The Saxons are probably in some disarray," added Iwan. "The defeat at Gwylan Canu and the death of General Ironfist would be known to them by now. This could be the perfect opportunity to use those white crystals of yours, Branwen, and to slip in among them and learn all that we can of their intentions. That way we would be doing Merion's bidding, and thwarting King Oswald's plans of conquest at the same time."

"And Chester is a great meeting of the ways, Branwen," Dera added. "Even if your one-eyed warrior is not there, in the streets of that old town we may learn news enough to send us on the right track."

"And we may meet up again with Gavan and his merry troop," said Iwan. "Were they not heading for the army camp outside Chester?"

"They were," said Branwen. "But we should avoid contact with them if they are there. Gavan would have no sympathy for our cause, and I'd not have our mission put into jeopardy by the likes of Bryn and his blundering friends!"

"The camp is huge," said Rhodri. "Far larger even than Doeth Palas. Many thousands of warriors are mustered there. We should have no trouble avoiding Gavan ap Huw."

"Chester, then?" Branwen said thoughtfully. "Yes, why not? The town lies little more than half a day's ride from the borders of Cyffin Tir, across a wasteland of forest and marsh." She looked up at the sun. "We could be there before nightfall, if all goes well." She straightened her back. "To Chester, then," she said. "Into the very mouth of the wolf!"

In truth, Branwen knew little of the lands into which they were encroaching—and all that she did know had been picked up from listening to old men and warriors swapping tales around the fire in the Great Hall of Garth Milain.

In her mind, Mercia was a land under perpetual nightfall—a land swarming with evil, a land of cold iron and fierce, savage people who looked upon Brython with hate-filled, envious eyes.

As a child, she had once joined in a rat hunt in the storage barns. The men had hunted the vermin by torchlight in deep evening. How old had she been? Five, six maybe—in among the legs of the tall men of Garth Milain, clutching a stick to beat at the filthy creatures. She had gone with the men into the back of a barn. A wooden winnowing pallet had been thrown aside—and a writhing and squirming nest of rats had been revealed! Branwen had never forgotten the disgusting, revolting sight; and that memory of the squealing and moiling rats had become over the years linked to all she had heard about the Saxons.

Rats and Saxons—they were one and the same.

Branwen remembered how she had screamed and beaten at the rats with her stick, frightened and enraged and sickened by them, lashing out wildly as the vile creatures had scattered in all directions—flooding through the legs of the hunters, tumbling and slithering, screaming as their backs were broken and their skulls were pulped. She remembered how the maimed and the injured rats had jerked in their death throes, all bloody and twisted and burst open on the ground.

A small fragment of the loathing and anger that she had felt came back to Branwen as she led her small band of followers beyond the lands she knew and into enemy territory.

Rats and Saxons.

Saxons and rats.

One and the same.

Deserving only of servitude or death.

And so, with Branwen's mind filled with such unpleasant images, they passed out of Powys and rode with heightened vigilance into the land of Mercia.

"Is that Fain?" Banon's long arm shot out, her finger pointing to a dot that wheeled just above the eastern horizon.

"I hope so," said Branwen, peering into the watery blue sky. "It's time he returned."

The falcon had been gone for a long while now, and Branwen was becoming worried that some Saxon bowman had shot him out of the sky. It had not been so long ago that she had thought him dead, and some of that anxiety remained.

The black shape floated above a forest of dark, glossy-leafed alders that spread itself out across a wide, shallow valley. Branwen's band had come to the eastern edge of a final hill, and in front of them the land dropped gently down to a seemingly endless plain.

From here Branwen could see far out to a blue haze where land and sky met. It was a strangely smooth land; it had no real headlands or ridges—no bones showing through its green and lush flesh—just a gently undulating ocean of moors and forest and peaceful, untilled lowlands empty of human life.

Odd. She had expected something different. A pall of darkness over the land? A countryside where rats might swarm in their thousands? Something less . . . *benign*?

"That's no falcon," said Blodwedd, her hands on Branwen's shoulders as she leaned forward to watch the solitary bird. Her fingers tightened, her nails digging in. "It's a raven," she said, her voice suddenly harsh. "And very large for its kind."

"A bird of ill omen," muttered Aberfa.

"Hush now," said Banon, seated in front of her. "It's but a bird."

"You do not understand," said Aberfa. "A wise woman spoke over my cradle when I was newborn. She told my mother that she should beware ravens if she wished to keep me from harm."

"Your mother is the greatest teller of tall tales in all of Gwylan Canu, and you know it!" Banon said. "Like as not she made up the whole thing to prevent you from straying."

"Think you so?" Aberfa said dubiously.

"I am sure of it."

"Ill omened or not, it is coming this way," said Rhodri, staring into the sky. "And Blodwedd is right—it's a mighty, big bird."

The raven climbed the sky, flying toward them but rising always higher until it was far above their heads, a threatening black cruciform shape cruising the air on stilled wings.

"There's evil in that creature," said Blodwedd, straining her neck to stare up at the slowly circling raven. "Deep, old evil."

Branwen didn't know about evil, but she did have the feeling that the bird's eyes were peering down at them. They were all staring up at the raven now, their eyes wide as though they had been transfixed by its appearance.

"It's watching us," hissed Dera. "Can't you feel it?"

"It's no ordinary bird, that's for sure," said Linette. "What do you think it wants?"

"The tales told by the Saxons say that Skur is always accompanied by a raven," Rhodri reminded them. "A raven named Mumir."

"The saints protect us!" murmured Banon.

"I'd test its mettle were it a little closer," said Iwan. "I'd launch an arrow, and we'd soon know if it had the protection of a heathen godling!"

The raven circled them, high above the reach of bow or slung stone. Branwen felt its presence like a spike driving into her mind. The tension made the air ring in her ears. A pain grew behind her eyes. Still she couldn't look away. It was as though the world had come to a halt—as though time was standing still, and nothing more would ever happen unless the oppressive attention of the steadily wheeling bird could be broken.

It *had* to be broken!

But the air was as thick as tree sap, and her limbs were leaden.

Summoning all her willpower, Branwen drew her sword and brandished it in the air.

"Do you see me?" she shouted up at the raven. "Do you know who I am? If you mean us no harm, then go about your business; but if you're a demon come to spy on us, return to your master and tell him we do not fear him! Tell him we are coming!"

A single, harsh croak sounded from above as though in reply to her challenge. Then the wide black wings flapped, and the raven sped down from the sky toward the forest.

Around her, the others gasped for breath and stared at one another as though they'd all snapped out of the same dark dream.

"Well!" breathed Iwan, giving a crooked smile as he looked at Branwen. "I will say this for you, barbarian princess, you don't shrink from defying the Saxon war-gods!"

Branwen gasped in relief as all the tension and the pressure was suddenly gone from her head. "Why should I?" she replied, filled with a sudden brash conviction. "I have my own protectors." She slapped the reins to get Stalwyn moving again. "And I have a great destiny!" she called back as her tall bay stallion went cantering down the hillside. "Didn't you realize, Iwan ap Madoc—I'm going to save the whole of Brython!"

Once out on the plain, she urged Stalwyn to a full gallop. Blodwedd's arms were as tight as vines around Branwen's waist, and the wind was shrill in her ears and cold and fierce in her eyes. A kind of madness was in her head, seething through her as rich as blood, clouding her mind and setting a wild fire in her heart.

She knew not from where this sudden frenzy had come, nor did she care as she utterly surrendered herself to it. The feeling was overwhelming and glorious! She felt as though with a tug of the reins she could foil the pull of the earth and lift Stalwyn up into the sky, to go galloping above the forest roof, up and up into the vault of the heavens until she might reach the sun itself and strike its disk with the blade of her sword as though beating a great golden gong!

She heard whoops and cries and the thunder of hooves as her followers came careering down off the hill, chasing headlong after her as she hurtled toward the forest.

"Branwen, what rash action is this?" gasped Blodwedd, her face netted by Branwen's whipping hair. "If a servant of Ragnar awaits us in yonder forest, we should approach him with care and caution, not rush at him like leaves in an autumn gale!"

"No!" shouted Branwen against the wind. "No care! No caution! If Skur is here, I will fight him even if Wotan himself, the father of all Saxon war-gods, stands over him!"

"What of our other mission: to find Caradoc?" gasped Blodwedd.

"What of it?" howled Branwen. She glanced briefly back at Blodwedd. "I must do battle with Skur! Don't you see?" She panted. "I *have* to know!"

"To know what, Branwen?" exclaimed Blodwedd.

"To know if I truly am the Emerald Flame of my people!" Branwen replied. "I have to prove it one way or the other. Kill or be killed! It's the only way!"

"And if Skur is there and you kill him?" asked Blodwedd. "What then?"

"Then I will become the thing that Gavan feared!" Branwen shouted. "All doubts will be gone, and I will know that I am Branwen of the Old Gods! Branwen of the Shining Ones!"

9

SLOWING STALWYN TO a canter, then to a trot, and finally to a snorting walk, Branwen led the others into the forest of alder trees. The wild abandon of her madness had faded, but her resolve was unyielding; it burned in her mind like a sword forged in white fire—firm and fierce and deadly.

Skur *had* to be real—and she *had* to fight him and defeat him.

The mythical Viking warrior's death would not only prove to *her* that she truly was a hero capable of saving Brython, but it would also send a warning through Mercia, and through her homeland—a grim portent to the Saxons and a rallying call for her own people.

Attack us at your peril! We are not easy prey! You will never defeat us!

"Tell me more about Ragnar," Branwen asked Blodwedd. "I'd know what powers he has."

"I know little of him," said Blodwedd. "Save that he is one of the fiends who huddle in Wotan's grim shadow. A god of deep darkness, I believe—and of trickery and malice and cruelty. I know of only one tale in which he features. He was challenged to an eating contest by the great giant Laufey. The winner was to be the one who could first devour one hundred humans. Laufey ate quickly, and soon all of his victims were consumed down to their bones. But Ragnar turned himself into flame and devoured the hundred, flesh, blood, and bone! Wotan declared Ragnar the victor, and Laufey was condemned to be tied to a rock and to have the corrosive venom of a poisonous snake dripped down upon his head for all eternity."

Branwen pondered this tale as they rode on. How things change! A few short moons ago she would have found this story an amusing and diverting piece of nonsense. A tall tale to be told around the fire on a winter's night. A tale of things that never really were and never could have been.

But these days she had no such confidence in what was real and what was not—no such certainty that demons and gods did not walk the world under the summer sun. The Old Powers were awakening from their long slumber. For good or for bad, things would never be the same again.

A flurry of wings suddenly filled Branwen's eyes. *"Caw! Caw! Caw!"*

Grinning, she raised her arm, and Fain came to rest on her wrist. "Where have you been, you truant!" she scolded gently, running a finger lightly over his chest feathers. "Do you not care how I worry over you?"

"Caw! Caw! Caw!"

"He has seen something in the wood," exclaimed Blodwedd, her words taking Branwen by surprise.

"Enemies?" asked Iwan, riding closer.

Fain gave voice to more harsh cries. Blodwedd listened intently, her head cocked to one side, her brows drawn down.

"Two people," Blodwedd translated. "A man and a woman. The man is huge—seven feet tall or more—and he carries a great double-headed battle-ax. He rides a mighty horse. His hair is the color of corn, and he is armed and armored with chain mail and with leather. The woman has long fair hair. She is on foot—tied by the wrists and held to the man by a rope knotted about his saddle."

"The raven," asked Rhodri. "What of the raven?"

Fain cried again.

"Yes, there is a raven," Blodwedd said. "It perches upon the man's shoulder and speaks into his ear." She looked at Branwen. "Fain says he has never seen such a bird before."

"Mumir!" breathed Dera. "So—Skur is real, and he is close by with a captive servant to do his bidding."

Her eyes narrowed. "What are we to do, Branwen? You must decide."

"Where are they?" Branwen asked Blodwedd.

"Not far from here," said Blodwedd. "Fain says that we are fast approaching a deep furrow in the land, like a channel cut by a long-dried river. The valley runs north to south athwart our path. The man and the woman are there."

"Heading this way?" asked Branwen eagerly.

"No. Their route will take them away from us."

"We can avoid them," said Rhodri. "There is no purpose in looking for a fight when we can quietly slip past them and go freely on our way." He looked anxiously at Branwen. "Don't we have danger enough ahead of us?" he asked. "Let others worry about Skur Bloodax."

"Mumir will have already told him of us," said Iwan. "He must know that we are coming this way. But will the raven know who we are—and what our purpose is in Mercia?"

"We must assume he *does* know," said Linette. "Why else did he watch us as he did?"

Aberfa shivered. "I can still feel the raven's wicked eyes upon me!" she said grimly. "And I do not forget my mother's warning!"

Branwen frowned. All eyes were upon her. "I agree that we are known to Mumir and his master," she said at last. "But I believe this meeting was destined to come! I have felt certain of it ever since the raven first appeared." She straightened her back. "I will fight Skur," she said. "News of his death will send a chill through the Saxon kingdoms." She set her jaw. "I will fight him alone! One on one!"

"While I draw breath and blade you will not!" exclaimed Dera. "I shall be at your side. Skur is protected by a god, Branwen!"

Branwen glared at her. "And am I not?"

"The Shining Ones cannot come to you here," said Blodwedd. "They are tied to their own lands." She shook her head. "Do not look for their help, Branwen. You are not in Brython now; Govannon of the Wood will not be able to save you when all seems lost as he did at Gwylan Canu."

Troubled by Blodwedd's words, Branwen looked at the others. She could see that all of them were determined to stand with her, come what may.

"We fight together," said Aberfa. "That is the way of it."

"But what tactics do we use?" asked Banon. "If Skur is protected by a god, how shall we come upon him unseen? We will be blasted by bolts of fire before we can draw our swords."

"My hope is that Ragnar will have limited power this far from his home," said Blodwedd. "He is able to enter this land by the leave of the Saxon war-gods, but the heart of his strength lies far away across the cold North Sea. It is the strong arm and sharp iron of Skur that we should fear, not the devilry of Ragnar."

"Fain will guide us," said Branwen. "We will set ourselves in Skur's path and see what comes! Rhodri, this will be sword against ax; and brave as you are, I wouldn't have you come into harm's way. When we attack, I want you to try and free the captive woman. Protect her if you can. Will you do that?"

"I will," said Rhodri. "But one day when we have time to pause in this pell-mell destiny of yours, Branwen, I'd be given some lessons in swordsmanship."

"That would be *my* pleasure," said Iwan. "If we survive this morning's entertainments . . . and if you have the heart to face me across the length of two swords, Master Runaway."

"If the one event proves true, the other will certainly come to pass," said Rhodri. "And in time it may even be that I will be able to teach you to use my right name, Iwan ap Madoc!"

The landscape of the deep forest was as Fain had described. Branwen and her band turned to the right, heading southeast by the sun, intending to come into the valley and to find some auspicious place where they could waylay the Viking warrior.

It was not long before the land began to dip under their horses' hooves, dropping in folds to a narrow defile thick with ferns that foamed about their horses' hocks like a green ocean.

"Do we lie in ambush or make a stand in the open?" asked Dera.

"There's little point in hiding," Banon said uneasily, pointing ahead. "Look there! In yonder tree. We are observed!" They followed the line of her finger to a tall tree on the slope of the valley leaning inward among many others.

It was a few moments before Branwen's eyes found the object of Banon's concern. A large black bird, perching in the underbranches, its head low, its eyes glittering as it stared at them.

"Mumir!" said Dera. She turned to Branwen. "I begin to think you were right, Branwen; I think your destiny has led us here. How else would that creature know where to lurk in wait?"

Even as she spoke, the raven took heavily to the air and silently flew away under the arching branches. Branwen watched until the forest swallowed him.

"We shall wait here," Branwen said, swinging down from the saddle. "The horses should be taken out of harm's way, and we will fight on foot."

She gave a few brief orders, instructing Aberfa and Banon to lead the horses away from the intended field of conflict, then sending Rhodri and Blodwedd up into the trees, ready to leap out and rescue the captive woman once the others had engaged Skur in battle. She stood ready in the middle of the valley, the ferns flowing around her knees, her shield up and her sword gleaming in her hand.

Iwan was at her right side, his sword sheathed, his shield slung over his back, an arrow ready on the bow. Banon was at his elbow, peering along the valley, nervously plucking the string of her bow. The sound was a bright, hopeful note in the low rustling and creaking of the forest.

Aberfa was on Branwen's left, a throwing javelin in her fist, two more thrust headfirst into the ground at her feet. Beside her were Dera and Linette, their faces grim behind their shields, their knuckles white around sword hilts.

And so they waited.

A fly buzzed in Branwen's face. She brushed it aside, annoyed to have her concentration broken by the errant insect. She needed to focus—to channel every fiber of her being into the coming fight.

The air was oppressively hot under the arching branches. Branwen felt sweat trickle down her back, and there was moisture on her top lip and forehead although her mouth was bone-dry. The trees loomed around them like spectators anxious for mayhem. Her eyes ached with staring along the valley. Her heart drummed in her chest.

"Will he never come?" murmured Dera. "He must know we are here! Why does he not show himself?"

"He'll come," said Iwan. "He sends fear ahead of him on the air. Hold steady! He'll come!"

Fear on the air. Yes, Iwan was right about that. The tension among them strained tighter than his bowstring, and with every beat of her heart Branwen felt the anxiety growing in her.

Come! By all the saints, come now!

A sudden sharp crackling sound came rippling along the valley—like a wind ruffling the ferns.

"What is that?" whispered Dera.

Then they saw it, a narrow red line moving arrow-swift through the vale, blackening and shriveling the ferns, sizzling like . . .

Iwan shot his bow into the running stream of red flame. The arrow was engulfed.

Branwen only just had time to lift up her shield to her face as the fire hit them. She was aware of heat and flickering light, and of her companions falling back, shouting and stumbling away from her.

But although the flames were all around her, she was not burned by them. They circled her, spreading to push the others back, leaving her standing alone in a blackened ring of scorched ferns. She was blinded by thick smoke. There was hot, searing air in her nose and throat. She stared into the gray murk, her eyes stinging and watering.

Something was coming!

The smoke began to whirl, coiling upward into the high branches—and then Branwen saw her enemy!

Skur stood before her—towering over her like a hill. His face was as pale and lean as bone, his eyes like dead blue pebbles under his knuckled brows, his mouth lost in a great bush of a beard. Thick yellow hair flowed from beneath a conical helmet of riveted iron. His shield was as large as a mill wheel, decorated with spokes of yellow and black, centered by a great boss of blue iron. He wore a tunic of red leather studded with iron rings. In his massive right hand he gripped the handle of his great double-headed battle-ax, its twin blades as wide as Branwen's shoulders.

"Greetings, Warrior Child." His voice was like thunder in her belly. "I am come to destroy you and to open the path to Brython's beating heart!" His cold blue eyes flashed. "But I am not without mercy, child—surrender to me and I will spare your life. Lay down your arms and kneel and kiss my foot, and you shall not die this day! What say you?"

Branwen let out a scream of pure rage as she flung herself at the giant Viking warrior. No quarter, no mercy—before this day's sun went down, one of them would be dead.

10

SKUR WAS A huge man, his chest like a barrel, his
arms and legs muscled like the boughs of great
trees. Branwen's plan was to surprise him with her
speed and agility—to leap high, to lift her sword arm
above the rim of his shield, and to thrust her blade
into his unprotected neck and down through flesh,
bone, and sinew to his heart. A single swift blow to
sudden victory.

*Such a creature will be slow to react and ponderous
in his movements. I shall destroy him before he can even
swing his ax!*

She heard the others shouting encouragement as
she sprang into the air. But Skur was quicker than she
expected; he stepped nimbly aside and struck at her
with his shield. The iron boss of the shield punched
into her stomach, doubling her up and sending her
crashing to the ground.

Her sword was jarred from her hand as she sprawled on her face. The pain in her belly was numbing and all consuming, making it hard for her even to draw breath. But instinct took over from thought, and her will to survive outweighed her agony. She squirmed onto her back clutching her shield in both hands, holding it over herself as the battle-ax came plunging down. The impact split the shield in two, sending a shock of pain through her arms and shoulders. But she was able to twist to one side so that the head of the ax sank into the ground a hairbreadth from her head.

Snarling and with muscles bulging, the great warrior struggled to wrench the blade of his ax from the hard earth.

Discarding the riven shield, Branwen writhed away from the stooping warrior and rolled across the ground to where her sword lay among the ferns. She snatched it up and sprang to her feet—but the agony in her belly betrayed her. She cried out in pain, clutching at her stomach, unable to stand upright.

Skur wrenched his ax from the ground and turned toward her, his face absolutely expressionless as he hefted the deadly weapon and strode forward.

"Branwen!" It was Iwan's voice, a frantic cry. "Branwen, run!"

Panting hard from the pain, she ventured a quick glance around. She and Skur were within a scorched ring of leaping fire. Where could she run? She was trapped unless she ran headlong into the flames.

She could vaguely make out the faces of her followers through the fire. Even as she looked, Aberfa hurled a javelin into the wall of flame. It flared white-hot and was consumed in an instant. Banon and Iwan were shooting arrow after futile arrow into the fire—none survived in it.

Screaming in rage and frustration, Dera was beating at the flames with her sword; but the fire held her back—as it held all of them back.

Branwen had wanted to fight Skur alone.

Now she had her wish.

She stumbled backward, bent over, one arm cradling her stomach, her sword shaking in her fist. Skur moved forward, the ax scything slowly to and fro in front of him, his face disturbingly tranquil, as though he were simply sweeping grass out of his path as he strolled through the forest. He hardly even looked at her.

He doesn't fear me at all. This is sport to him. Less than sport. The swatting of a fly.

The ax cut a lazy arc at head level, and Branwen only just managed to duck down and painfully scurry to the side to avoid it. She had her back to the wall of flame now. She could feel its heat on her shoulders, and her ears were filled with the roar and crackle of burning.

She edged sideways, putting more space between her and the huge warrior, circling him, getting her breath back, struggling to master the pain.

She had been a fool to fling herself at him like

that. She remembered what Gavan ap Huw had told her as they had sparred in the forest outside Doeth Palas. The old warrior had agreed to teach her the basics of battle. She had not done well.

Do not let your emotions rule you. The blood may be hot, but the mind must be always cool.

Her impetuous attack on Skur Bloodax had cost her dearly: she was hurt, and her shield was gone. Now she had to be calm and wise and cunning.

"Branwen! Hoi!" Aberfa's voice. A wild cry. Branwen glanced toward the sound, seeing the powerful girl hurl a javelin up and over the wall of flame. It arced and dipped and came down point first in the ground only a few steps away from Branwen. "Use it well!" Aberfa howled through the fire. "All the others are lost!"

Branwen darted forward, transferring her sword to her left hand. She ripped the javelin from the ground, spinning on one heel and raising her arm high, the javelin poised for the throw.

Skur lifted his shield to his blank eyes, the blue irises like ice, fathomless and impenetrable. Branwen feinted a throw. The eyes blinked and the shield was pushed forward. She almost forgot the pain in her belly as she danced sideways around the huge warrior, making him turn to keep his shield between him and the threatening javelin, jerking her arm every few moments so he could not be sure whether she was going to throw or not.

"The eye! Go for the eye!" that was Dera's voice.

Others were shouting their encouragement now as Branwen bounded around the ring of fire; but she blotted out their voices. She had to concentrate—she had to *think*.

Use your agility and your speed.

Gavan had told her that. Against power and weight, use agility and speed.

Branwen paused, breathing hard, faking weariness. Skur sensed his moment. He lunged forward, bringing down his ax like a lightning strike. Branwen stumbled sideways, the ground trembling from the blow. She fell to one knee; but the fall was planned, and her muscles were taut and ready. The arm rose and came down again, the biceps as thick as Branwen's thigh, the veins standing out like tree roots.

Branwen sprang up and jabbed the javelin down into Skur's outstretched arm. It pierced the flesh, sending the blood spraying. She leaned in on the long shaft, forcing the barbed point deeper, through flesh and muscle, until it emerged through his skin again in a gush of blood.

Roaring with pain, the Viking lashed out at her with his shield. But she was ready for him this time. Releasing the javelin, she snatched hold of the leather shield rim and rode the shield high into the air, her feet kicking, her fingers clinging on. She managed to bring up one foot onto the shield boss, using it to boost herself higher. And now she made her final move.

Pressing down hard on the shield with her hand

and her foot, she released her straining muscles and flung herself into the air. She twisted like a salmon, throwing her sword from her left hand to her right and using all the power of her arm and shoulder to cut downward as she leaped over her enemy.

The sword jolted in her hand as it hacked through the humped sinews at the base of his neck. Blood splashed high as she lost impetus and fell.

She landed behind him, coming down hard, bending her legs and turning her body so that she rolled over three times before coming to a halt perilously close to the surging wall of fire.

"Finish him, Branwen!" Dera's voice again. "Take my shield! Finish him now!" And so saying, Dera flung her shield high over the fire.

Branwen scrambled to her feet, a little dizzy and aching from her tumble but eager now to take advantage of first blood. Skur was staggering and roaring, still facing away from her, his wounded arm red to the elbow, blood cascading down his back from the wide gash in his neck.

Dera's shield spun against the dappled roof of leaves. Branwen stretched up, reaching for it with her left hand. But a black shape came careening out of nowhere, crashing into the flying shield, sending it whirling into the wall of flames, where it ignited and vanished.

"*Ragghh! Raggghhh!*" Mumir's cries tore the air as the bird banked and turned in a tight circle, his black eyes filled with rage as he flew into Branwen's face.

She fell back, her hands up to protect her eyes. She felt the sharp beak stabbing at her, the claws raking her skin. Hiding her face in the crook of her arm, she swung wildly and blindly at the bird with her sword arm. The raven's claws ripped at her hair, and the beak stabbed painfully at her head; and all the time the thrash of his wings was in her ears, and the raucous shriek of his voice pierced her brain.

And then there was another voice in her head, as wild and harsh and angry as the raven's—but this time it was a voice she knew well.

"Caw! Caw! Caw!"

Mumir's attack ceased abruptly, and Branwen was able to take her arm from her face. Fain and the raven were fighting in the air in a flurry of black and gray—beaks pecking, claws scrabbling, their wings no more than a blur as they rose higher into the trees.

"Fain! Be careful!" Branwen howled as the two birds became caught up in the branches and the desperate fight was lost behind a curtain of trembling leaves.

But it was a sound from much closer that made Branwen spin around. The sound of breath rattling in a throat.

Skur was looming over her, his face twisted with pain, his eyes burning. He had snapped off the javelin so that only the iron point was left, impaling his arm. He had dropped his shield and he was holding

107

up the huge battle-ax in both hands, the blood of his wound raining down as he balanced himself for the killing blow.

Branwen threw herself forward as the ax hurtled down. And as she came in under the blow, she gripped her sword in both hands and thrust upward into Skur's exposed belly.

Branwen put all her weight behind the thrust. The blade ripped through the red leather of Skur's tunic, scraping against the iron rings. The sword drove in to the hilt and Branwen went with it, her face crushed against the iron rings, the dark blood gushing out over her, thick and hot in her nostrils.

Pushed back by the force of her blow, Skur was lifted upright, his hands loosened from the hilt of his battle-ax, his mouth open in a bellow of mortal agony. For a moment he stood on his two feet, balanced, his head thrown back, his face to the sky.

Then, like a lightning-struck tree, he fell, crashing down onto his back, pulling Branwen helplessly along with him, her fingers still gripping her sword hilt.

She stood up, her hands slippery with his blood, the rusty iron smell of it filling her head. He was not dead. His chest rose and fell convulsively, the breath grinding and gurgling in his throat.

"Branwen!" She heard her name being shouted from all sides. "Branwen!" She stared dazedly around herself, hardly aware of what was happening. Then she saw that the wall of fire was gone and that her friends were running forward.

"*Caw! Caaaw!*" Fain came wheeling down from the canopy of branches, his feathers bloodied, his beak and claws dripping gore, but his voice triumphant. Of Mumir the raven there was no sign. Vanquished or fled, the evil old bird was no longer a threat.

Skur Bloodax gave a final great cry. Blood gouted thick and black from his mouth. His chest sank a final time. His eyes emptied of life.

The battle was over.

Ragnar's fire was quenched. His servant was dead.

Branwen arched her back, her arms spreading wide, her face to the sky, her mouth opening in a feral howl of victory.

She heard the voices of her followers as they gathered around her.

"Bran-*wen*! Bran-*wen*!"

The world was bathed all in red, as though a layer of thick gore clung to every surface, every shape and form. And it was inside her, too—the black blood boiling in her brain, the battle-lust running like madness through her veins.

"I am Branwen!" she shouted to the sky. "I am the Emerald Flame of my people! The Bright Blade! The Sword of Destiny!" Her voice rose to a scream. "Look on me and tremble, gods of the Saxons! You cannot stand against me! I am Branwen—Branwen of the Shining Ones!"

11

"BRANWEN? ARE YOU all right?"

Branwen hardly heard the voice as she stood exultant on the field of victory. Skur was dead, and she was sheathed from head to foot in his blood. It drummed in her brain and filled her eyes and glutted her to the very marrow of her bones. All the world was steeped in blood. There was nothing else—nothing but hot, smoking blood and the joy of the spilling of it: the glee in carnage, the overpowering glory of meting out death.

"Branwen?"

Another voice. Familiar. Concerned.

A face swam into view through the veil of running blood.

"Get back!" Branwen howled, swinging her sword. "Get away from me! Don't touch me!"

The figures surrounding her bounded back from her blade. Voices cried out in alarm and fear.

"Branwen—have you lost your wits?"

"Branwen—it is *us*!"

"Your friends!"

She snarled, seeing only more victims through the red haze. She delighted in the weight of the sword in her hands. She wanted nothing more than to sink the sharp blade into more flesh.

"She is mad!"

"It's the battle-frenzy—I have seen it before." One form stepped toward her. "Branwen?" She knew that voice. A calm voice. A voice calling her back from the Underworld. "Branwen—it's done. It's all over."

Her body was bursting with power and blood-lust. She was no longer human. She was a god now! A god of bloodletting and warfare. Freed from the shackles of humanity. Free to unleash slaughter through the world.

"Gently, now, Branwen. Gently now."

She blinked and stared at the figure through the red haze. Understanding dawned in the blood-soaked shambles of her mind.

"Rhodri?"

"Yes! It is I! Be calm, Branwen. It's over. The Viking is dead. All's well."

A hand closed around the wrist of her sword arm.

The pounding of blood in her head faded away. The crimson curtain fell from her eyes. She stared into Rhodri's worried face. She looked down at her sword arm. The blade was dripping blood, and there was blood caked over her hand and arm.

"Rhodri!" She dropped her sword and threw herself impulsively into his arms. He was a rock in the flood of her madness; he was an anchor in the swell; he was the only thing preventing her from being swept away on a brainsick tide of destruction.

"What happened to me?" She gasped, her face pressed into his chest.

His arms held her. "It was battle-fever," he said. "No more than that."

She looked up into his kind and compassionate face. "No. Something took hold of me, Rhodri," she breathed. "In my head—deep inside my head. Something that wanted to become me . . . or . . . or wanted me to become *it*! Something old and dreadful—something that enjoyed killing."

He dipped his head, his lips close to her ear. "Hush now!" he murmured. "You will scare the others with such talk. You are Branwen, still—*be* her!"

She looked into his eyes, fighting hard to gather together the scattered fragments of herself.

"Are you hurt, Branwen?" It was Iwan's voice.

She took a deep breath and pulled away from Rhodri. "I am not," she said. "A light-headedness took me, that was all." She turned and looked down at the gory corpse of Skur Bloodax, lying on its back in the ring of burned ferns. "So falls their great

112

champion," she said. "I would have the Saxons know of this victory."

"Aye, they should!" said Dera. "His severed head on a pole would do the trick!" She paced along his body, her sword ready.

"No, I'd take a less grisly trophy," said Branwen, looking away—heartsick now at the sight of so much spilled blood.

"His ax!" said Banon, running forward, gripping the great double-headed battle-ax with both hands and yanking its blade from the ground. "We should take his ax!" She hefted it in her hands. "By the saints! It's a heavy beast of a weapon! I can hardly lift it!"

"Arms like knotted twine you have!" said Aberfa with a slow smile, taking the huge battle-ax out of Banon's hands and swinging it around her head. "A worthy weapon for a champion," she said, bringing it to rest on her shoulder.

"And it has the mark we were told of," said Linette. "The raven in flight cut into the head. No Saxon seeing it will doubt that the Viking warrior is slain!"

Branwen looked at the engraving etched deep into the gray iron of the twin blades. It was Mumir to the very life: the wings spread wide, the eyes blazing, the claws extended, and the beak wide as though screaming defiance. A fine artist had done this work; and even though Skur was dead and the raven gone, the cruel image sent a shiver down Branwen's spine.

But it also brought something else to the forefront of her mind.

"Where is the woman he traveled with?" she asked, turning and staring along the valley. "And where is his horse?"

"We must find them," said Rhodri. "The woman may need our aid—and we shall at least have the pleasure of telling her that her master is dead."

"Rhodri, Blodwedd—come with me," said Branwen. "The rest of you, go fetch our horses. Strip this Viking of anything we may be able to make use of. The rest we will leave as carrion for the forest beasts to devour. Aberfa—keep charge of the ax for now, if you will." She looked up through the branches. The sun was halfway down the western sky. The day was wearing away. With Skur dead, she now had time to give thought to their other mission. "We have already been detained too long by this; I'd still have us in Chester ere nightfall, but we will need to travel more swiftly now, I think."

Blodwedd ran ahead of Branwen and Rhodri, racing lightly through the sea of ferns, her head turning from side to side, searching for some sign of the woman and the Viking's horse.

"Thank you," Branwen said quietly to Rhodri as they followed the owl-girl.

"For what?" Rhodri asked.

"For being yourself," Branwen replied. "For trusting that I was still your friend under all this gore."

"We have come through a lot, we two," Rhodri said. "Did you think I would lose faith in you?"

"Rhodri?" her voice was solemn now. "I truly felt that some power was trying to take my mind from me," she said. "What if Gavan was right—what if the Shining Ones are turning me into something . . . something other than human?"

"That will never happen," said Rhodri. "I will not allow it!"

"Really?" She was almost amused by this. "How would you prevent it?"

"Did I not tell you, Branwen?" he said, his eyes gleaming as he looked into her face. "I have gifts passed down the generations from my remote ancestors. The gift of healing for one, as you already know. And others I have not yet tested, I am sure." He arched an eyebrow. "I have Druid blood in me, Branwen."

She looked dubiously at him. "Rhodri . . . that cannot be true . . . !" So far as she knew, the Romans had eradicated the Druids five hundred or more years ago.

"It is true, or so my mother believed," he said. "I told you my father's kin farmed land by the sea in the west of Gwynedd, didn't I?"

"Yes, in Cefn Boudan—I remember. So?"

He smiled. "Cefn Boudan is but a short way by boat from the island of Ynis Môn—where the Druid priesthood made its last stand against the Roman legions in the ancient times. My kin fled the island

and renounced the old ways. But blood is blood, and I surely have powers enough in me to prevent you from turning to evil!"

Branwen stared at him, unsure whether he was telling her a true story or making up nonsense to take her mind off her troubles.

"How is it you never mentioned this before, Rhodri?" she asked, far from convinced.

"Why would I?" he replied. "The Druids worshipped the Old Gods, Branwen. You were at war with Rhiannon of the Spring when we met that second time in the forest outside Doeth Palas. You would not have wished to be my friend had you known I was descended from Druids, and I very much wished to be *your* friend." His eyes were cautious. "Only now that you have finally accepted the Shining Ones as your allies am I able to tell you the truth." He looked pensively at her. "Are we still to be friends?"

She frowned. "Do you have any other secrets I should know?"

"I hope not."

"Then we are friends." She shook her head. "And as for this Druid power you speak of—I'd say the blood of the Old Priesthood must have been thinned more than somewhat over the centuries, Rhodri. Were I you, I would not be too hopeful of working wonders in their name!"

"Perhaps you're right," he said. "In which case you will need to rely only on my friendship to save you if the battle-madness takes you again."

She smiled grimly. "That I *shall* do," she said. "And I would . . ."

"Here!" Blodwedd called, her voice breaking into Branwen's comments. "I see the steed!" The owl-girl had gone bounding away to the left, moving up into the trees that grew on the flanks of the valley. "And the captive human is here, too!"

They came upon the horse, tethered to a tree limb. He was a tall bay destrier—a powerful and muscular war-horse, black for the most part but with a white star on his forehead and feathery white hair around his fetlocks. His saddle was hung with leather and linen sacks, bulging with food and other provisions for the journey that Branwen's sword had cut short.

The captive was lying close by, bound hand and foot and with a linen gag wound around the lower half of her face. And she was a young woman, as Branwen now saw, but a few years older than Branwen herself.

Blodwedd knelt at the captive's side, stooping over her and untying the knots that held her gag. Branwen saw dread fill the young woman's eyes as she stared up into Blodwedd's face.

Of course! It was Blodwedd's inhuman eyes that filled the young woman with fear.

Branwen stepped forward. "Do not be afraid of her," she said. "She will do you no harm."

The young woman's eyes turned to Branwen just as the gag came loose.

She screamed, writhing on the ground as though straining desperately to get away despite the ropes that bound her wrists and ankles.

"Be calm!" Branwen said. "There's nothing to fear. Skur is dead—you are in no danger now!"

But the terrified captive just kept screaming, twisting and turning on the ground so that it was impossible for Blodwedd to work on the knotted ropes that held her.

"What is wrong with her?" Branwen asked, looking at Rhodri. "Is her mind gone? Has Skur destroyed her reason?"

"I suspect she thinks you are some demon from the depths of Annwn," Rhodri replied. "You are not a comforting sight, Branwen!"

"Oh!" Branwen looked down at herself. She was drenched in Skur's blood. It clung in thick clots in the folds of her clothes. It was sticky between her fingers. It clogged in her hair, gluing stray locks to her forehead and cheeks. It was on her lips, tasting and smelling of metal.

Yes, Rhodri was right—to the poor bound captive, she must look like something spewed up from the deepest pits of the Underworld!

"Blodwedd—come away," Branwen called. "We are scaring her. Let Rhodri minister to her."

As soon as Branwen and Blodwedd moved away from the young woman, she began to grow calmer, but her face was still full of panic, and her chest rose and fell rapidly as she stared at them with round, haunted eyes.

"I must find water to wash this filth off me," Branwen muttered.

Blodwedd lifted her head and snuffed the air. "I smell fresh water," she said. "Come away—I'll lead you to it."

"Look after her," Branwen called to Rhodri. Rhodri nodded, kneeling by the young woman's side. "There's nothing to fear now. You're among friends," Branwen heard him saying, his voice gentle and soothing.

Branwen followed Blodwedd along the steep slope of the valley side. The owl-girl seemed to have an unerring notion of where she was going, and it was not long at all before Branwen heard the first silvery chime of trickling water.

It was a small spring, cascading down a mossy rock face and splashing into a natural bowl formed by a hollowed stone. From there the pool of clear dancing water spilled over a green lip of rock and soaked away into the boggy ground.

Branwen knelt, scooping up the water in both hands. It was cold, but it felt good to splash it on her face and to feel the gore being washed away.

While Branwen cleansed herself, Blodwedd climbed onto a high point of rock above the spring and squatted there, gazing up into the treetops with a wistful look in her great amber eyes.

She misses her old life. She's not alone in that! This destiny of mine has pulled all of us up by the roots.

Branwen cupped more water, pouring it over her arms and her clothes, watching the congealed blood dissolve into carmine streams that dyed the moss at her feet a deep purple hue.

"Blodwedd?"

The owl-girl's round face turned to her, framed in tawny hair, the nose a sharp line, the mouth small and pointed—the eyes like golden suns.

"Yes, Branwen?"

"Do you think you made the right choice?" Branwen asked. "Do you ever wish you could take it back and be an owl again?"

"I wish it every day," Blodwedd replied. "I wish it when I hear the rustle of some small creature moving in twilight through the forest. I wish it when dusk comes. I wish it in the silent time before dawn. I wish it when I spy a bird on the wing, soaring high in the evening sky." She extended an arm, staring at it as if, for a moment, she did not quite know what it was. "I wish it when this stretched and brittle and spindly shape grows weary and cold at night." She lifted her hand to her face, flexing her fingers in front of perplexed eyes. "I was never cold at night till I was given this form," she said, her gaze turning suddenly to Branwen. "If not for Rhodri's warmth after nightfall, I think I might freeze to death." She pulled her dress up over her thighs, running her long white nails over her taut skin. "This is an unpleasant rind!" she said.

"Unbeautiful! Nasty to the touch." She sighed, covering her legs again. "I'd have my feathers back!"

Branwen knelt, dripping pink water, gazing up at her. "I'm sorry," she said. "I'm so sorry." She had assumed that the affection between Rhodri and Blodwedd might eventually lead to something deeper, but how could that ever be if the owl-girl found the human form ridiculous and human skin revolting?

Blodwedd's head tilted as she looked down at her. "You need not pity me, Branwen," she said. "Every choice must bear its burden; you of all folk should know that. It's true that I long to be what I once was, but I do not regret my decision. I did my duty by the land of my birth, and I accept the consequences." She pointed down at Branwen, her voice losing its melancholy air. "The blood is still thick in your hair—shall I help you wash it out?"

"Yes. Yes, please, if you will."

Blodwedd came bounding down the rock.

"And then we shall return to that pale creature and learn whether the sight of you unbloodied is more appealing to her," she said with a sharp and pointed smile.

"Let us hope so," said Branwen, stooping over the pool and letting her hair hang into the turbulent water. Her voice lowered to a murmur. "If I ever am truly cleaned of so much blood!" She closed her eyes as Blodwedd began pouring the icy water over her head. "So very much blood!"

12

"SEE!" SAID RHODRI. "What did I tell you—Branwen is no demon at all!"

Rhodri's words greeted the arrival of Branwen and Blodwedd back at the place where they had left him and the young woman. Branwen's hair and clothes were wet; but with Blodwedd's help she had managed to get rid of most of the blood, and she did not rue the exchange, especially on such a warm afternoon.

They found the frightened captive unbound, on her feet and looking much recovered.

"No," the young woman said hesitantly. "I see now that she is not." Her eyes turned to Blodwedd. "But what manner of . . . ?"

"Blodwedd is also a friend," Rhodri said quickly.

"I killed Skur Bloodax," Branwen said. "You need have no fear of any of us." She eyed the young woman curiously. "But what is your tale, lady? How did you fall foul of the Viking warrior?"

A few things Branwen thought she could already guess. The young woman was slender, her compact body lean and firm as if she was used to physical work. Blond hair curled to her shoulders; and her pale face was delicate, her dark blue eyes wide, her lips full, and her cheeks dimpled.

These were not the features of a woman of Brython. Her skin and hair were fairer than those of most of the Saxons Branwen had seen. No, if she were to guess, she'd say that the woman was also pure Viking stock—perhaps brought here from the Northlands to do Skur's bidding. Her clothing was certainly that of a servant: a simple gown of patched and threadbare gray, and worn leather shoes on her feet, the stitches beginning to come apart with age.

She did have one item of jewelry—a dull metal torque wound about her right wrist. Some family heirloom, perhaps, too lacking in value to have been worth stealing from her.

"My name is Asta Aeslief," the young woman said. "And Skur Bloodax was my abductor and my torturer, although it is not many days since I was happy and secure in my home, and much loved by my poor father."

"And where is your home?" asked Branwen. "Rhodri? Bring the horse—we shall walk as Asta tells us more. I would know how it is that you speak our language when you clearly hail from lands far from here."

As Branwen led the others down to the valley floor, Asta continued her tale. "My home these days is not so very distant. I live upon the island of Lindisfarne, which lies off the east coast of Northumbria. My father is a scribe—a great scholar and lore-master. It is he who taught me to speak your language, and the language of many of the folk who dwell here: Saxon, Angle, Jute, and Dane." She looked astutely at Branwen. "As you have guessed, I am not native to this land. My father brought me here as a child from our home in the Norselands. I was born in the kingdom of Vyiken; but on the death of my mother, my father took to the road, and me along with him. For some years we dwelt at the court of King Harhoff in the Danelands, till we took ship for Lindisfarne, where my father was to serve King Oswald as a translator of languages."

"And how was it you met with Skur Bloodax?" asked Rhodri.

Asta slowed, staring ahead and looking alarmed.

Branwen's companions were gathered a little farther along the valley; the sight of them seemed to have made Asta uneasy.

"They are my friends," Branwen assured her. "Come, be at ease; your tribulations are at an end."

Iwan and the girls of Gwylan Canu eyed Asta with interest as they approached. Branwen introduced them, but Asta's attention seemed fixed on the sprawling corpse of Skur Bloodax, the blood already blackening in his wounds.

Fain was on the ground close by, tearing with his beak at something gripped in his claws. Branwen chose not to look too closely at what meat the falcon had found to eat. There was nothing reserved about his appetite.

Aberfa and Banon stepped aside as Asta walked forward, her jaw set, her eyes glinting. For a few moments she stood silently over the fallen warrior, her body rigid, her clenched fists trembling.

"Monster!" she hissed at last. "May Sleipnir bear you swift to Hel's dark kingdom!" Then she spat upon him and turned away. "You asked how I came to be in his thrall," she said to Branwen. "It happened this way. We got word that a fearsome warrior had set sail from Oslofjord in the Norselands, summoned by King Oswald to be the spearhead of his attack on your lands. My father greeted Skur Bloodax well when he made landfall on Lindisfarne—little knowing that after he had dined and supped at his hearth, the vile cur would ride south with me as his unwilling servant!"

"Your father allowed you to be taken away?" asked Linette.

"He is old and frail," said Asta, her head bridling with sudden pride. "And yet he stood at the gate of our home with sword in hand and had to be beaten to the ground senseless before Skur could depart."

"That was a brave act," said Iwan, glancing at Skur. "I doubt that many men would have the courage to stand against such as he! And did your father survive Skur's attack, do you know?"

"I do not," said Asta. "His head was bloody when last I saw him, staring back in misery as Skur dragged me across the causeway to the mainland." Tears ran down her cheeks, but Branwen guessed these were more from anger than grief. "And it has been ten days and more since I was taken from him, and I have been forced to walk with my hands roped together while Skur rode at his ease into the south."

"And where was he heading, do you know?" asked Banon.

"His intent was to meet up with a thain named Horsa Herewulf Ironfist in a great encampment outside the town of Chester," said Asta.

"Then he would have been doubly disappointed!" said Dera. "For not only did he lose his right path, but had he come to that camp, he would have found General Ironfist absent—never to return!"

Asta looked puzzled.

"You have come too far; this place is to the southwest of Chester," Rhodri explained. "Another half a day of travel and you would have entered the kingdom of Powys!"

"And as for Herewulf Ironfist," added Iwan, "Branwen slew him in battle not two days ago!"

"And now she has also killed Skur!" said Asta, her eyes shining as she looked at Branwen. "I guess that you are more than you seem, Branwen. Little more than a maiden, you look—and yet you must be a formidable warrior!"

"Indeed so!" declared Blodwedd. "Branwen is the beloved of the Shining Ones. She has a high destiny, and all we who are gathered here are her faithful followers."

Asta stared around the band, her eyes wide, her lips parted in wonder. At last her gaze fell on Branwen again.

"And what *is* your destiny, Branwen?" she asked breathlessly.

"To rout the Saxons and to make the borders of Brython safe . . . ," Branwen said. She paused, allowing herself an embarrassed smile of self-deprecation. ". . . apparently . . ."

"You would be astounded if we were to tell you what she has already accomplished!" said Linette. "She has ferocious allies. Why, in the battle at Gwylan Canu, when all seemed lost—"

"We have no time for telling stories," Branwen interrupted her. "To horse, and away to Chester." She turned to Asta. "You are free to go where you will. It is a long journey back to your home, but I wish you well in it. You may keep for your own the Viking's steed and all the provisions he had."

Asta looked bewildered. "I do not know the way home," she said.

"Branwen, she is *Saxon!*" Dera said sharply. "Her loyalties are not ours; we cannot simply let her go on her way! She knows too much of us."

"I am not a Saxon," protested Asta. "I am . . ." Her voice faded suddenly away.

"A Viking!" prompted Aberfa, her brows lowered. "Yes, you are indeed."

"I mean you no harm!" Asta cried, staring around at them. "You rescued me from Skur; it would be mean-spirited indeed for me to repay you with treachery." Branwen frowned. Dera had a point. Asta was not of their cause; her loyalties must lie with her father's master, with King Oswald of Northumbria. And they were in enemy territory on a mission that only stealth and surprise would accomplish.

"We have killed an enemy and released his captive—only to find that she too is an enemy . . . of sorts," Iwan said, looking closely into Asta's perturbed face. "What are we to do? We cannot release her, and we do not have the time to take her to a place where she can be safely kept." He looked at Branwen, raising an eyebrow. "A weighty decision for a leader to make."

"We must be sure that she cannot threaten our mission," said Dera. "I see only two choices."

"And what are those, in your opinion?" Rhodri asked.

"She must be rendered harmless, or she must be killed," Dera said.

"No!" Asta wailed, backing away. Aberfa stepped up behind her and caught her by the elbows, her two strong hands holding her steady.

"That is a harsh sentence!" murmured Banon. "To save only to slaughter?"

"We cannot kill her!" said Rhodri, his voice shocked.

"How can we make her harmless?" Branwen asked, looking at Dera.

"If she has no tongue, she cannot tell our enemies of us," Blodwedd said, staring unblinkingly into Asta's frightened face. "And if that is not thought sufficient, her eyes could be put out. A dumb and sightless enemy is little threat."

"Blodwedd!" Rhodri looked at her, appalled. "We cannot maim her for fear of what she *might* do!"

"Would you rather we kill her?" Blodwedd asked, seemingly puzzled by his anger.

"Kinder to put a sword through her heart," said Dera. "But whatever we choose, it should be swiftly done. It's cruelty indeed to make her suffer more than need dictates."

Asta stopped struggling in Aberfa's powerful grip. She straightened her back, her chin up as she looked into Branwen's face. "I'll not beg for my life," she said, her voice firm but filled with fear. "Do what you will if you cannot put your faith in my gratitude! But if I am given the choice, a sword to the heart is my final wish."

"There you have it," said Dera. "A compassionate sword to end all doubt. She asks for it herself."

"We cannot kill her like this!" Rhodri was adamant.

"Silence!" Branwen snapped. "No more words." She paused, thinking hard, knowing she must assert her leadership before the dissent among her followers grew out of control. "The decision is mine to make," she said. "For our own safety we cannot let her go free, but I will not have her killed. There is another way to render the Viking harmless. Troublesome as it may be, we shall take her with us."

"Then she should be blindfolded and hobbled," Dera said doubtfully.

"Bind me and blindfold me if you must," said Asta with new hope. "But I can be useful to you. I have no experience in warfare, although I can shoot an arrow into a straw target. But in other ways than warfare, I will serve you well." She looked eagerly at Branwen. "I have skills that will be of use to you—all of you. I can cook, and I am able to patch and mend damaged garments. I speak the Saxon language—you may find that an invaluable gift in these lands."

"We already have tokens that will allow us to understand the Saxon tongue," Dera said.

"But not to speak it," Linette added. "If she can be trusted, a speaker of Saxon may come in very useful in Chester."

"*If* she can be trusted!" said Aberfa.

"It would be madness indeed to allow her to enter Chester with us!" said Dera. "One word from her and we'd have a whole army about our ears!"

"We shall not take her into Chester," said Branwen. "And she need not be bound if she is kept under constant guard."

"I will vouch for her," said Rhodri. "Put her in

my keeping. Blodwedd and I will see that she cannot escape."

"This is yet more madness!" growled Dera. "Would we welcome a scorpion into our midst to sting us to death in our sleep? Kill her now and be done with her!"

"No," Branwen said. "I won't have her blood on my hands without absolute need. She was brought here against her will. She is an innocent in the doings of this war." She turned to Blodwedd. "I put her into *your* keeping," she said to the owl-girl. "She will be your responsibility. Are you willing?"

"I am," said Blodwedd. "If she transgresses in any way, I will kill her."

"I know you will," said Branwen.

Branwen looked at the others. "Is anyone ill at ease with my decision?"

Dera pressed her lips into a thin white line but said nothing. Rhodri looked relieved. Iwan smiled, as though the whole affair had been put on for his amusement.

Aberfa let Asta loose. Rubbing her arms, Asta stepped up to Branwen, her face solemn.

"I will not betray you," she said. "My word on it!"

"To horse!" Branwen called, ignoring Asta as she strode toward where Stalwyn and the other animals stood waiting. "Enough time has been wasted! We ride to Chester!"

13

"I HAD NOT expected it to be so large," Branwen murmured as she gazed out from the summit of a long, forested fold in the land. "So many fires—so many lights! How many thousands must this place give shelter to?"

Night had come, swifter than Branwen might have wished; and they were still on their way when the sun set behind them and darkness swept the Mercian plain. But the news was not all bad—Fain had recently returned from a scouting mission with heartening tidings.

Blodwedd had translated his excited cries: ahead of them the land lifted in a long, gentle hill mantled in deep forest; but beyond that rise, the plain fell suddenly into a marshy valley through which a wide river flowed northward. And not far along the looping course of that river, as the falcon wings it, lay a great gathering of buildings. Chester, for sure!

The travelers had wound their way up through the trees and so had come within sight of the ancient town. Night softened and obscured its contours, but even at a distance Branwen saw by the multitude of lights that twinkled and flickered and shone in the darkness that it must be a formidably vast settlement.

"I told you it was big," said Rhodri, his horse close beside hers.

"You did," she agreed.

"What is our intent?" asked Dera, leaning over her saddlebow and peering at the faraway lights. "To slip into the town with the night as our ally?"

"I would not advocate such a course," said Iwan. "Daylight is a better friend to the thief than is the night."

"How can that be so?" asked Dera.

"Because a stranger seen walking the streets in broad daylight may have many innocent purposes," Iwan replied. "But an outsider prowling the town at dead of night is the more to be suspected of nefarious deeds."

"That's wise," said Linette.

"Of course it is," said Iwan.

"But won't Merion's stones protect us from being seen?" asked Banon.

"Not entirely," said Branwen. "And I agree with Iwan—it's too dangerous to enter by night. Far better to mingle with the townsfolk tomorrow and thus be in a position to hear their chatter. Our first purpose here is to learn of the one-eyed warrior. Who is there to overhear when doors are barred and only the guardians of the walls are abroad?" She shook her head. "No. We will sleep tonight in the forest and try our luck in the morning."

"And who shall enter Chester?" asked Dera. "There are only six stones, yet there are eight of us—seven if Blodwedd is to stay behind and watch over the Viking."

"I'll decide in the morning," Branwen said, tweaking the reins and turning Stalwyn away from the hill's edge. "We cannot risk a fire for cooking; it may be seen. But let us find a fit place to spend the night." So saying, she rode Stalwyn back under the trees. But even in the deep dark of the forest, the myriad lights of Chester lit a bright and sleepless fire in her mind.

Branwen dreamed that she was walking through the alder forest again, trudging up a long slope, her shoulders bowed, her body steeped in blood, her fingers and hair dripping red. Alone. Weary almost to death. Skur lay vanquished behind her in the valley, and it was night.

She recognized her surroundings although the scale was wrong: the hill was taller and steeper; the trees around her soared to impossible heights. And as she plodded up the hill, she left deep footprints that immediately filled with blood.

She came to that same spring of water and that same hollow stone where she had washed herself. But now the spring had grown and swollen to a waterfall, and the pool was a wide, round lake under the star-swept night sky. The full moon shone bright in the high middle of the sky, throwing down a perfect reflection of itself onto the lake. The hugest full moon that Branwen had ever seen.

Standing for a moment on the stone lip of the lake, she took a breath and dived into the water. It was cold and it stung, but she reveled in the way the blood was rinsed from her body.

She swam for a while, clean and refreshed. She turned onto her back and floated easily, gazing up into the pocked face of the moon, high above her.

"Branwen! It will not suffice!" A high, female voice.

Puzzled, she struck out for the bank and clambered onto dry land, her clothes clinging, her hair hanging in her eyes.

There was no one there.

She lifted her hand to pull the hair out of her eyes.

Her hand was covered in blood. Her hair was full of clots of gore. The water had not washed her clean.

She turned, diving in again, scouring her body with her hands, desperate to get rid of the blood.

She climbed into the air again, and still she was

smeared and stained with blood.

"That will not wash it away," called the high, piping voice. She spun around and saw a fragile silvery figure standing on a rock at the foot of the waterfall. A female, for sure, very tall but as slender as a child, her hair falling like white water to her waist, her delicate body clad in a dress so fine that it was like a mist.

"Then how?" Branwen called. "How do I get clean?"

"You do not," called the voice. "The blood is part of you now, Warrior Child."

"No! I don't want that."

"Blood is life; blood is strength; blood is a mighty river—it will not be denied. Own yourself, Warrior Child. Be who you have become."

"Who are you? What do you want?"

"I want to dance in the moonlight," called the creature. "My name is Nixie, but most call me goraig, if they name me at all."

Goraig? The goraig were the water goblins of her brother Geraint's old children's stories. Creatures that did not exist . . . that *should* not exist. But before Branwen had the chance to ask more of her, Nixie began to sing—a bright, lilting tune, her voice like the trilling of water over pebbles.

> *Oh, the cuckoo is a pretty bird, she sings as*
> *she flies*
> *She brings us glad tidings; she tells us*
> *sweet lies*

She flies the hills over; she wakes in the night
She pierces the heart through, with her
song of delight

She sucks the fair flowers, to make her
voice clear
She never stops singing, till the mountain
is near

Oh, the cuckoo is a pretty bird, in feathers
so gay
She sheds her bright plumage, at the close
of the day

And as she sang, Nixie began to dance, skipping featherlight over the stones that lay beneath the waterfall, pirouetting, twirling, springing from rock to rock, her slim body shining like a candle through the gauze of her dress.

Suddenly she leaped from the rocks and came down onto the black surface of the lake. Small moonlight ripples spread from her feet as she danced across the water. Branwen saw the undulations trouble the reflection of the full moon as it lay on the dark breast of the lake.

Nixie came dancing over to the reflected moon, circling it with delicate steps, her toes at its rim.

Branwen watched her in baffled delight, gazing at her bewitching, serene face, envying her airy grace and her blithe moonlit existence.

Suddenly Nixie stooped, reaching her two arms down into the lake. The moon exploded into glittering fragments as her hands clove the water. But a moment later she lifted her arms again, holding the white disk of the moon between her fingers as though it were a wheel made of pure light.

Branwen gasped as Nixie began to spiral toward her, the moon lifted high above her head, spinning like a silver coin.

She came to the water's edge at Branwen's feet. Bending low, she bowed her head, her hair tumbling forward, the moon held out toward Branwen.

"Take it," she said, lifting her head, her eyes radiant between the curtains of her hair. "It is yours. A gift from the Great One, to replace that which was broken."

Branwen reached for the moon disk—half expecting her hands to pass through it. But it was solid under her fingers, solid and cold like forged silver— the size of a shield.

"May it serve you well," said Nixie, rising to her full height, "as it served its old master."

"Who did it belong to?" Branwen asked. But Nixie was already dancing away across the lake. "Whose was it? What happened to him?"

"Remember the cuckoo!" Nixie called back. "She is a pretty bird, but her heart is taken by another. . . . She is not to be trusted. . . . Be wary of her. . . . Beware. . . ."

14

B RANWEN WAS AWOKEN by a hand on her shoulder and by Blodwedd's voice whispering in her ear.

"Something is afoot, Branwen," Blodwedd hissed. "Come. Swiftly."

Disoriented and with half of her mind still caught up in the dream, Branwen got to her feet and followed Blodwedd's padding footsteps away from the cloak-bundled, sleeping shapes of her companions and into the forest.

"What of Asta?" Branwen murmured, knuckling her eyes to wake herself up properly. "You were to watch her day and night." She saw that the light was gray. It would soon be dawn.

"She is deep asleep," Blodwedd replied. "She will not rouse soon."

"Caw!" A single sharp cry. Branwen turned,

looking up into the branches. In among the leaves she saw the gleam of Fain's eye.

"Hush now!" she called softly. "All's well. Stay and watch over the others!"

She caught up with Blodwedd.

"Why did you wake me?" she asked. "Where are we going?"

"Not far," said Blodwedd, turning with circular eyes. "Something waits for you."

"A shield!" Branwen gasped. "A white shield!"

"Then you dreamed it, too," said Blodwedd, her eyes glittering. "You are drawing ever closer to the Old Ones, Branwen. They are in your blood now."

Branwen stopped dead.

"What's happening to me?" she asked the owl-girl. "What am I becoming?"

Understanding ignited in Blodwedd's face. "Ahh!" She walked back, standing close to Branwen—the top of her tawny head the level of Branwen's chin—looking up at her. "You fear you will lose yourself."

"I do."

"You will not," said Blodwedd. "Am I lost under this absurd bag of bones? I am not." She smiled her pointy smile, her face more owl-like than ever. "Own yourself, Branwen. Become who you are."

"That is almost exactly what the dancing girl told me."

"I know. Come—do you not want your gift?" Blodwedd walked away. Hesitating only for a moment,

140

Branwen followed her.

They did not need to go far.

Daylight grew at Branwen's back. She saw something flashing through the trees—white as lightning, but circular. Something that hung in the branches of a solitary rowan tree.

It was a shield, dazzling in reflected sunlight.

The white shield from her dream.

"Take it and keep it," said Blodwedd, stepping aside as Branwen approached the dangling shield. "It is made from the wood of the sacred linden tree of Afallach, and over its face is stretched the hide of the White Bull of Ynis Môn. The boss is of white gold mined in Dolaucothi in the kingdom of Dyfed and forged by Gofi ap Duw."

"How do you know these things?" asked Branwen, narrowing her eyes against the glare of the sun-blazing shield.

"I know of its former master," said Blodwedd. "His name was Cudyll Bach of the House of Wyllt. He died long ago, and his shield and sword have been kept secret for many's the long year, waiting for a worthy champion. Be honored, Branwen of the Old Ones— the shield has chosen you! Take it for your own. It will bring you good fortune."

Her hands trembling, Branwen reached up and lifted the shield from the rowan branches. She slipped her hand into the grip, testing the weight and balance of the shield on her arm. "It feels good!" she said, smiling now. "What of the sword? Am I to receive that as well?"

"Be content," said Blodwedd. "The sword is for another champion."

Branwen frowned. "There's *another*?"

"There is."

Branwen was surprised and intrigued by this. And a little disturbed. Had the Shining Ones torn some other innocent from their home and sent them hurtling pell-mell along destiny's path? "Is it someone like me?" she asked.

"Like and unlike," said Blodwedd. "He does not dwell in Brython. His home is in the kingdom of Wessex, which lies to the south of Mercia. I can tell you no more of him. Come—a new day has dawned; the others are stirring."

Blodwedd strode off through the trees, and Branwen had to run to catch up with her. "Do you truly know nothing more about this other champion? Why have you not spoken of him before?" she asked, walking now at the owl-girl's side.

"I know only that he is a boy alive in the world," said Blodwedd. She glanced at Branwen, touching a finger to the middle of her own forehead. "I see in my mind a man in a cell of cold stone," she said. "A man named Thomas. But Thomas is not the champion—he merely writes of him. He is bent over—quill to parchment— scribbling frantically; he knows of the champion the boy will become. But when he writes, the champion has already slept for eight hundred years in the dark tower of Caer Rigor." A sharp edge came into her voice. "That is the extent of my knowledge, Branwen. Ask no more!"

Reluctantly, Branwen complied with Blodwedd's wishes and put no more questions to her—though Blodwedd's words were such a puzzle, she had nothing but questions. It was a long time before she was able to clear her mind of the notion that there was *another Warrior Child alive in the world.*

A boy.

A Chosen One.

Like her.

Branwen's companions were fascinated and awed by the appearance of the white shield—and even more so by the way it had come to her.

"A gift from the Old Powers," Banon breathed, barely daring to touch the hard leather rim. "This is surely a reward for the slaying of Skur Bloodax."

"Maybe so," said Rhodri. "Or a token that harder battles lie ahead."

"The gods of your people must love you dearly, Branwen," said Asta, gazing at the shield. "Might it not be wise for you to turn back now to give thanks? That is how my people do homage to our gods. We go to their sacred places and make sacrifices to them for their bounty."

"In due time, perhaps," said Branwen. "I don't

think Merion of the Stones would want me to turn from my path at this point." She looked at her gathered companions. The only one who stood slightly apart was Iwan, his arms folded, his eyes on her as though his head was full of unasked questions.

"I have made my decision about who shall come with me to Chester," Branwen said. "Aberfa and Linette will stay behind with the horses. With them we will leave our weapons and any other gear that will mark us as other than humble travelers come to do business in the markets of Chester. Asta will stay with them."

"I thought Blodwedd was to be the Viking's keeper," complained Aberfa. "I would go with you into Chester."

"Asta will be in *your* charge for this time," said Branwen. "It is pointless giving this task to Blodwedd; she would refuse it and give me an endless list of reasons why she must stay always at my side. I do not have time for such an argument."

"It's true," said Rhodri, his hand on Blodwedd's shoulder. "She would."

The owl-girl said nothing; but her eyes glowed like amber flames, and there was a glad smile on her face.

Aberfa frowned deeply but said nothing more.

"We will guard her well, do not fear," said Linette. "And as a reward, all we ask is to be in your vanguard when other dangers appear."

"There will be plenty of opportunity for that, I'm sure," said Branwen. "Let's get ready now. A quick breakfast is all we have time for, and then we must be on our way."

Once everyone had divested themselves of their war-gear, quite a collection of shields and swords and knives and bows were heaped up in the middle of their camp. Skur's ax lay on its own, as did a long knife that had been taken from his belt and his yellow and black shield.

"I wish you could take Skur's ax to Chester and display it so that all would know of their champion's death," said Linette.

"They shall learn of it soon enough," said Branwen. "The next time our two armies meet, we shall carry the ax with us, and our foes will be dismayed to see that their Viking warrior is slain. Maybe that will give us advantage in the field."

Iwan smiled at her. "You think like a general," he said.

"Perhaps," Branwen replied softly.

She turned and laid her white shield apart from the others, resting it against a tree trunk. She straightened up, noticing that Iwan was now looking at the shield and frowning.

"What's the matter?" she asked him. "You've hardly spoken since I returned. Are you envious that the gods have not favored you with such a gift?"

He gave a crooked smile. "I am conceited enough

to enjoy special treatment, I'll grant you that," he said. "And usually I deserve it. But I'm not sure that being a favorite of the Shining Ones is something I'd covet." He looked at her, and there was concern in his eyes. "Be careful, Branwen," he murmured, his voice oddly serious. "Be wary of the cost of such gifts. Do not let them . . ." His words trailed off.

"Say what you're thinking," said Branwen.

He was silent for a while as though choosing his words very carefully.

"I find your company mildly agreeable, barbarian princess," he said at length, the teasing tone back in his voice. "I would not wish for you to be changed overmuch by your contact with the Old Gods—for you to become more like them. I would not want to have to start worshipping you!" He laughed, turning and walking away from her. "At least no more than I do already!"

She stared after him, her throat suddenly tight, her heart skipping in her chest.

Why does he say such things? What does he mean by them?

But the riddle of Iwan ap Madoc would have to remain unsolved for now. Branwen had urgent matters to attend.

Fain came and perched on the rim of her white shield, cawing as if to let her know that he would guard her new gift with his life.

"Nobly done, my friend," she said, lightly stroking

the bird's chest feathers. "Keep your vigil here—I will not be overlong, and I cannot take you into the town. Such a lordly creature as you would draw too much attention." She turned and stared out over the plain. "And that is something we cannot risk—we few among so many enemies."

In the full light of day, Branwen found the age-old town of Chester and the army camp that sprawled at its side even more astonishing and impressive than she had when it had been no more than an unsettling cluster of lights in the dark of night.

She and her five companions made their way down through the grass and scrub of the low hill. They were more vulnerable, of course, without horse or sword, but also far less likely to cause comment as they moved in among the Saxon people. And in the thick of so many enemies, stealth and anonymity were their only real hope.

The land before them was brindled with woodlands, in some places forming wide forests, in others just a dappling of green where birches and alders and willows gathered. Close to the town they saw many coppiced groves where slender trees grew in cultivated thickets, providing timber and sticks and withies for the townsfolk. There were open tracts as well, cleared of trees for the grazing of sheep and goats and cattle, and other cleared strips of tilled land where wheat and barley and rye flourished.

I never thought of Saxons as farming the land. Foolish of me. Soldiers, I imagined—and the wives and children of soldiers. Never farmers!

The banks of the wide river were thick with reeds; and along the water's curving course, the land was a lush, sumptuous green that suggested wetlands and marshes.

Chester lay on the far side of a deep bow in the River Dee. Several ways led into its eastern gates, but from the west it could only be approached by a single wooden bridge from which a track of beaten earth wound northward along the course of the meandering river. Jutting out into the river at the side of the bridge were wharves and jetties for the loading and unloading of river freight.

A steady flow of movement animated the roadway, ox-drawn wagons and carts and many people on foot, all making their way from the northern villages and farms to buy and sell in the markets of the town.

No roads led to the west or south. It was two hundred years or more since the trade routes had closed between Mercia and Brython; and these days only soldiers took the westward ways, with murder and pillage on their minds.

The town was contained within a deep encircling ditch and ringed around by a wall of wooden staves, not unlike the palisade that had once protected Garth Milain. Except, as Branwen quickly noticed, here and there the wall was of stone, as though more ancient defenses had been incorporated into the timber fortifications.

Sprawled alongside the town was a huge and seemingly chaotic encampment of tents and huts crowding around a small knot of thatched wooden buildings that Branwen assumed must once have been a farmhouse and its outbuildings. Among the close-packed tents she saw enclosures for horses and open areas where men gathered like swarming ants. The great encampment of the dead general Herewulf Ironfist. An alarming sight that chilled her blood. This was the deadly crucible from which had poured forth the armies that had laid siege to Garth Milain and Gwylan Canu.

"I hoped never to see that sight again," said Rhodri, staring at the Saxon army camp. "How fate plays its tricks on me!"

It had been from this very camp that Rhodri had been fleeing when Branwen had first met him high in the Clwydian Mountains—a footsore runaway servant searching for a home in the west.

"It plays tricks on all of us." Branwen sighed. She looked fondly at him. "Have I told you what a fool you are to follow me?"

"Several times," Rhodri said with a sad smile. "And yet here I am."

"Yes. Here you are. Will you never learn?"

"A ship is coming," said Blodwedd. She pointed into the far north, where the coil of the river blended with the land in a blue haze.

Branwen peered into the distance but could see nothing.

"It lies low in the water, with wide bows and a high prow and stern," Blodwedd continued. "The sail is furled, and it is drawn downriver by oarsmen."

Iwan shook his head. "I cannot see it," he said, clearly impressed in spite of himself. "You have marvelous eyesight, Blodwedd."

She gave him a quick, strange smile. "Yes," she said, glancing from him to Branwen. "You would be surprised at the things I see."

"Are there men of war aboard?" asked Dera. "Is this maybe a lone survivor of the rout of the Saxon fleet at the battle of Gwylan Canu?"

"Did any ship remain afloat when the Old God came?" asked Banon.

"I think perhaps one did," said Dera.

"I cannot see who is aboard," said Blodwedd.

"It is likely as not a trading vessel," said Rhodri. "There is much coming and going of goods from Chester."

Branwen turned to look at the town again. With a pang, she recalled the tales told by the old men around the hearth in the Great Hall of Garth Milain. Tales of how the Roman conquerors had founded the town in the remote times when their power was like a raging fire. Deva, they called it, naming it after one of their goddesses. A great fortress it was in those days, filled with magnificent stone buildings so tall, it was said, that their towers scratched grooves in the face of the sun as it passed above them. Some said that the Romans were giants, others that they paid giants to build their homes for them. Either way, it had been a magnificent place, by all accounts, brought low in the end—as are all things—by the passage of time and the ceaseless gnawing of wind and rain.

When the Romans had departed, the people of Britain continued to live in the decaying town till the Saxon invasion drove them west. For many ages the town was buffeted by warfare, overrun by Saxons, retaken by the warriors of the Four Kingdoms—passing from one side to the other, while the farms grew rank with weeds and the houses burned and the women and children wept.

There had been a final great battle there ten years before Branwen's birth. Her father and mother had been part of the desperate last stand of the people of Powys against the war-hammer of the Saxons. But despite all their efforts, the Saxons had prevailed; and the people of Brython had drawn back behind their borders, licking their wounds, arming themselves in the few brief years of peace—watching and waiting for the onslaught they knew must come.

As Branwen and her band drew closer to the town, they descended the hill and came to the marshes that lined the river's banks. Now all that Branwen could see over Chester's walls were the thatched roofs of the larger houses and halls and the occasional curious stone construction that she did not quite understand. The ruined hulks of some great Roman building, she assumed, although she had never seen stone buildings that lifted so high in the sky.

The works of giants, indeed!

The six travelers had now come to the last piece of cover before the bridge: a huddle of willows with their roots in soft ground and their branches dangling in the steady northward flow of the Dee.

Thirty more paces and they would be in among the men and women crossing the river to enter Chester.

Branwen distributed five of the white crystals to her companions.

"Remember," she said. "They do not make you invisible. Keep quiet and do what you can to blend in. Although the stones will allow you to understand Saxon speech, it will not make your words clear to them, so keep mute if possible."

Banon held her stone up between finger and thumb. "How does the enchantment work?" she asked, staring at it. "What must I do to make it work?"

"Nothing," said Branwen. "Merion put her power into the stones; we must trust in their virtue to protect us."

"Much faith to put in so small a thing," said Iwan, holding his to the sun. "It is a pretty trinket, though, with a rainbow at its heart."

"Gavan ap Huw and his followers were making for

Chester," said Rhodri. "What if we encounter them in the town?"

"Remember what I said: make no contact if it can be helped," said Branwen. "Chester is a large town; with good fortune we shall not become enmeshed with them."

"Aye, a big town, indeed," said Dera. "How are we to quarter this town? As a group, or are we each to go our own way?"

"We shall divide into pairs," Branwen said. "Iwan shall be with you, Dera; Rhodri with Banon; and Blodwedd with me. That way we shall be able to spread through the town and learn more than if we remain together."

"That's wise," said Iwan. "So, we are to listen and watch for a one-eyed warrior. But what if we see and hear nothing? How long do we keep up this spying game? And how and when and where are we to gather again?"

"We should meet up here at day's end," said Branwen. "I do not think this is in vain, Iwan; Caradoc of the North Wind must be held in captivity by some great lord of the Saxon people. A Saxon nobleman with but a single eye should surely merit some mention. I have faith that we shall learn all that we need to know within the walls of this place." She closed her fist around her crystal. "So, we're done. Let us walk open eyed into the lair of the wolf. Good luck to us all! May the Shining Ones watch over us."

15

WHAT STRUCK BRANWEN most forcibly as she and Blodwedd crossed the echoing wooden bridge and came into the town of Chester was the overwhelming noise, the riot of smells, and the general sense of stress and urgency as the compressed crowds bumped and pushed and heaved in under the tall timber gateway.

Branwen had encountered large numbers of people before when she had entered the wealthy citadel of Doeth Palas, and she had found that disturbing and disagreeable; but it had not prepared her for this!

But there was nothing to be done—Branwen had to brace herself for the ordeal whether it was endurable or not.

There was good-humored shouting as friends greeted each other, angry exclamations and cries as the close-pressed people barged together, loud oaths when the wheels of two oxcarts became entangled. There was the bleat of sheep and the quarreling of herded geese, the creak and rumble of wheels, the snort and stamp of oxen. And under it all the loud babble and drone of endless voices, filling Branwen's mind so that she felt as if she had thrust her head into a beehive.

She kept her arm linked firmly with Blodwedd's, knowing how this crush and cacophony must distress the owl-girl and determined that the melee would not separate them. As was the case when they had infiltrated Doeth Palas, Blodwedd's face was shadowed by a deep hood. Even if the white crystals guarded them from close inspection, Branwen did not want to risk the owl-girl's inhuman eyes being noticed. From all she had been told, Saxons were a deeply superstitious people—even more so than her own folk; they would not react well to finding a demon in their midst!

Branwen caught sight of Rhodri and Banon making their way among the thatched buildings that pressed up against the inner side of the log wall of the town. She assumed Iwan and Dera were also somewhere nearby, moving cautiously through the slowly spreading throng.

The main thrust of people was heading along a wide thoroughfare—presumably to the main market square.

"This is our way," Branwen whispered to Blodwedd, pointing ahead. "People gossip in markets; we may hear things to our advantage."

As she allowed the tide of men and women and animals to take them deeper into the town, it seemed very curious to Branwen that she could understand what was being said around them. She could somehow tell that the people were not speaking her own language; but although the words and accents were foreign, the meaning of their words came clear in her head.

The thing that most surprised Branwen as she moved among these enemies of her race was that they looked not at all unlike the ordinary folk that she had met every day of her life in Garth Milain. She searched the faces—expecting to see cruelty and stupidity etched there, but finding nothing of the kind.

Stalls and open workshops lined the route, busy with trade.

"Eels, haddock, minnows, and pouts!" called a fishmonger from behind a row of filled wicker baskets. "Skate and lamprey, fresh from the river!"

"Are they today's catch?"

"They are, lady—clean and sweet. I cast my nets and my rods ere the sun was up!"

Women sat under an awning weaving and plaiting linen and picking out intricate embroidery on rich fabrics, their finished wares hanging at their backs. The whine and burr of a man working a pole lathe came to Branwen's ears, the craftsman busy turning handles for farm tools, his shop filled with wooden cups and bowls. There was an open smithy with a roof of slate, the sparks swarming high from the fire as two lads worked the leather bellows and their master beat the white-hot iron.

Voices cried out from all sides.

"Onions and cabbages, parsnips and carrots! Buy them by the shilling! Buy them by the penny!"

"Dyes and colorings! Madder and woad and club moss weld."

"Skins and pelts! Boar furs for a warm winter cloak! Cowhide for a pair of hard-wearing shoes!"

"A fathom of fine cloth to make a kirtle for a lady! Brocade by the thymel! Linen by the ell."

"New-baked rye bread! Wheaten loaves for the long in purse!"

The menfolk wore tunics of leather or cloth, dyed brown, blue, green, or red and held at the waist by leather belts from which hung the long-bladed Saxon knives known as seaxes. Only their beards set them apart from the men of her homeland. Branwen had been brought up with men whose chins were clean shaven and who wore the thick shaggy mustache that was traditional in Brython.

The women, too, were curiously similar—clad in floor-length linen kirtles and dresses, often with their heads covered by wimples. Their colorful clothes were adorned with jeweled pins and brooches, and many had pendants and chains wound about their necks and wrists.

If anything, it struck Branwen that these people were more prosperous than the folk of her homeland, and their love of color and jewelry at least rivaled that of the women of Powys. The wives and mothers of soldiers? They were that, it was true; but they were so much more than that. And again Branwen was puzzled that she had never thought of Saxon people living normal lives—and that their womenfolk would like to wear bright and precious stones at their throats and wrists.

This was turning into a day of unexpected revelations!

A man loomed up, dragging behind him a wicker cart on which lay a large barrel. He seemed surprised as he bumped into Branwen—as though he had not noticed her in his path.

The crystals were working their magic.

"A horn of beer, my merry maid!" the man shouted in her face. "We shall soon drink our beer from the skulls of the *waelisc* barbarians, so our lords and masters say; but for now a horn of beer will quench the thirst just as well!"

Branwen shook her head, gesturing to dismiss him as she gripped Blodwedd hard and moved away from the overbearing ale-monger.

Waelisc. She had heard the word quite clearly in her head, but the magic of Merion's stones gave it meaning: *foreigners*. It was clear whom the man had meant by "*waelisc* barbarians"—he had meant the people of Brython. The Saxon was referring to her people as foreigners!

"How are *we* the foreigners?" she murmured to Blodwedd. "They are the outsiders!"

"Humans have short memories," Blodwedd whispered back. "At first they come as raiders and pirates. Then they return as invaders and conquerors. And at the last they become settlers and lawmakers and kings, driving out those who came before them. It's always the way." She looked up at Branwen, and her eyes could just be seen as glittering points under her hood. "It is the restless nature of humans that the Old Gods fear," she confided. "Always on the move, never content—hacking and devouring their way through the land, leaving scorched earth in their wake—caring for nothing but themselves."

The marketplace was a maelstrom of buying and selling, but from what little Branwen could hear, much of the talk was of the war and the difficulties of feeding an army camped on their doorstep and how all the best goods and animals were being bought up cheaply by Thain Herewulf's quartermasters, leaving only scraps and dregs for the ordinary townsfolk.

"The warriors of the thain's household are bad enough," she heard one disgruntled woman say. "But the sooner the *fyrd*—those good-for-nothing common levies—are up off their backsides and across the river, the better. They eat us out of house and home! I wish to the earth mother, Nerthus, that this war would be over soon!"

"Aye," agreed her companion. "We give our husbands and sons to the great endeavor, but we see little good for all the blood that is spilt!" She lowered her voice, and Branwen had to strain to hear. "Leave the barbarian *waelisc* to their inhospitable mountains, I say. I'd not live there!"

"I could almost pity them," said the first. "King Oswald will not rest till the last of them is meat for the crows; and yet what harm have they done us, I ask? A poor, meager, uncultured world it is that they inhabit, Wotan bless their savage souls!"

Branwen was amazed and a little stunned by what she had heard. Brought up to believe that the Saxons were the aggressors, it was bewildering to hear two Saxon women speaking in such a way!

The two walked away from the heart of the market. "Well, this is a marvel such as I have never seen!" said Blodwedd. "What can it be?"

Branwen stared at the thing that had taken Blodwedd's attention. It was a huge, ruinous stone edifice—an immense ring of broken gray stone walls divided by thick rounded columns that jutted out like the trunks of huge trees. At their highest the crumbling stone walls reared up almost as tall as the hill of Garth Milain. It stood aloof from any houses, inhabiting a waste of rubble and unused land as though the Saxons feared it.

"Giants!" Branwen gasped, walking toward the impossible building. "It must be true that the Romans were giants!" Why else would the building be so huge?

"It fills me with foreboding," said Blodwedd, gazing at the noble ruin with haunted eyes. "It puts images in my mind!" She threw her hands over her eyes. "Dreadful sights! Impossible things!"

"What things?" Branwen asked.

"I see vast dwelling places where all the build-ings are as high as this, and higher still!" moaned Blodwedd. "I see houses of iron that rise up taller than mountains! They are polished like silver, and the sun strikes off their walls! Humans swarm in them like wasps in a great nest. Oh, Govannon, Govannon, let it never be!"

"Softly now, Blodwedd," said Branwen, concerned that the owl-girl might be overheard. But Blodwedd's voice rose to a frightened wail.

"I see arrowheads of iron high in the sky, gouging white furrows across the blue! Iron dragons breathe fire and smoke in the streets! The lights are bright and hard, and they do not flicker. It is the end of times! It is the death of all things!"

"Blodwedd!" Branwen pulled the owl-girl's hands from her eyes. "Calm down!" she whispered, looking anxiously around them. "You draw too much attention to us!" Fortunately, they had come to a place where there were fewer people to notice them. Besides this, as

Branwen now became aware, most of the nearby folk were turning their faces toward the market square and seemed to be listening to something that was being shouted through the streets.

"I am sorry," said Blodwedd, her face dreadfully pale. "Would that I never saw such things!"

"Shhh!" Branwen was straining to hear what was being shouted. A single word, possibly—or two short words shouted together, over and over. And as the chanting grew, so more people joined in, until even the folk around Branwen and Blodwedd were shouting out the same thing.

And now Branwen could hear what was being shouted.

"Iron-fist! Iron-fist! Iron-fist!"

A man came running along the street, his voice excited.

"Thain Herewulf has returned!" he called to anyone who would listen. "His ship has docked! He is entering the town! Let us hope he brings news of a great victory!"

"Iron-fist! Iron-fist! Iron-fist!"

"No! It isn't possible," gasped Branwen. "Ironfist is dead!

And then she remembered the ship that Blodwedd had seen on the river. A ship from the north—from the open sea. A ship such as had attacked Gwylan Canu.

Could it be that the Saxon warlord had survived the fall from the cliffs?

She had to know if her enemy lived or not!

She caught hold of Blodwedd's hand and, breaking into a run, swept along with the flood of people heading for the gates. All around her the exultant voices chanted till she could not tell the difference between their jubilant voices and the pounding of her own heart.

"Iron-fist! Iron-fist! Iron-fist!"

16

I T WAS ALL Branwen could do to keep a tight hold
on Blodwedd as the packed crowds drew them back
through the market square and along the narrowing street that led to the gatehouse. The noise of the
braying voices was deafening, the press and scrum of
bodies oppressive and overpowering. Branwen could
not have fought her way out of the excited mob if she
had tried. Keeping to her feet was challenge enough!

She managed to pull Blodwedd in front of her,
circling the owl-girl's thin body with her arms, pressing her mouth to the side of the down-drawn hood.

"All will be well," she cried over the blare of voices.
"Stay with me!"

Blodwedd's hand gripped her arm, the long nails
digging in like thorns.

Then the crowd came to a seething halt. They were

in the open space just inside the wooden gatehouse.

The mass of people were looking up, every one of them struggling for a better vantage point, every one of them chanting and stamping their feet.

"Iron-fist! Iron-fist! Iron-fist!"

Branwen's eyes were drawn to the top of the gatehouse.

A solitary man stood there, dark and imposing against the white sky, his feet planted firmly apart, his arms spread wide.

It was General Ironfist. Her great enemy had survived.

His fine red cloak was gone, as was his iron helmet with its silver and gold adornments. He wore still his coat of chain mail over the brown leather jerkin; but his clothes were dirtied, bloodied, and torn. And his face was terribly scarred, the right side of his face scored to the bone, his right eye socket a raw, red hole. The other eye, blue as ice, gleamed with twice the energy and mettle as though to make up for its lost companion. Nevertheless, he still carried with him the aura of power and command.

Branwen's mind fled back to the headland of Gwylan Canu, where she and Ironfist had fought. She saw herself—weaponless, in pain, lifting her shield in desperation as he lunged at her with sword swinging. And then there had come the shrieking and the clawing and the beating of ferocious wings.

Fain! Flying into the Saxon warlord's face, saving

her from certain defeat—from a bad death at the brutal general's hands.

So, these were the wounds that Fain had inflicted on him! *Good!* Branwen stared with a stony heart at Ironfist's injuries! *Good! I wish they had been worse!*

I wish they had been the death of him!

But no—he lived. Perhaps it was that his own gods had protected him. But whatever the cause and as impossible as it seemed, he had lived through the long fall from the cliff. Yes, now she thought again, at least one ship had survived Govannon's onslaught. Ironfist must have found the endurance to swim to it, curse him!

Bronze trumpets blared. Ironfist stepped to the edge of the gatehouse wall, his arms lifted for silence.

The crowd became mute. Expectant. Thrilling with anticipation.

"I bring woeful tidings, my people!" Ironfist bellowed. "By cowardice and treachery and by the use of sinister and fearful powers, the *waelisc* barbarians were able to cling for a brief time to their citadel on the sea!"

There were cries and murmurs of disbelief and distress from the throng. Ironfist silenced them with a gesture.

"Our warriors fell upon the savage enemy with stout hearts and stiffened sinews, each man prepared to give his life to defend our homeland!" cried Ironfist. "The *waelisc* cowards quaked at the sight of us, and the knocking of their knees as we approached was like the rattling of stones down a mountainside. Their strongest warriors quailed as we called out our honorable challenges, and many threw down their weapons and fell to their knees begging us for mercy!"

Branwen seethed with anger at this. Such lies! Such contemptible lies!

"We offered them fair and honorable treatment if they surrendered to us," Ironfist continued. "We told them that all their crimes against us would be forgiven if they laid down their arms and came forth." His voice rose to a roar. "Lifelong servants they would be— prisoners of war; but not one would be harmed, not one slain without cause, for are we not a humane and enlightened people? Are we not civilized? Are we not merciful, even to those who seek to do us great hurt?"

"Yes! Yes! Yes!" howled the crowd.

No! This is madness!

"For a time they treated with us, spinning lies and deceits as they delayed us at their gates," shouted Ironfist when the noise had subsided. "Would that I had better understood the sly and treacherous nature of the barbarian rats! Would that I had known what was to come!"

The incensed silence of the crowd was palpable now; Branwen could feel it like a brewing thunderstorm.

"All their cunning words had but one purpose," cried Ironfist. "To delay us until the spells and conjurations of their foul shamans were complete! For while we negotiated still at their gates, discussing terms with their leaders in good faith and in the hope that bloodshed could be avoided, there came down upon us from their black mountains a deadly army of demons and monsters!"

The crowd murmured angrily, and curses and threats rose up around Branwen.

If they knew who we were, they would tear us to pieces! Let us hope that Merion's stones do not fail us now!

"We knew it not until that moment, but one of the most terrible of their shamans was lurking behind the walls of their fortress! Like a girl she looks, dark haired and grim of feature, with eyes like sullen storm clouds and her mind a black gulf, filled with evil. Branwen ap Griffith is her name, curse the devilish powers that she worships!"

Branwen reeled at the sound of her own name, hardly able to believe the grotesque falsehoods that the Saxon general was spinning. She felt suddenly exposed and horribly vulnerable. Blodwedd pressed against her, trembling violently—petrified in this throng of angry enemies. The muttering of the crowd began to rise, but Ironfist stretched out his arms and lowered his hands, subduing the noise again.

"Even as the demons fell upon us from behind, I offered single combat with their greatest warrior, still hoping to save lives," shouted Ironfist, one foot coming up on the rim of the wall. "But it was the inhuman shaman, Branwen ap Griffith, who answered my call; and as we fought, so the demon hordes came among us, thirsty for blood, merciless and cruel! Almost I bested her, despite the great and dark powers she served, and in the end it was only by calling down a demon of the air upon me that she was able to escape my righteous wrath!" He gestured toward his ruined face. "These wounds it inflicted before I slew it! And I would have fought on and slain the evil shaman, but my men begged me to draw away from the field of battle, to take ship and to save myself so that I would be able to rally new armies and return again to defeat our enemy!"

There were shouts and oaths from the crowd, and this time Ironfist allowed them to voice their outrage for a short while before silencing them again.

"And so I return to you, bloodied but unbowed!" he roared, lifting his fists to the sky. "This is but a temporary setback, my good Saxon people! Too honest, too trustworthy we were! We shall not make that mistake a second time! When next we march upon the barbarians, their wickedness and treachery will not prevail! We will have victory! Full and final victory! And then we shall wipe even the memory of their cowardly race from the world! You have my word on that! You have the word of Thain Herewulf Ironfist!"

The crowd erupted, and for a long while Ironfist stood above them, his arms raised, urging them on till Branwen had to lift her arms from around the shivering owl-girl and put her hands over her ears to keep out the noise.

At last Ironfist waved his arms for silence.

"As you know, the seeds of our final victory have already been sewn," he shouted. "Even now the mighty warrior Skur Bloodax comes to us from his homeland across the North Sea! And as soon as Skur arrives, a new army will march forth from this place; and that time, my friends and my comrades, I will return to you with glad news!"

So saying, he stepped back and left his platform above the gatehouse while the crowds shouted and screamed and bellowed his name.

It took a while for the adoring throng to dissipate enough for Branwen and Blodwedd to slip away to a quiet place between two buildings, but at last they were alone and able to speak.

"I wonder the words did not choke him!" Blodwedd said, shaking her head. "Not one scrap of truth he spoke! Not one!" A cold grin spread across her face. "But in one case he lied despite himself! Skur will not come! That threat is lost on the wind, for sure and certain!" She frowned. "Branwen? What is the matter?"

"Didn't you see? His face?"

"Aye, torn in half!" Blodwedd chuckled, her spirits recovered now that she was away from the crowds.

"You told us that Fain came to your rescue! A goodly piece of ruin that brave falcon inflicted on the great liar! Ironfist will not quickly forget that encounter."

"He has only one eye!" said Branwen. "Merion told me I would know the one-eyed warrior when I saw him! She was right—I do! The one-eyed warrior is *Ironfist*!"

Amazement filled Blodwedd's face. "Can it be?" She gasped.

"It must be!" said Branwen. "But he would not take such a prized thing as Caradoc's prison with him into battle. It must be in the camp—in the Great Hall that he has made his headquarters!"

"Then we have come by good fortune to the very place Merion of the Stones wished," said Blodwedd. "But this means that to find the Shining One's prison, we must first pass through the greatest gathering of warriors that the Saxons have ever assembled!"

Branwen's eyes narrowed. "Then we shall," she said. "And may the Shining Ones look kindly on our endeavors!"

17

THE TOWN WAS alive with outrage as Branwen and Blodwedd made their way back to the marketplace, cautiously following a moving clot of people cheering Ironfist and his warriors through the streets. They were heading for the southern gate of the town, beyond which lay the army camp.

With the sheer force of his oratory, Ironfist had managed to turn the minds of the people from his defeat to the wickedness and deceit of their enemy. Branwen heard voices raised in fear and anger all around her.

By chance she came close to the two women whom she had heard speaking before. Ironfist's words had whipped them up into a seething rage.

"Under Wotan's grace, Thain Herewulf has returned to us!" said the first. "But did you see his poor face? So terribly hurt!"

"And yet they are noble injuries," said the other. "And against such evil!" She spat the words with a new hatred in her eyes. "I'd see that shaman girl's head hung above our gates! Death to Branwen ap Griffith! Why, I'd kill her myself were I a man!"

"I hope the thain can rally his men quickly," said the first. "It is our duty to hurl those wicked barbarians into the ocean!"

And theirs were not the only voices speaking Branwen's name and cursing it. All about her she heard the same thing.

Death to Branwen ap Griffith! Death to the foul waelisc *shaman!*

As she pushed her way through the people, Branwen clutched the white crystal tightly in her fist, more scared now than she had ever been in battle. To face an enemy with sword and shield was arduous and daunting; but to be surrounded by such disgust and loathing—and to be trapped among these people, unarmed and protected only by Merion's powers— was truly terrifying!

The knot of people surrounding Ironfist came to a sudden halt just inside the gate. Branwen lifted on tiptoe, trying to see the cause of the delay. But it was invisible among so many, and she could hear nothing above the cheering.

Blodwedd tugged at her arm, gesturing for them to move out of the main mass of the crowd.

"From there we will see clearer." The owl-girl

pointed to a tall thatched building that stood close by the outer wall of the town. Judging by its height, Branwen assumed it must be some kind of storage barn for grain; and high in the timber and white plaster wall she saw an opening and a winch for hauling up goods to a raised floor.

Blodwedd was right—from such a vantage point they could look down on the crowd and see what was causing the delay.

It was odd the way people would pause and stare around themselves as Branwen and Blodwedd pushed past. There was no doubt that Merion's magic was working. Occasionally someone would look directly into Branwen's face, as if startled to see her there; but a moment later the eyes would slide away, and it would be as if nothing had happened.

It was easy to slip into the barn unobserved. Its interior was dark and full of the smell of barley, but there was light enough for the two of them to move among the piled sacks of grain and to find the ladder to the upper floor.

They had to clamber over tight-packed sacks to find the opening under the thatched roof. As Branwen had hoped, the wide aperture allowed them to look right down into the crowded courtyard directly behind the gatehouse.

And from here the cause of the delay was quickly made obvious.

A small group of warriors had assembled to greet

Ironfist at the gateway, and among them was a young man who particularly caught Branwen's attention. He was tall and broad shouldered, and handsome in a fierce way: black haired, with a beard closely cropped and high, sharp cheekbones. He was finely dressed, with a scarlet cloak pinned at the right shoulder by a brooch of gold. The tunic was brown, embroidered at the wrist and hem; and about his waist was a belt studded with gold. A scabbard hung from the belt, also chased and adorned with gilding.

From his bearing, from the opulence of his clothes, and from the cold blue glint of his eyes, Branwen felt in no doubt that this was Ironfist's son, of whom Dillon had spoken: Redwuld Grammod—Redwuld the fierce, Redwuld the cruel.

And as if to confirm her in this opinion, Branwen saw a young woman standing at his back dressed in the simple, unadorned gown of a servant, her head bowed, her long chestnut brown hair hanging down past her shoulders. And even from this distance Branwen could see that the woman was a rare beauty—and that, although softened and reshaped, her features closely resembled those of Gavan ap Huw.

"Alwyn," Branwen breathed.

So even if Gavan ap Huw and the boys of Doeth Palas had found their way here, they had not yet had any success in stealing Alwyn away from her master. And how could they if she was kept forever at Redwuld's side? Branwen could imagine how the old warrior would chafe to see his child held in thrall to the Saxons; but it would take an army of thousands to assail Ironfist's camp. Even with all his hard-won skills and his desperate love for the girl, Gavan ap Huw's mission seemed to Branwen to be doomed to failure.

"Indeed, it must be she," murmured Blodwedd, close at Branwen's side. "And the other is Ironfist's son, come to greet his father. Do you see the ice in his eyes, Branwen?"

As they watched, Redwuld knelt before Ironfist, lowering his head as the general's hand came down on his son's shoulder. The crowd roared as Redwuld rose to his feet and father and son turned and walked out through the gate together, the band of warriors following close behind. The cheering of the crowd continued for some time, but eventually people began to peel away and return in twos and threes to their work; and at last the only people left at the gateway were the guards with their iron helmets and their long-hafted spears.

The opening at which Branwen and Blodwedd were standing was not high enough for them to see over the town's walls; but through the open gates, they had a narrow glimpse of the encampment with its huts and its tents and its busy workshops.

Even this restricted view showed them how crowded and full of activity the camp was. Iron was being forged into spearheads and swords. Tanned leather was being nailed to round wooden shields. Horses were being exercised; and in open spaces, men were training with bow and arrow and with javelins, while others were fighting together, watched over by the sheriffs and reeves of Ironfist's mighty army.

Moving through Chester unobserved was one thing—but passing through an entire army without being seen? Was that even possible?

"So, Branwen," began Blodwedd, as though voicing her thoughts aloud. "Do we dare cross this nest of snakes in broad daylight? And if Merion's powers are sufficient to hide us from prying eyes, how are we to find the place where Caradoc is imprisoned?"

"And how do we get that prison away from here?" added Branwen. "Merion said it might be a small thing—it could be a casket or a box of some kind, possibly. Marked by a lynx. But even were it something that could be carried between us, how are we to bear it away without being challenged?"

"I'd say this is a task suited more to the night than the day," Blodwedd mused. "At least in the dark of night many of the men will be asleep—and in shadows we may be able to perform deeds that the sun would make all too apparent."

Branwen slipped her crystal into its pouch and untied the golden key from her waistband. She held it on her open palm. "Or do we dare open the prison and let Caradoc go free?" she wondered. "I know Merion spoke against it, but it would make things much easier for us—and his powers might even aid us in our escape."

"You must not release Caradoc," Blodwedd said. "You do not know his power. I foresee death and disaster if you follow such a course."

"What could he do?" asked Branwen. "What powers does he have?"

"The power of all the winds of the world," said Blodwedd, her voice slow and solemn. "The ice wind from the north that cracks rocks and freezes the soul. The south wind that comes like a scorching dragon. The storm wind that scours over the ocean, bringing the flood and the lightning's fierce fork. The blizzard's blast and the snowy gale—all these forces he commands, Branwen. None can stand against him in his anger, nor none should dare to try."

Branwen stared at her. "How was he ever imprisoned if he's so powerful?" she asked.

"I do not know," said Blodwedd. "But it must have been a great and a fearsome incantation that trammeled him. Let Merion of the Stones calm his anger when he is released. Put the key away, Branwen. Do not think to use it!"

Branwen nodded, alarmed by the owl-girl's words. She leaned out of the opening, looking for the sun. It was high above, floating in a veil of thin white cloud. Half the day was already gone. "Let's go, then," she said. "We will meet up with Rhodri and Iwan and the others where we arranged—and we will plan for a night raid on Ironfist's camp."

Branwen climbed down the ladder and made for the door, her mind still full of the images that Blodwedd's warning had put into her head.

She opened the door into bright sunlight, and stepped out of the barn.

A group of five warriors were approaching. They stared at her, their faces grim.

One of them spoke. *"Hwaet la! Ceir aern plegestre leas gitung?"* The voice was angry, questioning. *"Astyntan! Gefylce aeht!"*

Branwen stopped in her tracks, taken aback to have been seen and horrified that the man's words were no more than a meaningless spew of sound in her ears. But then it struck her! *Fool!* She had slipped the white crystal into the pouch at her waist when she had untied the key. Too late she realized that its power must only work when she held it in her naked hand.

Worse was to come. Blodwedd stumbled into Branwen with a gasp, and the owl-girl's hood fell back, revealing her face.

"Wodena leoma! Hwaet yfel naedre!" shouted one of the men, pointing at Blodwedd with shock and fear in his voice.

Her eyes! They have seen her eyes!

They will not make you invisible! Those had been Merion's words to her in the cave. Now that the warriors had seen Branwen, it was as if the glamour of the stones had fallen entirely from their eyes.

Branwen was only dumbfounded for a moment. Realizing their danger, she leaped backward, bundling Blodwedd along with her, throwing the door closed in the faces of the Saxon warriors.

But there was no way to bar the door from the inside, and against the strength of five men it was impossible for Branwen and Blodwedd to hold it closed.

"Run!" gasped Blodwedd, fighting to keep the door shut as the men heaved on it from outside. "Go to the upper floor and jump! I will hold them back for as long as I can!"

"No!" Branwen dug in her heels, gripping the door with both hands, leaning back with all her weight. "You'll be killed!"

"Better one than both," insisted Blodwedd. "Your life is more precious than mine, Branwen! Do as I say!"

The door edged open, the timbers shivering and groaning from the strain. *"No!"*

The uneven struggle came to a sudden end. The strip of wood that Branwen had been holding split away from the door. She crashed onto her back as the door was wrenched outward, dragging Blodwedd along with it.

Branwen lay gasping as the five Saxon warriors entered the barn, their spears held ready, their eyes blazing.

18

BLODWEDD DID NOT hesitate for a moment. Like a wild animal she flung herself at the men, her hands curled into claws, her eyes blazing fury and her white teeth snapping.

Branwen was still struggling to her feet as she saw Blodwedd clinging to one man's back, her fingernails sunk into his face, her teeth at his throat as he staggered and choked and tried to throw her off.

Branwen thrust her fingers into the leather pouch at her belt, feeling for the crystal and pulling it out. It was too late to remain hidden, but knowing what the men were saying to one another might help in the fight.

Closing the fingers of her left hand over the crystal, Branwen took a firm grip on the piece of wood that had snapped off the door. It was about the length of a throwing spear, but much thicker and with a jagged, broken end. Not the ideal weapon against the iron-tipped spears of her opponents, but better than nothing.

Her battle-instincts took over, assessing the situation in a single moment, deciding on a course of action.

The townsfolk were gone from here, and the entrance to the barn faced away from the gate—which meant that if she could prevent these men from sounding the alarm, there was a chance of surviving the encounter and escaping.

Blood spurted from the neck of the man Blodwedd was attacking. He fell onto his knees, clawing at her, his face full of horror. Another man stabbed at Blodwedd, but she managed to twist herself and her victim around so that the spear sank into the kneeling man's shoulder.

The barn door swung slowly closed, shutting out much of the light, throwing the combatants into deep shade.

Good! That is to our advantage!

Three to one! Branwen had faced worse odds. She sprang forward, almost impaling herself on the thrusting spears, dodging from side to side as the leading man struck at her, parrying the lunging spears with her improvised weapon. She used all her moving weight to bring the sharp point of the length of timber into his face.

She felt the shuddering impact but avoided looking

at the damage she had caused. She felt none of the euphoria of the battle with Skur. There was no red mist before her eyes. No wild cyclones in her brain. This was just a job that had to be done as quickly and efficiently as possible. For her and Blodwedd to live, these men had to die. It was harsh, it was brutal, and it was very simple.

The first man fell with a choked cry, his hands coming up to his ruined face. Branwen turned, crouching low, her bloodied weapon jabbing at the two remaining men.

She heard a muted cry from behind her. Blodwedd's voice—pained, cut off short. Branwen gritted her teeth. Her attackers were coming closer, their eyes hard, their spear points aimed at her heart. She risked a glance over her shoulder. Blodwedd was sprawling on the ground, the lower part of her face a mask of Saxon blood, hissing and spitting as the second man prepared to stab down at her. She writhed away from the spear, but the man's foot came stamping down on her chest, pinning her. Her arms and legs flailed as he raised his spear for the final thrust.

Branwen swung around, falling to her knees as she flung her weapon at the man's head. It struck him a jarring blow on the temple, knocking him sideways so that he came staggering up against the wall of the barn.

But before she could turn back to defend herself, Branwen felt a heavy blow to the small of her back. Not a spear point—that would have finished her;

it must have been the butt end of a spear crashing viciously into her spine. She was flung onto her face, the air beaten out of her. In trying to save Blodwedd she had doomed herself. A savage kick to her side spun her onto her back, a fierce pain raging under her ribs. A booted foot came down on her throat. Enraged eyes stared down at her from beyond the barbed iron tip of a spear.

"No! Don't kill her!" called one of the other men. "Better to take them alive! I'd know what they are doing here—and what *that* is!"

He clearly meant Blodwedd. The owl-girl was on her feet again, thick drops of blood dangling and dripping from her chin. The soldier was holding her at bay with his spear, and the only way for her to get to him would be by throwing herself onto the point of his weapon.

"I am death that comes on silent wings!" cried Blodwedd, spitting blood. "I am the raking claw! The stabbing beak! I shall swallow you whole and cough up your bones! Come—I long to taste your flesh!"

"It's not human!" gasped the man, thrusting toward her with the spear. "It's some *waelisc* demon!"

The man looming over Branwen pressed down harder on her breastbone with his boot, crushing her into the ground, making it difficult for her to draw breath. "What is that thing? Do you control it?" He brought the spear point close to her face. "Answer me!"

Branwen glared up at him. She could see her death

in his angry face. She would need to do something sudden and shocking if she wished to come through this.

"Release me or you will suffer all the torments of Annwn!" She gasped. "I am protected by powers you cannot comprehend!"

The two men stared down at her. "What is she saying?" asked the one with his boot on her. "Do any of you speak this barbarous language?"

"Do you not know who I am?" Branwen snarled. "Run from me, Saxon curs! I am the Emerald Flame of my people! Have you not heard my name? I am the mighty shaman of the *waelisc*! I am Branwen ap Griffith!"

The man jumped back as if from a sudden fire. Even if they did not understand anything else she was saying, they recognized that name!

"By Welund's blade, it is the sorceress Thain Herewulf spoke of!"

"Kill her!" howled the second man. "Before she casts a spell on us! Kill them both!"

Gasping for air, Branwen rose to her knees. She lowered her head, grimacing at the two men, staring balefully at them through veils of hair. She had hoped to throw her attackers off balance for a few moments—for long enough to fight back—but it seemed she had underestimated the terror she instilled in them.

Both men raised their spears, drawing back their arms, ready to throw.

Branwen braced herself, watching the spear points, chancing all on her ability to evade the coming attack. Expecting to die.

A sudden flood of bright light struck the two men, dazzling them as they threw. Branwen flung herself on the ground as the spears whirred over her. She heard the familiar whiz of an arrow—and then another. Two cries cut short. A noise from behind her and the grunt of a man in pain.

She heaved herself onto her feet, not understanding what had happened.

For a moment the three figures outlined against the sunlit open doorway were just a dark blur. But then she heard a voice.

"Bryn—finish that man!"

It was Gavan ap Huw. Branwen narrowed her eyes against the glare. Gavan stood just inside the barn door, his sword in his hand, bloodied to the hilt. The man who had been holding Blodwedd at bay was crumpled at his feet.

Bryn was crouching over the other man with a knife in his fist. The man whom Blodwedd had first attacked. A quick, silent slash across the throat and it was all over.

Padrig was also there, bow in hand, a third arrow ready.

Gavan drew the door closed, and the barn became dim again. He looked into Branwen's face, pointing to the man she had struck first—the man into whose face she had thrust the broken piece of wood. He lay curled up on the floor, staining the earth with blood from his wound, his breath rasping.

"He's alive still," Gavan said grimly. "Finish the task!"

"How did you come here?" Branwen gasped.

Gavan did not look at her as he replied. "Think you I have no skills in the hunt?" he said. "I saw you right enough, standing in full view up in yonder hatchway!" He gestured to the ladder that led to the upper floor. "Do you think yourselves invisible that you showed yourself thus? Any of a score or more men could have shot you down from there!"

"They could not see us," said Branwen. "We were protected from their sight by . . . certain *gifts*. . . ."

"I can imagine the nature of the gifts!" said Gavan. "You need not speak more of them." He pointed to the dying man at Branwen's feet. "Give him peace, child! Do your duty to him!"

Branwen looked down at the helpless man. His face was turned away from her, but she could tell from the blood that soaked into the hard-packed floor that he was dreadfully hurt—hurt probably to the death.

She stooped and pulled his seax knife from his belt. A single cut across the windpipe and all would be done. But she could not do it. Not in cold blood.

Grim-faced, Gavan strode across to her. He snatched the knife from her hand and crouched to draw it across the man's throat. There was a choking gurgle, then silence. Branwen looked away, shamed that she had been unable to kill for mercy as Gavan had done. The old warrior wiped the blade on the man's tunic and then stood up, slipping it into his own belt. "Padrig—guard the door; give the word if any come nigh this place. Bryn—strip the dead of their weapons; we may find use for them."

Obediently, the two boys did as they were told; Padrig went to the door and peered out through a crack in the timbers while Bryn went from one Saxon corpse to another, taking their seaxes and spears.

The eyes of Branwen and Gavan met in the gloom.

"There's no mercy in letting a dying man suffer needlessly," Gavan said. "Or maybe mercy is no longer of interest to you, Branwen?"

Branwen stared at him, her jaw clenched. "We would maybe have died here if not for you," she said at last, looking briefly at Bryn and Padrig. "You have my gratitude, if it means anything to you."

Bryn's sullen, beefy face was as impenetrable as ever; but Padrig had a fierce, uneasy light in his eyes. Branwen guessed that the two Saxons were his first kills—he seemed both proud and alarmed by what he had done.

"Your thanks are not needed," said Gavan. "I'd not see even a Powys brach die under a Saxon sword."

A brach! Is that what he thought of her—no better than a female hunting dog?

She and Gavan ap Huw had once been pupil and

master—there had been trust and affection between them. But now they stared at each other like rival wolves meeting in disputed territory. No trust. Just suspicion and tight-lipped enmity, despite the fact that Gavan's intervention had almost certainly saved her and Blodwedd's lives.

"I have seen your daughter," Branwen said hesitantly, her eyes moving from his face, a flush rising in her cheeks.

Gavan nodded. "I, too, have seen Alwyn," he said. "We were at the gate when Ironfist met his son." His eyes narrowed. "The great general of the Saxons is not dead, as you thought."

"Maybe not," said Blodwedd, coming to stand at Branwen's side, wiping the blood off her mouth with her sleeve. "But Skur Bloodax is dead—defeated and slain in mortal combat. Be not so haughty, Old Warrior, when you speak to the Chosen Child of the Shining Ones—she has done great deeds since last we met."

Bryn's face darkened, and Padrig gripped his bow tightly, as though the owl-girl's bold words annoyed him.

"Defeated by witchcraft, no doubt," said Gavan without looking at Blodwedd.

"No! By muscle and sinew and good iron, with a sharp mind and a cunning eye behind!" said Blodwedd. "You taught her well, Old Warrior; rejoice that she was such an apt disciple." Her eyes glowed. "Or would you wish that she had died in the combat?"

"Hush, Blodwedd," Branwen murmured, not wanting things to become more difficult than was already the case.

"Do I wish she had died?" said Gavan as though testing the words in his mouth, still avoiding the eyes of the owl-girl. "No, I do not wish her dead. But you may wish it, Branwen, ere the Old Gods are done with you; and I'd wish with all my heart that you could see the truth clearly and return to the love of your people."

"We have spoken of this before," Branwen said quietly. "My mind has not changed, and neither has yours. Let's have no more of it." She met his eyes again. "How have you managed to keep hidden in this place? There are few men here with shaven chins."

"A deep cowl hid my features for the most part," said Gavan. "A wrap of fox fur about my chin did the rest. And the boys needed no disguise with their hairless faces. But gaining entry to Ironfist's camp is another matter. I speak little Saxon, and the boys none. Yet I must and I will find a way into the heart of the camp. I will not leave this place without my daughter. I have made a vow on that!"

"Where are the others?" Branwen asked. "Andras and the boy?"

"They are safe outside the town, with the horses," said Gavan. "I did not think it prudent to bring Dillon into Chester—his face may be recognized. And what of your followers? Is Dera ap Dagonet with you still, or has she seen sense?"

"Some are here, and Dera is among them," Branwen said, not rising to his bait. "They are protected by the same enchantment that hides us from Saxon eyes. The rest are in the forest atop the hill on the far side of the river." She looked keenly into Gavan's eyes. "Tell me, Gavan ap Huw—what would you do to bring your daughter safe from this place?"

Gavan frowned at her, his eyes like gimlets. "I'd walk unarmed through every black pit and foul trench in Annwn," he growled. "I'd pluck the horned god Cernunnos himself by the beard! I'd spit in the face of every demon from here to the fabled court of Math ap Mathonwy! I'd do all a man can do and more besides!"

"Would you ally yourself with me and mine?" asked Branwen, watching his face carefully. "Would you use the gifts of the Shining Ones to set her free?"

She saw Gavan flinch. She was not sure why she had made the offer. To prove to Gavan that the Shining Ones were not as deadly as he believed? Hardly that; she was quite sure they *were*! To offer the hand of friendship—in the hope of retying the bonds between them? Maybe. Simply to *help* him? She hoped her motives were that pure.

"We don't need their help," said Bryn, looking distastefully at Branwen.

"Be silent!" said Gavan, his eyes riveted on Branwen's

face. She could see the conflict in his mind.

Branwen opened her left palm and held up the white crystal to Gavan's eyes. Even in the darkness of the barn, she could see the rainbow coiling at the white stone's heart. "This and five others like it I have carried with me for many years," she said. "They were given to me by my brother, Geraint, although he did not know the power that they could contain."

Gavan stared uneasily at the stone, his eyes narrowed.

"Merion of the Stones gifted us with the ability to go unseen among enemies while we hold these crystals," said Branwen. "Do you still think I do wrong to follow the Old Gods when so much of my life has been bound to them?"

Gavan didn't respond to her question, but she could see doubt and disquiet in his gray eyes.

"With Merion's stones, we will be able to pass through the ranks of the enemy like a night wind through the trees," murmured Blodwedd. "They will know nothing of our coming nor of our going. Can you do the same, Old Warrior?"

Gavan's face contracted into a scowl. "In battle a man will use whatever weapon comes to hand," he said under his breath. "My mind speaks against it, but my heart will not be denied." He glowered into Branwen's face. "But why would you wish to help me? What is my daughter to you?"

"I'd help you because once you were my friend," said Branwen. "And I too have business in Ironfist's Great Hall. Maybe it is that we will help each other." She lifted her chin. "Make your decision! I offer you my aid, if you will have it. If not we will go our separate ways; and you will take my good wishes with you, despite all the bad that you think of me."

She was aware of Padrig and Bryn watching Gavan closely, and it was clear from their faces that they hoped he would refuse her offer.

"To save my child, I will risk all," Gavan said at length. "Yes, Branwen of the Old Ones, I will join with you for a time—if the gifts of your gods will work for an unbeliever."

"Oh, they will, Old Warrior; do not fear on that account," said Blodwedd, her eyes shining. "The bounty of the Ancient Ones embraces even the most reluctant of their children."

"I am not a child of the Old Gods!" snarled Gavan, finally looking into her face.

Blodwedd smiled, and there was blood on her teeth. "Oh, but you are," she crooned. "Do not fool yourself, Old Warrior. We are *all* their children, whether we acknowledge it or not."

Gavan turned away, but not before Branwen saw a look of profound dread disfigure his features. Blodwedd's words seemed to have cut him to the very soul; and if not for his hunger to save his daughter, Branwen felt sure he would have quit that place and never once have looked back.

"Then it's settled," Branwen said. "We should hide these bodies among the sacks so they are not quickly found. And then we should leave this town and gather our forces and await nightfall."

19

"A GLORIOUS SUNSET to herald a night of dangerous endeavor!" said Iwan, coming suddenly to
Branwen's side as she stood on the breezy hilltop,
gazing out over the darkening plain. The lights of
Chester and of the army camp that grew like some
poisonous tumor at its side were beginning to ignite.

Iwan was right. Behind the forest at her back,
high banks of cloud burned scarlet and orange, as
if the western sky was aflame. And above her purple
scuds of cloud hung impossibly still against the grainy
blue of dusk. In the distant east a rich velvet darkness
crawled imperceptibly across the world, obliterating
everything.

Branwen had been thinking of her mother, wondering whether, in the midst of her labors, Lady Alis
had taken the time to lift her eyes to the glory of the

dying day and whether it was possible that at that moment she was thinking of her errant daughter and offering her blessings for Branwen's safekeeping.

Branwen looked at Iwan but said nothing, struck by the way the fading light complemented the shape of his face, highlighting the curve of his mouth, the shadows under his cheekbones, the glimmer of his dark eyes.

He smiled, cocking his head to indicate the people and horses gathered just under the eaves of the forest. "A merry bunch we are, to be sure," he said, his eyes twinkling with private amusement. "Do you see how Bryn glowers at everyone, like a hunting dog desperate to be unleashed on a flock of chickens!"

"Does he ever look otherwise?" Branwen sighed.

"No, I dare say not," Iwan said, laughing softly. "But can we trust them, Branwen? I think Gavan hates and fears you in equal measure. Is it wise to take him with us into Ironfist's camp?"

"We have had this debate, and the decision is made," said Branwen. "There are six stones—and six people have been chosen." She raised an eyebrow. "Unless you would give up your place to someone else? Rhodri, perhaps?"

"By no means," said Iwan. "Let him and the others stay and keep watch over that Viking maid."

Branwen frowned. He meant Asta, of course. "Why will no one use her name?" she asked.

"Perhaps because she is not of our blood, Branwen."

He looked thoughtfully at her. "Can I speak of Rhodri without angering you?"

"I don't know. Do you have that ability?"

"He is a good fellow, I believe," said Iwan. "And I dislike him less than I show; but he is half Saxon, Branwen. I'd rest easier if I thought you understood what that means."

"You'd hold his divided parentage against him?" said Branwen, surprised and a little annoyed. "He has proved himself a friend many times over. Why do you trust no one, Iwan?"

"I trust but one person," Iwan replied. "I know for certain of only one man who would willingly give his life for you." His voice lowered to a soft whisper. "A thousand times over."

Branwen looked away from him, staring out over the wide plain, hoping he could not hear the way her heart was pulsing. She swallowed, the pounding sensation growing under her rib cage.

"What man is that?" she asked, her voice cracking.

There was no reply. She turned. Iwan was walking away from her under the trees.

Bringing the two bands together without conflict had not been easy, and at the very best a hostile truce was all that existed between Gavan's boys and Branwen's followers. After some brief initial antagonism, Bryn and the others virtually ignored Iwan, obviously thinking their former friend and companion beyond the pale with his new allegiances. Iwan found this all too obviously amusing, which only made the other boys of Doeth Palas more peevish. And none of them would even look at Blodwedd; skinny Andras positively shrank away if she came close to him. All the while, Dillon kept to himself, silently watching with huge eyes.

It had not taken long to hide the bodies of the dead Saxons in among the barley sacks in the barn. A length of sacking had been torn away to provide a wrapping for the spears and knives that Bryn had taken from their corpses.

Their departure from Chester had passed without incident, Gavan's Brythonic features hidden under his cowl, Bryn clutching the looted weapons in the wrap of sacking. Once across the river bridge, they had slipped south off the road and made their way to a huddled glade of willows, similar to the one in which Branwen had made her final plans before entering the town earlier that morning.

Here they had found Andras and Dillon and the five horses; and here they remained for the afternoon, hardly speaking, Branwen and Blodwedd sitting together, and Gavan and the boys keeping their distance. To pass the time, Gavan had arranged mock sword fights with the lads. Branwen watched with a critical eye. Padrig was a good shot with a bow, but although he was light-footed and quick-witted, his sword work wasn't up to much in her opinion. And Andras was all but useless, more likely to trip up and stab himself in the foot than to do damage to an enemy. The only truly dangerous fighter among them was Bryn, and his abilities were due more to weight and force than to anything else. But there was a cold look in his eyes as he fought of which Branwen had taken particular note.

He'd kill without a second thought. I could never bring myself to like him, but he would be a good man to have at your side in a desperate situation.

Branwen had managed a private word with Gavan while they waited for the others. She felt he had a right to know the full nature of their mission, to give him the opportunity to break their alliance if he found it too disturbing.

He had listened in stony silence as she told him of Merion and of the imprisonment of Caradoc of the North Wind. When she had finished, he made only one comment.

"If I find Alwyn and have the means to escape Ironfist's camp with her, I will do it," he had warned her. "Whether your mission is fulfilled or not."

"And if I find Caradoc's prison, I too will depart the place," Branwen had responded. "And I will not wait for you or yours."

"Then we understand each other, Branwen."

"Yes. I think we do."

Rhodri and Banon had been the next pair to appear

from Chester, heading toward the place Branwen had suggested for their gathering and drawn to this new hiding place by a shrill whistle from Blodwedd and Branwen's beckoning arm.

Rhodri had accepted the appearance of Gavan and the boys without comment, but Branwen had not forgotten that these were the lads who had cornered and beaten him when he had been captured in Doeth Palas. She guessed his forbearance was due more to not wishing to cause her problems than to having forgiven the boys.

Rhodri and Banon had little to report that Branwen had not already known. They had heard Ironfist's speech and had been as disgusted by it as Branwen had been. They had then moved among the townsfolk, listening to much the same kinds of conversations. But Rhodri had used his knowledge of the Saxon language to manage to buy some food for them.

"How did you come by the money?" Branwen had asked.

A slow grin had spread across Banon's face. "I played cutpurse, and relieved an overfed wheat monger of it," she said. "He did not even notice the loss! 'Tis a quick way to gain coin, although my mother would not approve!"

As the afternoon wore on, Iwan and Dera had also appeared. Dera had not hid her disapproval of the new alliance that Branwen had forged, but her antagonism had been restricted to glowering looks. Iwan had been hugely entertained by it, and his mockery of the boys almost brought him to blows with Bryn. Only Gavan's intervention prevented them from fighting. After that, the boys of Doeth Palas hardly spoke to their onetime friend and companion. Not that Iwan had seemed to care.

Now that they had all come together, they headed up the forested hill to join with Aberfa and Linette and Asta. There had been more awkwardness, with Aberfa and Bryn facing off, sullen face to sullen face; but in the end Branwen and Gavan had managed to convince everyone to hold to this temporary truce— at the very least until their tasks in Ironfist's army camp were done.

Asta had prepared a meal for them all while they awaited nightfall. She moved quietly among them, her eyes lowered, handing out bread and cheese and parcels of fish stuffed with herbs and cooked in the embers of a smoldering fire too small to be seen from afar.

Gavan had questioned Asta about Skur, and the answers she had given him were the same as those she had given to Branwen when she had first been rescued. Gavan approved of the decision not to let her go free, but Branwen could see that he also sympathized with the Viking maiden's plight despite her being of foreign blood.

One last decision had been needed.

Six stones.

Twelve people, not including Asta or Dillon.

Who would go with Branwen and Gavan into the camp?

In the end Branwen chose Blodwedd, Dera, Iwan, and Bryn.

And so, all choices having been made, Branwen had walked from their small camp under the trees to watch the sunset and to think of her mother—only to be interrupted by the perplexing and unsettling appearance of Iwan.

At the last moment before the six departed for Ironfist's encampment, Branwen sought out Rhodri for a quiet word alone.

"I don't want you to be concerned that I chose Iwan over you for the mission into the Saxon camp," she said.

"I'm not," Rhodri said. "Iwan is the better fighter; if you fall into bad luck, he's more likely to get you all out safe than I." He smiled. "And I have my own skills," he added. "Who better to tend the wounded when you return?"

Branwen was relieved. "Good. Exactly." She looked into his face. "You are my truest friend, Rhodri—and the voice of my conscience, whether I like what it tells me or not. I don't want any misunderstanding between us. I'd not upset you for all of Brython. Please remember that."

"I shall." He touched his hand to her arm. "I'm not concerned for your safety; Iwan will make certain that you do not come to harm."

She looked at him, puzzled by this. "Why Iwan? I would have expected you to have named Blodwedd as the one to keep me from danger."

"Blodwedd would fling herself into fire for you," said Rhodri. "But I think Iwan might just do more." He smiled a knowing smile. "I believe that under all his bravado and mischief, he may possibly cherish you almost as much as you cherish him."

Branwen almost choked, embarrassed that her attraction to Iwan was so obvious and desperate to deny it. "What do you mean? He's a valued companion to me. No more."

Rhodri's smile widened. "Don't try to dupe me, Branwen; I know you too well. I have seen the fond way you look at him when you think no one can see."

Branwen felt her cheeks burning. "I have no idea what you mean," she said. "And if we're speaking of ardent gazes, Rhodri—what of the mooncalf eyes you make at Blodwedd!"

A look of pain crossed his face. "She is an owl, Branwen," he said. "She can never love me."

Branwen winced to have hurt him. "I'm sorry; that was unkind," she said gently. "And I hope she will prove you wrong. But you are mistaken about my feelings for Iwan, and his for me. He is conceited and artful and annoying! He could never love another as deeply as he loves himself! I would need to be a great fool indeed to harbor affection for one such as he."

Rhodri looked thoughtfully at her, leaving a silence, it seemed, into which she might pour more words. But she had nothing more to say.

"Your fellows await you," Rhodri said at last, and Branwen had the disturbing feeling that he had seen through the shield of her thoughts and had looked into the hidden rooms of her heart.

She turned, glad to bring the conversation to an end.

On the edge of the forest, five people stood waiting. And as she walked toward them, she saw Blodwedd hold up her crystal to the rising crescent moon, and she saw the rainbow heart of the stone blaze out through the owl-girl's fingers in shafts of ever-changing many-colored light.

Branwen took from her pouch the two crystals she had still to distribute, along with two slender lengths of linen.

It had been Rhodri's idea to enfold the stones in linen strips and to tie them around the wrists. That way the stones would be in constant contact with skin, but the hands would be free.

Already, Branwen, Dera, and Iwan had on their linen wristbands—and Blodwedd had removed her stone from hers only for a few moments to watch it shine in the moonlight.

"They must be constantly against your flesh,"

she warned Gavan and Bryn. "Their power will fail if they are not. And remember—they do not make us invisible. . . . They merely give us the ability to go *unnoticed* so long as we do not draw attention to ourselves."

She put the first crystal into the linen strip and made to tie it to Bryn's wrist. But at the last moment he drew away, his face tight with unease.

Gavan offered his arm. "Here, tie mine first," he said.

Branwen looped the cloth around the warrior's wrist, the crystal snug in its folds. She wound it twice and tied it tight.

"See, boy?" Gavan said gruffly. "I'm not burned nor struck down by dark sorcery. Now—wear a stone or I'll pick another and leave you to tend the horses!"

With great reluctance Bryn allowed the final stone to be secured against his wrist, but Branwen could see how it disturbed him to have the thing touching his flesh.

"Are you content?" she asked him.

"It is cold," he mumbled, tugging fretfully at her knots.

"It is," she agreed. "The stones are always cold. But likely enough you'll have other things to occupy your thoughts before long."

Soon enough, they would have plenty of other concerns.

This time they were planning to enter a Saxon

stronghold armed and ready to fight if they must. All six bore shields and weapons, as well as armor of leather and chain mail.

Branwen turned to those they would be leaving behind, drawing her sword and lifting it in a final salute. Fain was perched upon Rhodri's shoulder, the bird's black eyes reflecting the crescent moon. Rhodri's hand rose in response to Branwen's gesture, his skin white in the moonlight.

And so, silent as a night breeze, the six companions stepped off the hilltop and began the long walk to General Ironfist's encampment.

20

AS THEY APPROACHED the bridge over the river,
Branwen saw that the gates of Chester were
shut fast for the night. Torches burned brightly on
the walls, the light reflecting ruby off the helmets
and spear tips of the guards who patrolled the town's
outer defenses.

Moving in complete silence, they filed across the
bridge, keeping to such shadow as there was. Branwen
went first, warily watching the guards high above her,
praying that no head would turn toward them in sudden interest.

There was a clatter at her back, and she froze,
turning, her face grim.

Bryn had dropped his spear.

"Do not move!" Branwen whispered.

They all became as still as roosting shadows.

Gavan's voice was a soft growl. "Fool of a boy!"

Branwen turned her head and peered up at the wall. One guard was leaning over the timber palisade, staring down at the bridge.

She heard a voice.

"Sighard? What is it?"

"I thought I heard a noise—but I see nothing."

"Likely it's one of the thain's drunken louts falling into the river! There's a great feast in the hall tonight, curse our luck."

"Aye, I know; and I'd rather be quaffing ale than wearing away my feet up here on the watch! What enemy would dare assail us here, Eanfrid, with Ironfist's entire army clamped to our side? It would be sheer madness, and even the mountain rats of the west are not such fools. Why, they would need to come here in their thousands to even . . ." But then the guard moved away from the edge of the wall, and Branwen could no longer hear what passed between him and the other.

A great feast? Interesting. In honor of the return of General Ironfist, no doubt—although Saxons needed little excuse for debauched carousals. But it might work in their favor—it was during one such revelry that Branwen had previously caught Ironfist unawares. Maybe she could work the trick a second time?

She gestured for the others to move again. Even in the darkness she could see the deep flush on

Bryn's face. *Good! Maybe it will teach him to be less clumsy in the future!*

They slid across the bridge and then came down off the road and followed the outer line of the walls alongside the soft bank of the river. It was slow work to find firm ground in all the reeds and bog, but Branwen brought them to the southwestern corner of Chester's walls without anything worse than muddy boots.

Now they could see the army camp, and hear the shouting and laughter of the wakeful men. Torches and bonfires blazed among the canvas tents and huts. It seemed that the entire army was celebrating the homecoming of their great general.

"But Ironfist lost the battle," puzzled Dera. "Many ships foundered—and hundreds of warriors were slain. Why do they rejoice?"

"This is not an expression of gladness," growled Gavan. "This is the frenzy of a joyless debauch. Ironfist whips them into a fever for the battles that are to come. Yet it is in our favor. Drunk by night, the majority of Ironfist's army will be lying like pigs in the mire ere sunup. But they will have guards walking the perimeters—and those guards will be sober. We'd best lie low and judge the number of watchful sentries before we seek to enter."

Branwen glared at him. She had been about to give the same order, but he had not allowed her the time.

He returned her look with eyes as cold and unreadable as gray pebbles.

"Would you have us act differently?" he asked.

"No."

She crouched in the reeds, watching the great camp. Gavan had been right of course—there were armed sentries at several points within sight; but none were patrolling, and Branwen saw that not a few of them were leaning on their spears and talking at ease with others, and some were even swigging from ale horns.

It seemed that the guards here were of the same opinion as those Branwen had heard on the walls of Chester. Why miss out on the revels? The *waelisc* barbarians would need to be absolute fools to attack!

Good. All to the good.

She turned to the others huddled together in a low dip at her back.

"The sentinels are inattentive," she said. "We should have no trouble passing them. But we must not speak once we are in the camp." She glowered at Bryn. "And we must move in absolute silence. Remember, the power in the stones cannot hide us from a man once we have drawn his attention. We shall move in single file, keeping always to the line I take. When we come to the Great Hall, Iwan, Bryn, and Dera will wait outside—you three will be backup if things go badly—either to enter the hall to help us if we are seen or to help cut a way out of the camp if that becomes necessary." She looked at Gavan. "Your desire is to find and rescue your daughter, and as far as possible we will aid you and Bryn in that. But *our* task is to find the prison in which Caradoc is confined and to bring it away with us." She glanced from Iwan to Dera to Blodwedd. "No one life is more important than our mission. If I fall or am trapped or caught or hurt, do not linger to help me. And the same goes for each of us. Those still standing must escape with Caradoc at all costs." She stared into Blodwedd's eyes, knowing how the owl-girl must hate such an order. "Promise me you will do this."

"I promise to do all that I can to ensure that Caradoc is brought safe from Saxon hands," Blodwedd said. "But if you are captured or wounded, Branwen, and unable to escape, I will leave Caradoc of the North Wind in the keeping of others, and I will return here, though ten thousand bar my way; and I will not leave again without you."

"It won't come to that," said Iwan. "No one is going to be left behind; I'll see to that. Let's get on with it, by your leave, barbarian princess, while the night is still young." He moved out of the hollow and came up close to Branwen. "I'll not be outdone in courage by a plucked *bird*," she heard him mutter under his breath.

She could almost have smiled!

Branwen stood on the outskirts of the camp, taking a moment to try and calm her nerves.

Merion will protect me. I know this. She stared into

the massed throng of carousing men. *I need have no fear. And yet . . . and yet, it feels as though I am about to walk into a furnace.*

She was trembling. She tried to suppress it, desperate for the others not to notice how she hesitated. She stood absolutely motionless until the shaking in her legs subsided. Her muscles knotted and cramped. She must move on!

She offered a last prayer, her fingers running over the lump in her wristband—the small hidden stone that was all that stood between her and certain death.

Do not desert me!

She took a final breath, bracing herself for the plunge. She didn't look back at her companions—they must not see the fear in her face or they would not follow.

And so, with her stomach like a ball of lead in her belly, she took the first step and came in among the tents, her mystical white shield held up against her chest, her right hand gripping her sword hilt.

She walked slowly, watchfully, trying to keep clear of the revelers, always on the lookout for a suddenly turning head or a pair of seeing eyes, expecting to be discovered at every moment.

The place was fomenting with activity and noise. Bonfires crackled and roared into the night, sending red sparks spinning upward, bathing the long canvas tents of the soldiers as red as blood. In open paddocks, mounted men raced their horses to and fro, beating at one another with sticks and howling with laughter if one went tumbling from the saddle.

Others gathered five or more deep around barrels of ale, filling their drinking horns and cups and wooden mugs again and again, their mustaches dripping foam, their beards streaming with the thick brown liquid.

They sang, their voices like the bellowing of animals: songs of death and destruction and of cold iron and hot blood. Songs of warfare and slaughter. Songs to chill the soul.

> *Wild is the blood, high the heart*
> *Glad the eye to see our enemies slain*
> *Like a field of corn laid low by the scythe*
> *Their heads roll, their eyes stare up, ripe*
>   *berries for the crow*
> *And our kinsfolk sleep among them*
> *Blessed in noble death.*
> *Come, do you hear the walkyrie song?*
> *They ride from Walhal*
> *From the empty wine cup and the gnawed*
>   *bone*
> *They ride by threes, the warrior women*
> *Urth, Verthandi, and Skuld*
> *Maiden, mother, and crone, drawing down*
>   *the moon of war.*
> *The boar paws the ground, snorting, tusks*

sheathed in blood
The raven's wings darken the sky
The hammer and the sun wheel, the symbel
   and the husel
Symbel for valor, husel for strength
They ride, they ride, Mogthrasir's children
Singing as they split the storm asunder
Come to bear us to the wide tables and the
   flowing mead
The honeyed cups of Walhal
We dead on the battlefield
We blessed ones who died in war
Come, death, let us die in battle
Death, we welcome you
Walkyrie on the wind, carry us home
Carry your heroes home!

And as they sang their songs of death, they stamped and danced and beat hide drums till Branwen's head was raging with the dreadful clamor of it and her blood ran cold in her veins.

They love death. Their fondest wish is to die in battle. How do we fight such people? How do we stand firm against such reckless madness?

On into the great camp Branwen walked, her anxiety growing rather than diminishing as she threaded her way toward the group of thatched buildings with the Great Hall in its midst. Every step was like a step into greater danger. Like walking alive into the black bowels of Annwn.

Men pranced around bonfires, urging dare-devils on to hurl themselves across the flames, their cloaks snapping as they hung for a moment in the air wreathed in sparks. Iron rang from mock sword fights. Two wrestling men came tumbling across Branwen's path, almost tripping her as they swore and fought and tore at each other's clothes.

The heady smell of roasting meat hung in the air. Men gnawed at gobbets of red meat skewered on their seaxes, the juices clotting in their beards, the fat glistening on their lips and cheeks.

Some few lay snoring or belching on the ground, the ale draining from overturned mugs, their eyes glazed with drunkenness.

Now Branwen was moving among the buildings. The Great Hall loomed up, its doors wide-open, lights blazing within, voices shouting and roaring. Men squatted and stood outside the doors, eating and drinking, their faces bloated, their eyes swimming.

By the saints! Do we even need Merion's stones among such excess? I swear, not one of these drunken swine would know friend from foe at this time!

The thought comforted her a little, but she knew the worst ordeal still lay ahead. Herewulf Ironfist was within these walls—and would even Merion's enchantments keep her hidden from his one good eye? She half feared that his hatred for her would give him the power to cut through all falsehood, to pierce the veil of the stones and to leave her standing helpless and all too visible in front of him.

"It is the waelisc *shaman girl! Kill her. Kill her!"*

No! No! It does no good to think such things.

Clear the mind of fear. Focus on the task at hand.

She stepped over the legs of a man sprawled in the doorway and stared at last into Ironfist's Great Hall. The reek of roasting meat and spilled ale struck her, mingled with the smell of burning fat and cooked herbs. And with it came the roar of the feasting Saxon warriors, General Ironfist's chosen few, selected to join him at the festive board.

Like and unlike the halls of her own people it was. Similar in that a fire blazed in a hearth of stone in the middle of the long main chamber, but strange because the feasters sat on benches at trestle tables rather than on the rush-strewn floor. Similar in that the timbered roof soared up high above, strange in that there was a raised gallery at the far end of the chamber, reached by a wide ladder, where wicker partitions formed private rooms. Similar in that the firelight was augmented by wall-mounted torches and thick tallow candles, different in that the stooping servants who moved among the drinkers were men and women of the Four Kingdoms—Branwen's own folk, captive from childhood like Rhodri or abducted from their homes as Dillon had been. Similar in that the lord of the hall sat upon a throne at one end under awnings of draped battle flags. Different in that the design on the flags was the white dragon of the Saxons and that the man who sat enthroned was a deadly enemy.

The last time Branwen had seen Ironfist like this was when he had been sprawling on the seat of the lord of Gwylan Canu, deep in drink and slow of mind. But he did not look like that now; he was sitting hunched forward, one hand gripping the arm of the chair so that the fingers were white. The other clutched a wine horn, but it hung at an angle and seemed empty.

Malevolent and sinister he looked now, like some monster of legend, brooding among his minions, his one blue eye horribly alert as it darted to and fro over the carousing warriors of his court. His mouth was set in a grim line, his brows furrowed. The raw wound burned red in the firelight, and the lost eye was a pool of crimson.

Another man sat on a low stool at his feet wrapped in a scarlet cloak, staring silently at a slender form who moved among the drinkers balancing a large ewer on her hip and pouring out ale to all who needed more refreshment.

It was Alwyn—Branwen recognized her at once. She stood out from the other servants with their drab, shabby clothes and their matted hair. Alwyn was wearing a gown of bright yellow, clasped at the shoulders by jeweled brooches and girdled with a sash of blue silk.

Silk? What's this now? Do the Saxons dress their servants in silk? I've never heard it so. She must be a favorite to be adorned so—and look at her hair!

Her brown hair was plaited and drawn back from her face, held in place with sparkling pins and netted with bright strings of jasper and malachite. Very beautiful she looked, gliding among the drunken throng; but Branwen noticed that none abused her or snatched at her or even made eyes at her. Strange! Drunken men of all races had sport with pretty servant girls at the feast. And yet she may as well have been a haggard crone for all the notice Ironfist's warriors took of her. It was as if they dared not. As if . . .

And then Branwen remembered Dillon's words: *". . . one woman stood out from the others. Redwuld had brought her with him from the north. Very beautiful, she was, with flowing chestnut brown hair and big eyes like a doe; and Redwuld treated her as a favorite. . . ."*

So, that explained it. Alwyn was his alone, and none dared look at her for fear of his anger. That was not good—if Redwuld never took his eyes off her, how were they to rescue Gavan's daughter?

21

B RANWEN HEARD A sudden breath drawn behind
her. She looked around. Gavan was there, at her
back, staring at his daughter as she moved along the
trestle tables pouring ale for the feasting warriors. A
conflux of emotions choked his features: anger, long-
ing, love, loss, remorse, hope, determination—all
were there in his face.

Branwen brought her mouth up to the side of his
head. "We must wait till she is alone," she whispered.
"We have no hope of escape with her among so many."

He nodded.

But what are we to do next?

She looked more closely at Ironfist, searching for
some box or cask or flask or bag close by—something
in which a god could be confined. There was nothing. Her eyes moved upward to the upper half floor
above his head. Private rooms lay behind the wicker

screens. A sleeping chamber, perhaps, where a man might keep the most prized of his possessions?

Blodwedd was now standing at Gavan's side, her eyes disgusted as she looked in at the Saxon feast. Branwen remembered the owl-girl saying to her once that of all the foul attributes of humankind, the one she found most repulsive and impossible to understand was the desire to pour down their throats a liquid that had no purpose but to steal away their reason!

Well, that might be so, but at this moment that attribute was working in their favor. She gestured to Gavan and Blodwedd—discreet hand movements to suggest that they should keep close to the walls and make their way along the hall to the ladder, and thence to the upper floor.

Gavan nodded. Branwen was about to move from the doorway when Ironfist's body suddenly tensed and he half rose from his seat, his brows drawn down, his eye seeming to stare straight at her.

She froze, her heart clubbing at her ribs. All along she had known Merion's powers would not fool him! She was hideously aware of the white disk of her shield—bright as the full moon—shining out like a great silver coin. Drawing Ironfist's attention to her.

But there was something curious about the way he stared—as though his eye was not quite focused on her but was looking straight through her. As though his attention had been caught by something beyond her. And then he sat again, his face puzzled, his head tilting and angling as though he was trying to fix his gaze on something half hidden.

He senses me, but he does not see me. Dare I move? If I shift a finger will I be seen?

For a long, horrible time Branwen stood frozen in the doorway, well aware of Gavan chafing at her back but not daring to stir a muscle in case it gave them all away.

Then when she felt she could no longer stand the strain, the tension was suddenly broken. Redwuld rose to his feet.

"A song!" he cried. "Come, Alwyn, give us a pretty song!"

The noise of the feasters subsided. Obediently, Alwyn put down the ewer and glided to the far end of the hall, her head down, her face oddly serene. She curtsied to Ironfist and then turned to face the hall.

Redwuld's act had broken Ironfist's concentration. This was the perfect moment to slip in and along the wall, while everyone's attention was on Alwyn.

Gavan's daughter clasped her hands together, lifted her head, and began to sing.

> Oh, the cuckoo is a pretty bird; she sings as
>   she flies
> She brings us glad tidings, she tells us
>   sweet lies . . .

Branwen paused, startled as the sweet melody rippled across the silent hall. It was the same song that she had heard in her dream-vision. The song that the goraig of the lake had sung to her: Nixie's song of the beautiful bird filled with trickery and deceit.

Branwen stared at Alwyn. What did this mean? Was it a coincidence? Surely not! Had she been forewarned by the goraig? Was Alwyn the pretty cuckoo that they could not trust? And what did that mean for her rescue?

Her mind surging with conjecture, Branwen continued to walk softly and silently along the wall behind the rapt Saxon feasters. They obviously knew better than to talk or make undue noise while Redwuld's favorite was singing. And as Alwyn sung, Branwen saw the young man's eyes on her—not filled with love, she thought; it was a look that a man might give a prized possession: greedy and jealous hearted.

Branwen came to the foot of the ladder and began to climb. Gavan came up after her and Blodwedd at the rear. The wooden rungs of the ladder creaked a little under their feet, but no one seemed to notice.

The three of them had just assembled on the lip of the upper floor when the song came to an end. There was a tumult of cheering and stamping and hammering of fists and mugs on the tables.

"A tune!" someone shouted. "We'd have a merry tune!"

And more voices called out in agreement.

"A lively tune!"

"Let her play something upon the harp!"

"Yes! The harp! Fetch down the harp!"

"So be it!" shouted Redwuld. "Alwyn, go fetch your harp! We'd hear a pretty tune to beguile the night and to remind us of hearth and home!"

Alwyn bowed her head and moved to the ladder. Branwen and her companions drew back from the edge.

"She comes up here!" hissed Blodwedd. "By Govannon's horns, this is good fortune!"

"But how are we to make our escape with her?" asked Gavan, his face desperate now, his eyes almost pleading.

"You shall give her my stone," said Blodwedd without hesitation. "It will shield her from their eyes."

"No! What of you then?" said Branwen.

"Do not fear on my account," said Blodwedd. "I'll give them a fine race." She smiled her sharp smile and looked into Branwen's eyes. "Remember on the cliffs outside Gwylan Canu? Remember how I ran and how they could not say if I were a dog or a hare or a deer of the mountain?" She touched Branwen's arm. "Do not fear. I will mislead them long enough to get clear of this place."

"Very well," agreed Branwen. "I see there is no other course. And perhaps Alwyn will lead us to Caradoc's prison and save us the search."

"It is to be hoped so," said Blodwedd. "But I will

begin to look nonetheless while you show yourselves to the girl and reveal to her the purpose of our entry into this grim place."

There was renewed noise from below, the feasters taking the opportunity of a break in the entertainment to shout for more ale and to sing raucous snatches of song as they continued their debauch.

Blodwedd unwrapped her wristband and gave it and the stone to Branwen before slipping away among the screens. Branwen looped the band through her belt and tucked the stone in with her own for safekeeping.

"How are we to reveal ourselves without frightening her?" Gavan asked, and Branwen was astonished to see that his hands were trembling. "It has been many years. Will she remember me?"

"Of course she will," said Branwen. "Be calm, Gavan ap Huw! We will do this together. Wait till she is out of sight of those below, then I will throw my hand across her mouth so she cannot scream, and you will show yourself to her. It will take her no more than a moment to understand that we are here for her good."

Gavan nodded, and Branwen saw him pause and gather himself. For the first time she realized how much this moment meant to him. Fearless in battle, he shook like a windblown sapling to think that he was so close to being with his child again.

Alwyn came to the head of the ladder and stepped

out onto the timber floor. Entirely oblivious of them, she walked to one side, passing behind a screen. Branwen laid down her shield and slid soft footed after her. This was a narrow chamber with a simple fur-strewn mattress on the floor and a wooden chest at its side. Against the far wall stood a small triangular beech wood harp, carved and engraved by a master craftsman, its twelve horsehair strings held taut by pegs of white bone. It was a beautiful instrument— Branwen could see that—a harp such as might once have been played by the great bard Taliesin himself.

As Alwyn passed alongside the mattress, Branwen struck. She caught the young woman from behind, one hand clamping around her waist, the other coming up across her mouth. She spun her so that she was facing her father.

Gavan rested his hands on Alwyn's shoulders, staring into her face.

"Alwyn! Know me! See me! I am your father!"

For a few moments the young woman continued to struggle.

"Alwyn! Have no fear! I am here to release you from servitude! *Alwyn!*"

Suddenly Alwyn became still, but Branwen could feel the tension thrilling in her body.

"Do not cry out! Speak softly!" Branwen hissed. She took her hand from Alwyn's mouth.

"Father . . . ?"

"Yes. It is I."

"But . . . but how . . . ?"

"There is no time for explanations, my beloved child," murmured Gavan, his eyes glowing with love, his shaking hands touching her cheeks and hair as though he needed the contact to prove that this longed for moment was real. "We must slip away swiftly, before they come in search of you." He turned to Branwen. "Wrap the cloth about her wrist—give her the stone. Hurry!"

Alwyn's face clouded, and she pulled away from her father. "No!" She gasped. "No! What are you doing here?" She twisted her head over her shoulder, scowling at Branwen, who still held her around the waist. "Release me, you *waelisc* pig!" she hissed. "I shall call the guards! You will die for this effrontery!" She took a deep breath; and even in her amazement, Branwen had the foresight to realize she was about to scream. Her hand came slapping over Alwyn's mouth, silencing her.

"Alwyn?" cried Gavan. "We are here to rescue you from your servitude! Do you not understand, child? I am come to take you home!"

Alwyn writhed in Branwen's arms, her face furious, her arms flailing. Gavan managed to snatch hold of her wrists and force her arms down to her sides.

"Your daughter is moonstruck, I think!" panted Branwen as she struggled to hold Alwyn still. "Ow!" Teeth bit into her fingers, and she jerked her hand away in pain.

Alwyn took another breath, but Gavan's hand came up and struck her across the cheek so that the air came hissing voiceless out of her mouth. Staggering, Alwyn glared at him, her face suffused with anger, a red weal blossoming across the side of her face.

"Be still, child!" growled Gavan, his voice desperate. "What is this now? Are you out of your wits?"

Alwyn back kicked Branwen, taking her by surprise, her heel hammering painfully against Branwen's knee, sending her limping backward. Branwen's heels caught on the edge of the mattress, and she tumbled over.

"Alwyn!" Gavan snatched at his daughter's arm, catching her as she made to run from the chamber. The young woman pivoted in his grip and came to a sudden wrenching halt.

"Get away from me! I will not be abducted! Redwuld will have you killed for this!" Alwyn's face was ferocious as she dug the nails of her free hand into Gavan's arm. She ripped down his forearm, clawing red grooves in his flesh. Gavan stifled a cry of pain as Alwyn twisted her hand free.

A small, slender shape came up behind her; one thin arm was raised, something gripped in the hand. The arm fell sharply, and the object struck Alwyn a glancing blow on the back of the head. Even as Branwen was scrabbling to her feet, Alwyn let out a low moan and dropped to the floor.

Blodwedd stood over her, gripping a gold statuette of a wolf in her hand.

22

BLODWEDD'S EYES SHOWED her confusion. "What is happening?" she asked, staring down at the fallen woman. "Why does she fight us?"

"I do not know," said Gavan, ignoring the blood welling from his wounds as he knelt at his daughter's side. "Fear, perhaps. Or madness. I do not know!" He turned her, cradling her head on his knees.

"'Tis good they make so much riot below," said Blodwedd. "Else we'd have been embattled by now."

"All the same, we have to move quickly," Branwen said. "They will soon wonder over the delay." She knelt beside Gavan, grabbing Alwyn's limp arm and twisting the linen strip around her wrist. She tucked the stone into the wrap, looking up at Blodwedd. "You've done us good service," she said. "We would never have got her out of this place awake. Let's trust

228

that she remains stunned long enough for us to get her clear of the camp." She stood up again. "We still need to find Caradoc's prison," she said. "And we have little time."

"I believe I have found it," said Blodwedd. "Come. I will show you."

Branwen followed the owl-girl into another of the small chambers. It lay alongside Alwyn's—larger and more opulently appointed, with swords and shields hung from the walls and with red silk draperies across the low mattress. Several golden ornaments stood on a wooden shelf, a gap showing where the gold wolf had rested.

Blodwedd pointed to a small casket that lay under the shelf. It was of polished oak wood, strapped with silver and held closed by a richly ornamented silver lock. Branwen dropped to her knees, drawing out the small casket. "Yes!" she breathed. There was an engraving carved into the wood on the curved lid—a prowling cat shape with a blunt face and tufted ears, and with a long body and a short, thick tail.

She looked up at Blodwedd. "It is the lynx," she said. "As Merion said it would be." She lifted the casket in her hands; it was not heavy, being about the length of her forearm and as deep as her stretched hand.

She held the casket to her ear, listening. There was no sound. What had she expected, she wondered? A howling wind? The boom of trapped thunder? The sizzle of contained lightning? "How can we be sure?" she asked. "What if we free the lock but open the lid only a small amount?"

"No!" Blodwedd said adamantly. "We would die; have no doubt of that!"

"Then I must trust that Caradoc is within," said Branwen, getting to her feet, the casket held gingerly between her hands. She walked back to where Gavan sat with his unconscious daughter draped across his lap.

"Gavan ap Huw? Can you carry her in your arms?"

"I can." The old warrior gathered his daughter and stood, one arm under her knees, the other cradling her back. Her arms and legs trailed, her head lolling, hanks of rich brown hair hanging loose, spilling jewels. Gavan's face was grim and grieved as he held her—Branwen knew this was not how he had expected his daughter's rescue to play out.

"Go swiftly!" urged Blodwedd. "I will remain for the moment. Do not wait for me no matter what you hear. If all else fails, I will meet you in the forest. Go!"

Branwen nodded, hardly able to look at the owl-girl. Now her own words came back to haunt her.

No one life is more important than our mission. If I fall or am trapped or caught or hurt, do not linger to help me. And the same goes for each of us. Those still standing must escape with Caradoc at all costs.

They came to the head of the ladder. The Great

Hall was a cauldron of noise—of eating and drinking, and of loud speech and raucous laughter. Only one man seemed impatient that Alwyn had not yet returned with her harp. Redwuld was staring up at the ladder, his brows drawn down.

Like a spoiled child being forced to wait for a treat! Branwen thought.

She helped Gavan to lift the supine form of his daughter over his shoulder so that both hands were free. Slowly and carefully he descended the ladder. Branwen watched Redwuld's eyes. As Gavan climbed down with his burden, she noticed that Ironfist's son did not take his eyes away from the top of the ladder.

Good! The charm is still working.

She turned, looking back to where Blodwedd stood in cover behind a screen. The owl-girl was standing quite still, her fingers curled like claws, her shoulders drawn up and her head lowered. There was a fiendish smile on her face. Her uncanny eyes stared through the thick tumbled locks of her hair, burning like the fires of Annwn. A demon in human form.

Branwen shuddered at the diabolical sight. Sometimes the owl-girl seemed almost human—but at moments such as this, Branwen was starkly reminded that not one drop of human blood ran in her veins. Branwen turned again and stared out over the hall. Gavan had reached the floor and was edging along the wall behind the feasters. Branwen waited till she saw him reach the far doorway, intending to give him and Bryn a head start in their escape.

Picking up her shield and slinging it onto her back, Branwen stepped down onto the ladder, the casket tucked under her arm. It would not be easy to climb encumbered by the casket, but with care it was possible.

Redwuld's voice rang out over the uproar. "What is keeping the girl? Go—someone—fetch her down! I'll not be kept waiting!"

A young warrior from a table near the ladder stood up and began to climb.

Branwen halted, staring down at him in consternation. The man was climbing quickly. She had only moments to react.

Clutching the casket against her armpit, she brought her free arm around behind the ladder. Gripping the rung tightly from behind, she swung herself sideways off the ladder. She grimaced, her arm and shoulder taking her full weight as she hung off the back of the ladder. It was agonizing, the strain burning in her shoulder and wrist. Already she could feel her fingers slipping. The man came stamping up. Very nearly he trod on her fingers as he passed her and made his way up off the ladder.

She tried to hook her leg over the ladder again, to pull herself back onto it, but the angle made it difficult. She looked down between her feet. There were barrels beneath her. It was not a long fall, but she feared for the noise she would make as she landed on the lids of the barrels.

But her hesitation did not last long. There was a blood-chilling cry from above. It was drowned out by a scream, not of pain but of animal rage: a feral, savage scream the like of which Branwen had never heard. But she knew it had issued from Blodwedd's throat.

A moment later the man was hurled down off the high deck, bright red blood spilling from his torn-out throat.

He landed with a crash almost at Ironfist's feet.

Pandemonium erupted. Tables were overturned as men surged up from their benches. There were shouts of shock and anger. Ironfist rose from his throne, drawing his sword, staring upward.

"A demon!"

"A *waelisc* devil!"

"Shoot it down!" Ironfist bellowed. "Kill it!"

Branwen let go of the rung and dropped down onto the barrels. Any noise she might have made was lost in the tumult that filled the hall. Unobserved, Branwen raced along the wall, the casket cradled against her chest.

At the door she looked around. Blodwedd stood on the lip of the raised floor, her arms stretched out, her mouth open in another terrible scream. Arrows and javelins cut through the air, but none hit her.

She'll die here! By the love of the Three Saints, no! I cannot let her die alone!

But Branwen had the casket in her arms. Her first duty was to get it to safety; otherwise all they had done here was in vain.

She ducked out through the doorway, narrowly avoiding colliding with men who were running in to find out what was happening within.

How long can the stone hide me in this mayhem? Surely I shall be seen, and then all will be lost.

Iwan and Dera were pressed against the outer wall, keeping away from the inrush of warriors.

"Take this!" hissed Branwen, thrusting the casket into Iwan's hands. "Go, now! I will follow if I can."

"I'm going nowhere without you," said Iwan, pulling his hands away, refusing to take the casket from her. "What's happened? Where is Blodwedd?"

"She's trapped in there. I'm going back for her," snapped Branwen.

"By the saints, you are *not*!" said Dera. "You are the Chosen One—you cannot sacrifice yourself like that. Iwan! With me!"

"No!" Branwen tried to rip herself free as Dera and Iwan caught hold of her arms.

Iwan leaned in close. "Another shout like that and the Saxons will hear us and we will all die here!" he hissed. "You *will* come with us, Branwen!"

More warriors were running toward the open doorway of the Great Hall now, swords drawn, spears at the ready, alerted by the continuing uproar within.

Branwen twisted her head as she was pulled away

from the hall. "I cannot leave her," she murmured. "Don't make me do this!"

"You cannot save her," hissed Dera. "All you could do is die at her side."

"Then I'd do that."

"Be silent!" whispered Iwan. "That is the last thing Blodwedd would wish! If we—" A running warrior crashed into him, sending him sprawling. The man reeled, staring around himself in confusion. Then his eyes turned downward, widening in sudden realization. He could see them!

His mouth opened, but the only sound that escaped him was a dull grunt. Adder-quick, Dera had thrust her sword deep between his shoulder blades. The man dropped like a log.

No one needed to give the word—none of the three moved a muscle. Men rushed past them, missing them by hairbreadths as they made for the hall.

"What's this with Beroun?"

"Drunk as a thain, I'd say! Leave him where he lies!"

"What is happening in the hall?"

"Some wild thing has got in there."

Iwan slowly got to his feet. Branwen stood staring back at the hall, the casket hard against her stomach, her every instinct urging her to race back and help Blodwedd. But she knew Dera and Iwan would not allow it, and she could not risk an argument that would result in them being seen—not while they were surrounded by so many enemy warriors.

Iwan beckoned and they moved again, slipping away between the tents, halting when Saxons came too close, hardly breathing. Waiting. Moving again. Gradually making their way to the outskirts of the encampment, where the terrible screams of the owl-girl could no longer be heard and where the men still ate and drank and sang, unaware for the time being of the commotion at the heart of the camp.

At last they were beyond the negligent sentries and in among the reeds at the riverside.

Branwen halted, staring back the way they had come. "I will rot in Annwn for such a betrayal!" she said. "She will die alone and unaided. She deserved better of me!" She glared from Iwan to Dera. "You should have let me stay for her!"

"She would not have wanted that, Branwen," said Iwan.

"She may yet survive," said Dera. "She is not helpless."

"She will not." Branwen groaned, her heart aching with grief and reproach. "I know it. She will not. And it is my fault. This venture was ill planned from the outset! Only five of us should have come on this mission—and we should have kept the sixth stone for Gavan's daughter. I am no leader! I should have thought of this before we set off!"

"Do not reprove yourself, Branwen," said Iwan. "None of us thought of it. It is pointless to despair over things that cannot be altered."

"Is that the thing we came here for?" asked Dera, looking uneasily at the casket in Branwen's arms. "Is that where Caradoc of the North Wind lies?"

"I believe it is," said Branwen.

"Then Blodwedd will be glad of her sacrifice," said Dera. "She gave herself up to save one of the Old Gods that she serves. Could such a creature have a worthier death, Branwen?"

"Shall we get across the bridge before we speak more?" said Iwan. "I'd be well away from this place before the alarm is sent that the mountain rats are among them! And it will! The loss of the girl and the casket will be proof enough of that."

"What of Gavan?" asked Branwen.

"He went on ahead with his daughter slung over his shoulder," said Iwan. "Bryn went at his heel, like a faithful hound. Did the girl faint? There was no chance to speak with him."

"She did not faint," said Branwen grimly. "But more of that later. You are right—let's get away from here." She looked one final time back to the Great Hall beyond the tents and huts of the encampment. Angry tears pricked her eyes. "Farewell, Blodwedd," she murmured. "And how am I to break the news to Rhodri? This is one thing for which he will never forgive me." She shook her head as she turned away. "Nor shall I forgive myself!" she murmured under her breath. "Never!"

* * *

"What is that?" Iwan turned back the way they had come, peering into the distance, across the river, toward Ironfist's encampment. He pointed to a dark smudge low in the sky, hanging over the camp like a plume of black cloud.

Branwen stared hard. "Smoke, perhaps?" she said. It was hard to tell *what* they were looking at— the night was dark, but the thing above the camp was darker still, like a clump of shadow just above the horizon. "Is the Great Hall aflame?"

"I see no sign of fire," murmured Dera. "I cannot make it out. It is too distant and the night is too deep." She tilted her head as though listening. "Do you hear that sound?"

"Yes," breathed Branwen. A strange sound on the very brink of hearing: a high-pitched sound, like the faraway babble of children's voices, or maybe more like the sound of many knives being sharpened on whetstones—shrill and thin, now that Branwen listened more intently, frenzied and somehow unpleasant.

"Is it an omen?" murmured Dera. "Some portent of doom?"

"Perhaps," said Branwen. "But for whom?" She shuddered, turning away and continuing up the long slope of the hill.

A portent of doom.

As if she needed sinister portents to darken her mood!

23

BRANWEN FELT NO sense of triumph or achievement as she approached the camp in the high forest. She knew that they had done all that they had set out to achieve, but the success of their efforts was overshadowed by the cost; and as for Gavan, she feared that the rescue of his beloved daughter would bring him a deeper heartache than he could ever have imagined.

As they drew near to the camp, Branwen, Dera, and Iwan could hear the young woman's raised voice piercing the night.

"Take me back! I demand you take me back! Redwuld will flay you alive for this insult! You will not escape his vengeance, no matter where you flee! His wrath will come down on you like the hammer of Thunaer! Take your hands off me!"

"Alwyn is awake then," said Branwen.

"And in fine voice!" added Iwan. "We'd best find a way to quieten her; they'll hear that racket all the way back in Chester, else!"

"It seems her father has little control over her," said Dera. "This could prove a greater burden than we may have thought!"

"A cuckoo in the nest," Branwen wondered aloud. "Let's hope it's not so."

An uncomfortable scene met their eyes as they passed in under the trees and came to the small camp. Linette, Aberfa, and Banon were gathered together to one side, Asta sitting on the ground at their feet. Andras and Padrig and Dillon were standing apart from them, the horses tethered at their backs. Between the two groups stood Bryn, gripping Alwyn's upper arms from behind, holding her back while she shouted and raved into her father's face.

Rhodri stepped out from among the horses as Branwen's small band came into the camp, his puzzled eyes questing for the friend who was not with them.

"You are sick in your mind, my child," Gavan said gently. Branwen had never heard his voice so kindly or so distressed.

"I am not your child!" stormed Alwyn.

Gavan's head lowered in sorrow. "No, you are not. Forgive me." He looked again into her flushed, angry face. "But you are my daughter, though you have become a woman since last I saw you. And as your father, I tell you that your wits have become distracted, Alwyn. Cease this foolishness—you are free now. Free to go home."

"Home?" spat the enraged young woman. "What home is that? The rat holes of Brython—is that where you'd take me?" Her eyes blazed. "I have lived in a king's hall, I have dined off gold plates, I have worn silk! And what do you offer me? A reed-strewn floor where the mountain rats gobble their food among the dogs and the vermin! I will not go with you to live like a swine in the muck!"

The faces of the onlookers showed confusion and discomfort—and also a growing dislike for the young woman. But no one spoke as Gavan gazed unhappily into her face.

Branwen had no time for these hysterics. She stalked across the clearing and confronted the disheveled woman. "Listen well, Alwyn ap Gavan," she said. "I do not care why you abuse your father so, but know this: you *will* return with him to Brython—even though you travel slung over the saddle with a gag to your mouth and your arms and legs tied! Whatever seductions have turned you from your own people, forget them! Your life among the Saxons is ended."

A cold smile slithered over Alwyn's face. "Is it?" she said, her voice calm now but filled with pride and spite. "I think Redwuld, son of Herewulf Ironfist, will have something to say on that matter." Her chin lifted. "You think I am no more than a servant to him? I am very much more. He has proposed marriage, and I have accepted. Once this war is done and you people are crushed forever, we will return to my lord King Oswald's palace in the North, and we shall be wed!" She looked venomously at Gavan. "Now what do you think of your chances of bearing me away? Redwuld will send an army to bring me back safely." She stared around at the others. "All of you will die for this act! Redwuld's anger will descend upon you like . . ."

"Oh! For the love of Saint Dewi, Saint Cynwal, and Saint Cadog, be silent!" Iwan burst out. "Must we listen to this demented banshee till doomsday? Gavan ap Huw, you are her father—gag her for pity's sake! Do we not have enough to bear without the witless braying of this deluded fool?"

Gavan looked sternly at his daughter. "Alwyn, I hold more love for you than for life itself, but you must reconcile yourself to what has happened." She opened her mouth, but he lifted a hand to quieten her. "Be silent, daughter, or I *will* have you gagged."

Alwyn fell into a glowering silence, one hand moving up to pull a draggling lock of her wrecked hair off her face. A jeweled pin dropped into the grass.

"And as for any thoughts you may have had of marrying Ironfist's son, forget them," added Iwan. "Are you truly so addled in your mind that you think a great thain of the Saxons would let his eldest son marry a servant woman? You have been duped, madam! You have been a plaything to Redwuld, and nothing more."

Alwyn's eyes narrowed in hate, but she turned away from him without making any retort.

Rhodri came up to Branwen, his face worried. "Where is Blodwedd?" he asked.

Iwan looked compassionately at Rhodri. "We had to leave her," he said gently, before Branwen had the chance to speak. His eyes flickered toward her for an instant. "It was no one's fault."

Rhodri's forehead contracted, his eyes on Branwen. "You *left* her?" There was disbelief in his voice. "You left her in Ironfist's camp?"

"We had no other choice," said Dera. "I know you had affection for her."

Rhodri's face drained of color. "She is dead?" he breathed.

Branwen swallowed, finding it hard to hold his distressed gaze. "Yes, I think so."

Rhodri looked from one to the other of the three. "Did any of you see her die?"

"No," said Iwan. "But she was in Ironfist's hall— surrounded by hundreds—and she gave up her mystical stone for Gavan's daughter." He frowned, sympathy for Rhodri deepening in his voice. "She could not have escaped."

"But you did not actually see her killed?" asked Rhodri.

"We did not," said Dera.

"Then she is alive," said Rhodri. "I would know

if she had died." His eyes burned into Branwen's. "I would know!" He turned and walked toward where the others were preparing the horses.

Branwen had the urge to chase after him, to catch his arm and to beg him to forgive her. But she dared not. She could not let the others see her weeping in Rhodri's arms. She would have to endure the guilt and the loss on her own.

Fain suddenly appeared, floating out of the trees on stilled wings and coming to rest on Branwen's shoulder. Caressing his feathers, she looked up into the sky. Clouds veiled the moon and hid the stars. "The night is not half gone, and we could all do with rest," she said. "But we cannot stay here. Alwyn ap Gavan is correct in one thing: we will be pursued—but not for her rescue. Rather, for this!" She held up the casket for all to see. "This is the prison where Caradoc of the North Wind is held. We have done as Merion of the Stones asked—and now we must hasten to return to her. We will ride through the night." She looked at Gavan. "Shall you ride with us now?"

"We shall," he replied. "For the moment."

Branwen nodded. "There will be no sleep now, till we are back in Brython. Make everything ready; we leave at once!"

It was a subdued and uneasy group that rode out of the western fringes of the forest in the deep watches of the night and made their way back toward Cyffin Tir.

They were all aware now that Blodwedd had been sacrificed so that the oak wood chest could be brought safely away from Ironfist's camp. Gavan's lads seemed indifferent to the loss—or maybe even a little relieved to be rid of the inhuman thing. Of all the girls of Gwylan Canu, Banon seemed the most upset; and Branwen saw tears in her eyes as she rode tandem with Aberfa. She and Blodwedd had bonded in the hunt, and Banon took the loss of her new friend hard.

Rhodri rode silent and a little aloof from the others, keeping to the rear of the column, constantly looking back, as though he was convinced that at any moment Blodwedd would appear in their wake.

Iwan and Linette rode together again, although this time Branwen was hardly even aware of it, save for the constant whisper of words between them. Alwyn rode with her father, seated behind him, his cloak over her shoulders, her features crabbed and hostile. Dera was astride Skur's great destrier with Asta clinging on behind. The dead Viking's huge battle-ax hung from a harness on the saddle—the spoils of a victory less costly than that which had won them the casket that was now strapped to Branwen's saddle.

A great pity that Alwyn has not taken to our forced company as Asta has, Branwen thought, one hand rising to her shoulder, her fingers gently stroking Fain's chest feathers. *Soon I shall need to speak with Gavan ap Huw and learn his purposes now that his errand in Mercia is fulfilled. Our ways will part, I think; and we'll all be glad*

245

of that, I have no doubt. I shall call a halt soon, come the dawn—a brief rest will do us all good; and once the sun has risen Fain can patrol the skies at our backs and warn us of any pursuit.

The clouds slid away as they rode, and now the night sky was full of stars. The crescent moon hung low over the murmurous dark smear of a wind-ruffled forest. There was the trill of running water from somewhere nearby, a lively counterpart to the steady thud of hooves and the creak and jangle of harnesses.

Branwen was drowsing a little in the saddle, her head nodding every now and then. Fatigue was getting the best of her. She felt hollowed out, drained both physically and emotionally. The rippling of the water was almost like a melody in her weary mind. Like the song of the goraig . . . seeping gently into her head.

The cuckoo . . . yes . . . I will be wary of Alwyn . . . but what harm can she do to us. . . . She is her father's burden, not mine!

The hollow, eerie hooting of an owl brought Branwen to her senses. It had come from the rear, floating like a melancholy moan on the dark air.

"Blodwedd?" It was Rhodri's voice, calling out into the night.

Alert now, Branwen turned in the saddle. Rhodri's horse had stopped, and he was twisted around, looking back the way they had come.

The rest of the band halted as well.

"She will not come," called Dera. "It is but an eagle owl waking in the forest."

"She is there!" shouted Rhodri, sliding down from the saddle and running helter-skelter through the tall grass. "I know she is!"

Iwan snorted. "Our runaway is moonstruck if he truly believes that was Blodwedd! Shall I fetch him back, Branwen?"

"No. I'll do it." Branwen tugged the reins, turning Stalwyn around. Fain flew from her shoulder and found a nearby branch. She set Stalwyn at the trot, passing the other riders. Rhodri was running like a mad thing, calling all the time.

"Blodwedd! Blodwedd!"

Branwen urged Stalwyn into a canter.

Rhodri had vanished into a grove of aspens. Branwen brought Stalwyn up short, jumped from the saddle, and ran after Rhodri into the deep darkness under the trees.

"Rhodri?"

There was no sign of him, nor any sound of footsteps under the trees. Branwen walked slowly forward, listening intently, trying to make sense of the deep darkness. Something glinted—ahead of her and high above the ground. Two disks of pale light that stared unblinkingly down at her.

She met the stare and moved toward it.

An owl sat on a high branch, veiled by leaves, staring down at her.

She swallowed, strangely disturbed by the silent creature.

Blodwedd's ghost—come to haunt her?

By the saints, I pray it is not so, though I deserve no better from her!

More eyes ignited in the darkness. With a shiver of apprehension, Branwen realized that there were owls all around her, perched in the trees, watching her, their heads turning slowly as she passed, their eyes shining eerily.

They mean to kill me. For vengeance!

Then she heard a whispering voice.

Rhodri's voice, chanting softly.

> *Blessed healing spread, blessed healing grow*
> *And sickness disappear, and sickness be*
> > *laid low*
> *Be gone thou withered weal, and let this*
> > *soul be healed*
> *Begone, begone forever, thy eye be opened*
> > *never*
> *No burial for this pretty maid*
> *This healing token have I made*
> *To guard thee from all hurt and harm*
> *To make thee hale, I speak this charm*

There was a pause—a yawning silence—and then Rhodri's voice again, trembling, speaking quietly.

"Blodwedd? I have you. All is well. I have you now."

Shaking in every limb and with a hooked claw clenching in her belly, Branwen moved deeper into the trees. She saw Rhodri kneeling on the ground with his bent back to her. A pale, slender shape lay in front of him.

Her throat as tight and painful as knotted twine, Branwen circled Rhodri, her heart thumping.

Blodwedd lay on her back, bleeding from many cuts, her dress torn to tatters, her huge eyes closed. For a moment Branwen was certain that she was dead, but then she saw the faint flutter of her chest.

She knelt, aware of a score or more round eyes watching her from above. Judging her. Condemning her.

Rhodri was running his blood-wet hands over Blodwedd's frail body, chanting softly under his breath, tears running from his eyes. He seemed unaware that Branwen was even there.

She did not speak.

She *could* not speak.

What was there to say?

Branwen knelt listening for a long while to Rhodri's whispered charms, then, at last, she reached out and touched her fingertips to the back of his hand.

He started, lifting his head to look into her face.

"She is hurt almost to the death," he murmured. "But I will save her. By the healing powers of Frigé, she will not die!"

"How did she get here?"

"I don't know."

"Did she follow . . . on foot . . . all this way . . . hurt as she is . . . ?"

Rhodri didn't reply, but his hand turned under Branwen's, and he gripped her fingers tightly. "I shall not let her die," he said, a fierce light in his eyes.

Branwen heard movement through the trees. Iwan and Dera emerged out of the gloom.

"By all the saints, she escaped the Saxon camp!" said Dera. "I would not have believed it possible. And yet she lives!"

"Barely," muttered Iwan, his eyes narrowing in concern as he looked down at Blodwedd's blood-streaked face. "She needs a practitioner of medicines, I fear, or we shall yet lose her."

"Rhodri is a healer," said Branwen. "He will tend her."

"Can she be moved?" asked Dera.

Branwen tightened her grip on Rhodri's hand. "Can she?"

"Yes. With great care. I will need herbs and roots—and fresh running water."

Iwan rested his hand on Rhodri's bent shoulder. "I will help you carry her. There is a stream close by—I heard it as we rode."

"Dare we linger?" murmured Dera, gazing east-ward through the forest. "Will we not be overrun by our pursuers?"

"I don't care," said Branwen. "I will not abandon

her a second time—not if all the armies of Mercia should fall upon us!"

"Then let's to the river and prepare to fight if needs be," said Dera. She looked into Blodwedd's face. "So great a sacrifice deserves our solicitude, far from human though she be!"

Rhodri gathered Blodwedd's limp and bleeding form in his arms and got to his feet, Iwan keeping close with his hands ready to help.

"There is no need," said Rhodri, gazing down into her face. "She weighs nothing."

But as he began to walk, Blodwedd moaned softly, her head turning from side to side.

"Beware!" she muttered, her lips hardly moving, her voice the ghost of sound. "Beware the black bird. He comes. On darkling wing and with a heart filled with old evil, he comes. Beware the raven. The harbinger of death! Beware Mumir . . . beware his ancient eye!"

24

THE STREAM FLOWED through a deep, mossy culvert between rising banks of willow. The dawn was not far off, but night still cloaked the land as Rhodri laid Blodwedd close to the water and began to wash her wounds.

The owl-girl was restless, muttering constantly of the black bird and the peril he represented.

Leaving Blodwedd to Rhodri's tender ministrations, Branwen gathered Iwan and the girls of Gwylan Canu to her. They needed to make plans for keeping watch while they lingered here, and for how they might defend themselves if they were attacked.

They were deep in these discussions when Gavan approached.

"We should not stay here," he said. "This is not a good defensive position. There's higher land close by; we should make camp there, if we must break our journey." He looked coldly at Blodwedd. "*If* we must."

Branwen turned to him. "We shall remain in this place until Rhodri tells me that Blodwedd is fit to be moved," she said. "But you and yours are under no obligation to stay with us, Gavan ap Huw. Depart now, if you wish."

He looked thoughtfully at her for a few moments, and she saw the scar on his jaw move over a jumping muscle. "It would be reckless for us to divide our meager forces while we are still in Mercia," he said at last. "But I would speak with you alone, Branwen."

She nodded. "Iwan, Dera, Linette, and Aberfa— you know what is needed. Go, be our eyes and ears in the forest. Banon shall stay to guard the camp. Come the dawn I will have Fain patrol the skies at our back, but for now we need keen eyes on high ground so that we'll have good warning if enemies approach." She walked away from them with Gavan at her side.

"You have become a worthy leader," he said. "I see great changes in you since we first met."

"I have learned a lot in a short time," Branwen replied.

"But you still have much to master," he said. "And a little knowledge can lead down false paths, if confidence is not tempered with humility."

She halted some small distance from the others, under the hanging branches of a green willow. "What did you want to talk about?" she asked tersely, not liking the implied criticism in his words. "The parting of our ways, I assume? What is your plan when we come to Powys again?"

"To travel on the Great South Way to Pengwern," he said. "It may be futile, but my duty to Brython requires me to offer my services to King Cynon now that Llew ap Gelert's treachery is revealed. And maybe there Alwyn will return to her senses. In any event I will stay with the king, if he will have me, and I will help to defend Brython from enemies both without and within." There was a glint in his eyes that suggested something left unsaid.

"Am I an enemy within, in your opinion?" Branwen asked.

"That I cannot say," he replied. "But you are in the service of ancient powers whose true desires neither you nor I can possibly know." He looked sharply at her. "It is your destiny, so they say, to raise up an army against the Saxons. Such a destiny would earn you the gratitude of all the folk of Brython, if it were fulfilled."

Branwen could hear the hesitation in his voice. "But . . . ?"

"But King Cynon rules in Powys, as does Maelgwn Hir in Gwynedd and King Dinefwr and King Tewdrig in the other two of the Four Kingdoms of Brython," Gavan said portentously. "Is it your destiny to raise warriors in Powys under Cynon's flag? For if not, I see only civil war and brother set against brother as the result of your actions. The king will not allow an army to grow in his realm that does not accept his overlordship—and yet I have heard nothing from you that suggests the Old Gods wish you to ally yourself to the king." He paused as if to let this sink in. "So? What is it to be, Branwen of the Old Gods? Will you stand alongside the king, or are you entirely the creature of the Shining Ones?"

Branwen didn't reply. She had never considered the politics of her actions, nor the impact her destiny might have on those kings and lesser lords who ruled over Brython.

Gavan nodded as though her silence confirmed some belief he already had. "The Old Gods lead you down dangerous pathways, Branwen," he said, an urging tone entering his voice. "You have it in you to be a great leader of men," he continued, and Branwen could hear his excitement building as he spoke. "Come with me to Pengwern, Branwen. Make this destiny truly your own—give your allegiance to the king, help him to throw down the traitor Llew ap Gelert, and then unite with him to raise an army that will deal such a blow to the Saxons that they will leave us in peace for a thousand years!" He put a hand on her shoulder. "Be true to your destiny and be true to your own people, Branwen—and we shall fight side by side. You do not need the wayward devices of forgotten gods to do this thing!"

She looked into his slate gray eyes. They were powerful and compelling, offering her a safe path: the companionship of noble men and women—a great and true calling under the standards of the four kings of Brython.

"Do it, Branwen," he said, his eyes gleaming. "Throw the casket into the river and come with me to the king. Shed the encumbrances of the gods. You don't need them or theirs. Be rid of them all."

He spoke a fraction too soon. If he had kept silent a little longer, she might almost have agreed. "The encumbrances of the gods?" she repeated. "And what are they, Gavan ap Huw? Is Blodwedd one such, in your estimation?"

"She is a demon in human form," said Gavan.

"No! She is not," said Branwen. "She is an *owl* in a human skin—and she is with me out of loyalty and choice. What would you have me do? Hurl her into the water along with the casket that she almost died to help me recover?" She shook her head. "No, for good or bad, I will follow the Shining Ones."

"Despite all that I have said?"

"You do not know their true desires," said Branwen. "But I cannot believe they mean anything but good for Brython and for all its people."

Gavan's face became stern and grim. "Then you are lost to me," he said. "I will waste no more words on you. We shall ride together till we come to Cyffin Tir, then our paths will be sundered forever." He turned and began to walk away from her. But suddenly he stopped and looked at her over his shoulder. "I hope we never have to face each other in battle again, Branwen, because if we do, it will be because you have come into conflict with the king of Powys. And if that happens I shall not hesitate to kill you."

"Nor I you, Gavan ap Huw," she replied, although it broke her heart to say this.

Trembling with pent-up emotions, Branwen walked under the arching willow branches and down to the lip of the small, bright stream. She needed a few moments alone to gather herself before facing the others. She hated to have disappointed and distressed the old warrior, but she had learned enough to know that no good would come of turning her back on the Shining Ones. And she could never betray Blodwedd like that—not when so much harm had already been done to the faithful and valiant owl-girl.

Standing and gazing into the purling waters, she heard the rustle of someone moving through the tangle of branches.

She turned. It was Asta.

The Viking girl nodded to Branwen and gave a nervous smile. "Rhodri sent me to seek for comfrey and yarrow," she said.

Branwen looked behind her. "And you are wandering alone?" she asked sharply.

Asta came up close to Branwen, a frank and open

look in her eyes. "I wish only to help," she said. "You have treated me kindly, although I know my presence among you is not welcome."

"It's hard on you, I know, when you are blameless in all that has happened," said Branwen. "But I cannot release you."

"I understand," said Asta. "Truly, I do. It would be foolish to let an ally of the Saxons go free. But if I am to stay with you for the time being, I'd make myself useful." She grimaced. "I'd not be such a burden as the daughter of Gavan ap Huw! I have some small knowledge of herbs and healing unguents, and I would do all that I can to help bring Blodwedd back to full health." Her smile strengthened a little, deepening the dimples in her cheeks. "I am allowed to wander alone because your followers are busy making sure we are guarded from attack. But I will return to Rhodri's side, if you so wish."

"No." Branwen looked into her pale, eager face, searching her dark blue eyes. She saw only honesty and gentleness in them. "You must not return empty-handed. I have not seen any yarrow, but there is comfrey in plenty along the riverbank. Come, we'll gather it together."

They followed the river a little way, picking up sprays of white comfrey as they went.

"I wish I could set you on the path back to your father," Branwen said as they headed to where the others waited. Branwen had even managed to find some yarrow, and both had their hands full of white flowers. "But you would need a horse to travel so far, and I cannot spare one. When we come to my own lands, I will ask Gavan ap Huw to take you with him to the king's court in Pengwern. You may have to stay there a while, but I believe you will be well treated. The king is a good man, so they say; and he will do you no harm when he knows your story."

Asta looked at her. "I'd rather stay with you, Branwen," she said. "If I can earn your trust, that is."

"I'm on a hard road," Branwen replied. "You'd find more comfort and ease in Pengwern, trust me on that."

"Nevertheless, it is you who saved me from the brute Skur. I'd ride by your side, if you are willing. I may have no battle skills, but I can be of use in other ways." Her forehead creased. "I'd pay back the debt I owe you, Branwen. My father would wish that of me."

"We shall see," Branwen said kindly. "How was Blodwedd when you left her?"

"Quieter," said Asta. "Not asleep, but more restful. I hope she lives."

Branwen sent up a silent prayer. "As do I," she said. "But Rhodri knows what he is doing. He won't fail her. You'll see. All will be well."

Branwen only became aware that it was dawn because of the way the light grew in Blodwedd's face. She had not left the owl-girl's side since she and Asta had come there with the yarrow and the comfrey. She had helped Rhodri beat the flowers to pulp and had watched anxiously as he and Asta had applied the resultant poultice to Blodwedd's wounds.

Now that the blood had been cleaned away, it was easier to see the hurts done to her by the Saxons. She had several shallow slashes on her arms and legs and body, as though from the glancing blows of sweeping blades. There were also puncture marks of arrows or spears—some deep and worrying, others just small round holes where the blood had already clotted. The worse of her wounds were bound with linen, the others Rhodri and Asta laved with water steeped in comfrey while Branwen dabbed gently at her forehead with a damp cloth.

Under the lids, Blodwedd's eyes darted restlessly, as though she was lost in nightmares; and now and then her lips would tremble as if she was trying to say something.

With the coming of daylight, Rhodri sent Asta in search of other flowers and roots, and Branwen was content for the Viking girl to forage alone. She did notice Gavan looking askance at the young woman as she headed up and away from the culvert. And she saw him say something to Bryn, after which the big lad trailed along in Asta's wake. Padrig, Andras, and Dillon were nowhere to be seen—Branwen assumed Gavan had sent them into the woods to be his own scouts.

As the light burgeoned, Branwen sent Fain out to watch at their rear for any approaching Saxons. She knew that Gavan fretted at the delay; and neither was she at ease with their present situation—in fact, the only person who seemed to be glad of it was Alwyn. The horses had been unsaddled; and she sat on a saddle in the grass, twining her fingers agitatedly in her hair, her face turned continuously to the east as though hoping at any moment to see Redwuld Grammod come riding out of the trees to bear her away.

She's a witless fool. Iwan was right—there'll be no marriage bed for her in Mercia! Ironfist's son would never marry a . . . what are we? Mountain rats! I hope Gavan's wish is fulfilled, and she comes to her senses in the end. Otherwise, theirs will be a bitter reunion, indeed.

Her thoughts were broken into by a high-pitched scream from somewhere above the narrow cleft cut by the river.

Branwen sprang up, staring into the trees, trying to pinpoint the direction of the scream. Others were also watching the tree line, and some already had swords and spears at the ready. Gavan ran forward, his sword in his fist.

"That is Asta's voice," said Rhodri, pausing in salving a wound in Blodwedd's arm. "She's in danger!"

25

BRANWEN RAN UP the slope, her shield on her arm and her sword in her hand. Willow fronds brushed her face and shoulders as she lunged through them. She was aware of Iwan and Banon and Gavan close by, keeping pace with her, but gradually spreading out among the trees.

Asta had not screamed again.

Dead? Let it not be so! Can I never protect my people?

She saw Bryn first. Lying on his face in the dirt, his sword not even drawn.

Expecting at any moment to be attacked, Branwen moved through the hanging willow branches warily now, her eyes darting from side to side.

She paced soundlessly forward to where Bryn lay. She came down at his side on one knee, her nerves tingling, the knuckles of her sword hand white.

He lay unconscious, but she could find no wound on him. She heaved him onto his back. No. There was no sign of sword or arrow on him, although he had a raw graze across the side of his face as though he had been struck by some heavy object.

Gavan came to their side, sword ready. His voice was curt. "Is he slain?"

"No. A blow to the face has rendered him senseless, that's all."

Banon ran out of the dangling branches. "I see no Saxons," she hissed. "Have they taken Asta?"

Branwen stood up. What had happened here?

She heard a movement to one side.

"Hail friends, do not attack!" It was Iwan's voice, and a few moments later he came into view. Asta was at his side, her shoulders held in the curl of his arm.

"What has occurred?" asked Gavan.

There were tears streaking Asta's frightened face. "I did not mean to hurt him," she choked. "But he would not let me go!"

"What are you saying, girl?" growled Gavan. "Did Bryn attack you?"

Asta turned and buried her face in Iwan's chest, her shoulders wrenched with sobs.

Iwan gave Gavan a caustic look. "Have you no control over your followers, Gavan ap Huw?" he asked. "Or is assaulting women part of their training now?"

"It is not!" exclaimed Gavan. "And well you know it, so keep your sharp tongue between your teeth,

Iwan ap Madoc." Gavan stooped and caught Bryn by the collar of his tunic. "Wake up, boy!" he bellowed. He sheathed his sword and slapped Bryn's beefy face. "Wake now, you lummox!"

Bryn came to his senses with a gasp and a look of shock and disbelief. The old warrior dragged him bodily off the ground and set him on his feet.

"What happened here, boy?" Gavan growled.

Bryn tottered, his hand coming up to his injured eye. "I did nothing, sir," he mumbled, his head down, his eyes on Gavan's shoes. "It was but in jest. I meant no harm by it."

"You meant no harm by *what*?" snapped Branwen. "By the saints, if you sought to do injury to her, I'll . . ."

"It was her bracelet," Bryn burst out. "That was all. I wanted a closer look at her bracelet."

Asta pulled her face from Iwan's tunic. "He snatched at my arm," she said, wiping the tears from her eyes with the heel of her hand. "He tried to pull it off my wrist." She glared at him. "It is all I have to remind me of my father!" she cried. "And you would steal it from me!"

"I only wanted to look at it," blurted Bryn. "I'd have given it back!"

"Oafish lout!" said Banon. "Lucky you did not try such tricks with me or you'd have lost your fingers!"

"I don't doubt it," Iwan said, taking his arm from around Asta's shoulders. Now there was a tone of mockery and amusement in his voice. "But the question that intrigues me, friends, is how it came about that Bryn should end this encounter stretching his length on the ground with his meager wits knocked out of him." He smiled at Asta. "And you not half his size and as slender as river reeds."

"I was angry," Asta said. "I struck out at him with a rock in my fist."

"That was well done, child," said Gavan. He glared at Bryn. "And you deserved worse, you fool! Get out of my sight before I darken your other eye for you!"

His shoulders slumping, Bryn stumbled away without another word, although Branwen did see him give Asta a bad-tempered look as he went.

"My apologies, maid," Gavan said to Asta. "The boy means no real harm; but he keeps his brains in his britches, and sitting so often upon them has numbed his wits." He glanced at the dull metal bracelet that wound around her wrist. "May I see your torque, maiden?"

Asta put her hand behind her back, her face suddenly wary.

"I shall not attempt to take it from you," Gavan said. "I wish only to look at it. I had not thought of it, but it is of an unusual design—one that I have not seen before."

Asta's face cleared and she stepped toward Gavan, her arm held out. "Likely you have not," she said. "It comes from my homeland and was given to me by my father when I was but a child."

Gavan reached out, but Asta pulled her arm away. "Please do not touch it," she said mildly. "It is a silly thing, I know, but I do not like others to handle it."

"Indeed, maid, I shall not."

Branwen had never really paid any attention to Asta's bracelet, but she leaned in now as Gavan examined it.

The torque was an open loop of tarnished bronze, dented and scored by the years and designed in the form of a triple-twined plait. Its two ends were shaped to resemble the stylized heads of birds that came together, almost beak to beak.

"What birds are those?" asked Branwen.

"They represent the gyrfalcons of Freyja," said Asta. "They have long been the symbols of my family. They offer us protection from evil."

"They must have been drowsing when Skur took you," said Iwan, peering at the torque over her shoulder.

"Perhaps," Asta said with a smile. "Or perhaps it was foreseen that I should be brought here . . . for some special reason."

Branwen looked at her. Could it be so? All that she did seemed bound up with the actions of gods; how unlikely was it that Asta's fortunes were braided with her own? The Viking maid was brave enough in a pinch, that much was obvious; and slender as she was, she had been strong enough to lay Bryn out with a single blow. Perhaps when time allowed she would give Asta some lessons with the sword, and learn whether a warrior's spirit lurked behind those gentle blue eyes.

Footsteps came pounding toward them, along with rasping breath. Bryn burst through the branches. "My lord Gavan!" he gasped. "It is Alwyn! She is gone!"

"How did it happen?" roared Gavan, his face thunderous. "Was she not being watched?"

"Only the half Saxon and the demon-thing were there when I returned," Bryn gasped, meaning Rhodri and Blodwedd.

"She must have taken the opportunity of us all being called away to effect her escape," said Iwan. "But she cannot have gone far. We should spread out. She will be heading east, I fancy—back into her lover's waiting arms!"

Gavan flung a deadly look at Iwan, clearly stung by the casual mention of his daughter's feelings for Redwuld Grammod.

"She should be hobbled about the ankles with strong ropes when we find her," said Banon. "It is a wayward and an obstinate child you have there, my lord Gavan."

They ran through the trees, gradually fanning out along the hillside, heading back into the perilous east.

Branwen darted between the drooping willow branches, angry with herself for not having thought to tell someone to stay with Gavan's daughter when they had all run to Asta's aid. She had assumed they were under attack—but that was no excuse. A good leader must give thought to all possibilities. Perhaps Gavan was right: she was overconfident in her abilities, and she was making mistakes.

Sad that things were not different—sad that she and Gavan could not work together, and that she could not learn more from him.

She heard Alwyn before she saw her.

"You're hurting me, you filthy sow! Take your hands off me!"

"I'll hurt you a deal more if you struggle! By the saints, I've a mind to take out my sword and beat you black and blue with the flat of the blade!"

Branwen slowed to a walk. The second voice belonged to Dera.

She came upon them within a few steps. Alwyn was on her knees, with Dera standing behind her. Dera had hold of Alwyn's arm and was twisting it against the shoulder joint so that Alwyn could not rise or pull herself free.

"See what woodland pooka I have snared!" said Dera as she caught sight of Branwen. "Running pell-mell to keep tryst with Redwuld Grammod, I deem!"

Alwyn writhed, letting out a scream as Dera twisted her arm more fiercely.

"Be still, woman!" said Dera. "I'll take off your

arm at the shoulder ere you'll get free of me!" She glowered at Branwen. "If not for the sake of her father's renown, I'd suggest we rid ourselves of this burden once and for all. But say the word, Branwen, and I'll snap her neck!"

Angry as she was, Branwen knew Dera's threats were only meant to subdue her captive. Dera was of too noble a spirit to kill a helpless captive—even one so aggravating as Alwyn.

Branwen came down on her haunches, reaching out and lifting Alwyn's furious face by the chin. "What ails you, Alwyn?" she asked quite calmly. "Are you sick in the head? Does it mean nothing to you that your father has come all this way just to bring you home? Do you care so little for him that you'd spit in his face?"

"What do you know of it?" snarled Alwyn. "He was no father to me. Always away at the wars—never at home for more than two nights at a time, and away year after year while spring turned to winter and winter to spring!"

"Not through choice," said Branwen. "He was needed to defend our country. He loves you, Alwyn. Can you not see that?"

"Then he should have been with us when they came!" howled Alwyn, her face burning red. "He should have been at our side when they murdered my mother and bound me and dragged me away behind their horses! He should have *been* there! I shall never forgive him for that! Never!"

Branwen stood up. She could almost sympathize with the distressed woman. Such a miserable fate as Alwyn had suffered might have crushed the strongest of souls. It seemed that the rescue of Gavan's daughter was only the first step in bringing Alwyn safe and whole back to her home. Branwen sighed and turned away. The old warrior had heartache in plenty ahead of him.

Branwen and Dera returned to the camp with Gavan's troublesome daughter to find that a good thing had happened in their absence. Banon was at the riverside with Asta and Rhodri and Blodwedd—and the owl-girl was awake and sitting up in Banon's arms.

Iwan stood apart from them, his arms folded, gazing into the trees as though Blodwedd's recovery was of little interest to him; but Branwen remembered his concern when they had found her and was not fooled by his feigned indifference.

Branwen ran down to the river, her heart leaping to see Blodwedd's great amber eyes open again. She came crashing down in the grass at Blodwedd's side, snatching her out of Banon's arms and clasping her tightly.

"I thought I had left you to die," she gasped, tears running down her cheeks. "I thought I'd never see you again."

"Gently, gently," said Rhodri, touching Branwen's

shoulder. "You'll break her in two with your gladness!"

"Oh! I'm sorry!" Branwen drew anxiously back. "Have I hurt you?"

Blodwedd smiled. "No, you have not. Did I not tell you that the Saxons would not catch me? Although I will admit that the nature of my escape was not something I had looked to."

Dera gazed down at her. "How did you prevail against so many?" she asked. "And you without sword, spear, or shred of armor."

"I did not do it alone," said Blodwedd. "I had the help of many brothers and many sisters."

Branwen frowned at her. "What do you mean? Who was it that came to your aid?"

"An army of hundreds," said Iwan. "An army that answers the riddle of the dark cloud we saw hovering over the Saxon camp as we departed."

Branwen knew what he was referring to, but it still made no sense to her. An army in the form of a black cloud?

"Owls!" said Rhodri. "Owls by the hundred!"

Branwen's eyes widened. "Owls?"

"I did not call to them, but still they came," said Blodwedd, her eyes full of a deep amber luster. "From north, south, east, and west they came, sensing my distress, flooding the skies above the Great Hall like the waters of a mighty deluge. With wing, beak, and claw they fell upon the Saxons, driving them back, their glad and fearsome voices lifting high as they came to the place where I was embattled."

That sound they had heard from across the river—the eerie, high-pitched noise that had set Branwen's teeth on edge! It had been the screeching of a sky full of owls!

"I was in sore need by then," Blodwedd continued. "And even in my uttermost peril, I was joyous indeed that my kindred had not forsaken me despite the human form that is now my cage. I had lost count of the Saxon eyes I had put out and the throats I had torn open, but I was badly wounded and surrounded on all sides. But the owls beat back my attackers, and the greatest of them plucked me by the clothes and the hair and the limbs and drew me up into the sky."

"Wonderful! Wonderful!" gasped Branwen. "Oh! I wish I had seen such a sight! I wish I had *known*!"

"I must have fainted then from my injuries," said Blodwedd. "Because when I woke again I was here, and Rhodri was tending me." She reached out and took his hand in hers. "My dear friend."

"And are you able to move yet?" asked Dera. "We would stand around you with a shield wall till doomsday if we must, for the part you have played, but we'd fare better on horseback and riding hard for Powys."

"I can ride, I believe," said Blodwedd. She looked at Branwen. "Do you remember what I told you when first we met? I heal swift or not at all."

"Yes, I remember," said Branwen. "But you must

be weak still. You've lost a lot of blood." She looked at Rhodri. "Is she fit to travel?"

"We *must* travel, and quickly, too," said Blodwedd, tightening her fingers around Branwen's wrist. "I am uneasy in my mind. In my fever I have seen visions and portents that cannot be ignored." Her eyes became fiery. "The black bird laughs at us, Branwen! I have heard his voice in my mind. He mocks us and speaks sinister words into my ears."

"What black bird?" asked Dera.

"Mumir the raven, which bird else?" said Branwen. "I'd hoped we were rid of that pestilence; but if Blodwedd speaks the truth, he has returned to plague us again."

"What did he say to you?" asked Iwan.

"'*She will betray you,*'" said Blodwedd. "Those were his words. '*She will betray you. She will bring death and disaster upon you. The mountain will be broken and all that live shall be devoured.*'"

"The Aesir protect us!" Asta gasped, her hands to her face. "That is a terrible prophecy indeed!"

Branwen gazed into Blodwedd's face, disturbed that Skur's raven still haunted them, and horribly aware of who the *she* was of whom he had spoken. But how were they to defy or escape such a dreadful foretelling?

Blodwedd pointed toward Alwyn, who was standing close by with Gavan at her side. "Surely it is *she* of whom the raven spoke!" she cried. "She is the cuckoo in the nest!"

"By the saints," said Dera, closing her fingers around the hilt of her sheathed sword and turning to stare at Alwyn. "But this is a prophecy that can be overturned in a moment with a sharp blade."

Gavan stepped in front of his daughter, his own sword snaking from the sheath in a swift, fluid movement. "You will not harm her, Dera ap Dagonet," he said, his eyes deadly. "Not unless you come to her over the corpse of Gavan ap Huw!"

In a moment Dera's sword was also bared and ready in her hand. "So be it!" she cried, lunging forward before Branwen could move to stop her.

26

"NO!" SHOUTED BRANWEN, jumping to her feet. "Put up your sword, Dera!"

She stepped between them, her own sword still sheathed, her arms outstretched to ward off both of them.

"There shall be no bloodshed between the peoples of Brython!" Branwen exclaimed. "If we fight among ourselves, who will reap the benefit but the greater enemy?" She looked from Gavan to Dera. "Blodwedd heard the laughter of Mumir; would you hear the guffaws of every Saxon in Mercia?" Her voice cracked like a whip. "Dera! Sheath your sword! Alwyn will not be killed!"

"Is this wise counsel?" muttered Dera, and for a moment Branwen feared that the fierce girl would defy her. Then Dera shook her head and put away her sword. But her eyes were baleful as she looked at

Alwyn, the girl's frightened face half hidden behind her father's shoulder. "Live on for now, Alwyn ap Gavan," Dera said. "But I am watching; and when the time comes that you betray us, I will strike you down."

Gavan's voice was calm and low, but filled with authority. "Branwen of the Old Ones," he said, "you'd best tell your people to keep away from my daughter, for I'll put to death any who touch so much as a hair of her head."

"No one will do hurt to her; you have my word," said Branwen. "Blodwedd is able to travel now. We should get to horse and speed our path from this land." She looked into his glowering face. "And when the first hoof of the first horse enters Powys, we shall part, Gavan ap Huw; and I will be glad to put distance between us. Your daughter is not to be trusted, and heavy prophecies hang about her."

"I give little heed to omens conjured by the Old Gods," Gavan said contemptuously. He turned away from her. "Bryn! Go into the woods—call back Padrig and Dillon and Andras. This pointless sojourn is done!"

As she too turned to walk away, Branwen glanced sidelong at Alwyn and was disturbed to see a cold smile curling on her lips, as though she delighted in the conflict that she was causing.

Almost I wish I'd let Dera have her will in this. But no. Gavan's daughter cannot be killed for fear of what she might do. We are close to our homeland. On the sacred soil

276

of Powys we shall sever this bitter alliance and ride our sun-
dered ways, and let doom and disaster fall elsewhere as it will
while we take the straight road to Merion of the Stones.

It did not take long to assemble the rest of Gavan's
and Branwen's followers; and as though some strange
animal sense brought him to them, Fain came wing-
ing out of the east just as Branwen was mounting
Stalwyn, ready to leave the riverside.

He alighted on her wrist, cawing loudly.

Blodwedd was close by, seated in front of Rhodri,
her thin body circled by his arms. She was pale and
weak, but her eyes were bright as she listened to Fain's
news.

"None follow close behind," Blodwedd reported.
"The east is clear of foes."

Branwen frowned. "That is good news, but puzzling also," she said, her hand coming to rest on the
curved lid of the stolen casket. "Why are they not
close on our trail?"

"Perhaps because they have the wisdom to have
ridden hard to block the way ahead of us," said
Gavan. "Ironfist is a canny soldier; he well knows how
to outflank an enemy. Mark my words, if they are not
behind us, it is because they plan to lie in wait for us
on our road."

"They have not had the time," Branwen said stub-
bornly, refusing to be schooled by him. "And they
do not know which path we will take." She lifted her

voice. "Ride now!" she called. "The straight road to Powys! The straight road to home!"

"That is not wise," said Gavan. "A winding path is the less easily tracked."

"But takes the longest," said Branwen. "No. The flying arrow reaches its mark the soonest." So saying, Branwen pressed her heels into Stalwyn's flanks, and the final stage of the ride to Powys began.

As much as Branwen desired a speedy exit from Mercia, she knew the horses could not be ridden at the canter for long periods without exhausting them. And so as the sun burned down on their backs from midway up the morning sky, they slowed their flight and took their horses at a brisk walk through groves of alder.

A wide, dense forest lay ahead; and in the far west, the mountains of Brython rose in brown sawtooth ridges and were seen often now as they came to higher ground or found a break in the canopy of the trees.

It would not be long before they came to the wilderness that formed the eastern flank of Cyffin Tir. Branwen could almost hear the calling voice of home in her mind as she rode. But the joy of going to Garth Milain and seeing her dear mother again, that would have to wait on her duty to Merion.

Fain was far behind them, sweeping the skies, watching for pursuit. He had instructions to fly to them like an arrow if he saw so much as a Saxon horse coming out of the east.

Rhodri and Blodwedd were to one side of Branwen; Iwan and Linette rode together on the other. Gavan was some way ahead, with the stony-faced Alwyn at his back. The boys of Doeth Palas rode together and apart from the warrior maidens of Gwylan Canu, and there was clear tension between them. Branwen would be glad when the time came for them to part, and not only to be rid of Mumir's grim prophecies.

"And you say Asta knocked Bryn out with one blow?" said Rhodri, grinning at Branwen's tale. "She must be stronger than she looks. Very much stronger."

"I think she is," said Branwen, looking ahead to where the Viking girl rode behind Dera on the tall destrier. "She'd make a fine warrior! She is reconciled to the fact that she cannot go home yet awhile. But when I told her I'd have Gavan ap Huw take her to Pengwern, she said she would rather stay with us."

"Did she, indeed?" said Iwan. "And did she give a reason for such a strange choice?"

"Is it so very strange?" asked Linette. "We ride with Branwen—why should she not?"

"Because she is not of Brython," said Iwan. "Her homeland is far away. Why should she wish to be involved in our troubles?"

"She feels she has a debt of honor to repay," said Branwen.

"Ahh—a debt to the slayer of Skur Bloodax," said Iwan with a nod of understanding. "And while we speak of axes, Branwen—what would you have done with Skur's battle-ax? Are we to keep it with us, or will Gavan ap Huw bear it to Pengwern as a war-gift to the king?"

"I have not decided yet," said Branwen. The truth was, she had not even thought that far ahead. Escaping Mercia was the one focus of her mind.

"We should keep it," said Linette. "It will draw warriors to our cause from all parts of the Four Kingdoms."

"And away from the courts of the four kings," Iwan said thoughtfully. "Is that what you want, Branwen—to set up a rival court in Powys to King Cynon's?"

"For the moment my intent is to bring the casket to Merion and to see Caradoc of the North Wind set free," said Branwen, uneasily aware of how closely Iwan's question echoed the concerns that Gavan had expressed earlier.

Blodwedd spoke softly. "And when that deed is done, the Shining Ones will light our farther path," she murmured. "Do not doubt that, Iwan ap Madoc."

"To be sure," muttered Iwan. "And what next tightrope would they have us walk, blindfolded and hemmed about with sharp iron?"

"We have survived thus far," said Rhodri. "What

of faith, Iwan ap Madoc? Do you have none?"

"I prefer a clear road ahead of me, Master Runaway; that is all," Iwan replied. "But have no fear; I will not turn from the path I have chosen."

"Then we are marvelously blessed," Rhodri said caustically.

"Indeed you are," said Iwan with a laugh. "More than you deserve, I suspect!"

Their conversation was broken by Gavan turning his horse and riding back to them.

"The straight path ahead will take us into a heavily wooded vale," he said. "It is too easy a place for an ambush. We must take the prudent way: skirt the forest and come to the border of Powys through open land."

Branwen looked sourly at him, irritated by the peremptory tone in his voice. Ever since they had been together, he seemed to have done all that he could to undermine her authority. And still he was giving orders!

She could feel the eyes of the others on her, waiting for her to respond. A quiet voice inside her told her to swallow her pride and follow the old warrior's advice. He had fought many campaigns in his life, and he knew all there was to know about the tactics and strategies of war. But her anger and displeasure shouted louder in her ears. It was because of Gavan ap Huw that fearful prophecies hung over their heads. It was his disbelief and disdain that made her constantly doubt herself—and doubt her destiny.

No! Enough and more than enough! He has not gathered to himself all the wisdoms of the world! I will do as I see fit!

"We go the straight way to be in Powys the quicker," she said, hardly able to keep the resentfulness out of her voice. "The forest is too large for us to ride around without too great a delay, and I would rather have the forest to shield our movements from prying eyes than be caught in the open."

Gavan stared unspeakingly into her face. For a moment he hesitated, as though deciding whether to argue against her; but then he nodded curtly, turned his horse again, and rode off ahead.

Branwen felt concerned eyes on her from all sides. The decision had been made, and she could not back down now. Only by unwavering faith in herself could she keep the headstrong likes of Iwan and Dera on her side. If she showed signs of hesitation now, she might lose them—and if they deserted her, the girls of Gwylan Canu must surely follow.

Unspeaking, she urged Stalwyn on, and the small group rode into the trees and down the long slope into the last forested valley in western Mercia.

They had not been long under the thick shelter of the overarching trees when Fain came flying in from the east. Branwen lifted her arm for him, and he landed in a flurry of wings and a ferment of sharp cries.

"Saxons!" Blodwedd translated. "Many hundreds

strong. At our backs. Riding hard. Ironfist is at their head."

"At last they come!" said Iwan. "How far distant?"

Fain cried again.

"They're not yet upon our heels, but they are moving quickly," said Blodwedd.

"Then I chose the better path," said Branwen, trying not to sound too relieved. "They are at our backs, and not ahead of us as Gavan ap Huw would have had us believe!" She ran a finger over the falcon's chest feathers. "Go again, my friend. Keep watch behind. Let us know if they are gaining on us."

With a single cry, Fain sprang up and sped away again through the trees.

Branwen lifted herself in the saddle, calling out to where Gavan and the boys rode. They were some distance ahead, following a narrow trail that wound along the valley's floor.

"Gavan ap Huw! Ironfist is on our track! Fain has seen him riding hard with an army of hundreds in his wake!"

Gavan turned to look at her.

You were wrong, Old Warrior, and I was right!

But even as that thought rang in her head, Branwen heard the sound of voices howling and roaring from the trees all around them. Moments later the air was thick with volleys of arrows skimming in from all sides. A shaft struck Stalwyn in the neck. He reared, screaming in pain, his hooves striking the air.

As she struggled to keep balance and to draw her sword, Branwen heard the alarmed shouting of her followers. Stalwyn twisted in his agony and came crashing down onto his side, his legs kicking wildly. Branwen was thrown headlong from the saddle, and her head was dashed with brutal force against the trunk of a tree. As red lights exploded in her mind, she heard a triumphant chanting coming out of the forest.

"Redwuld! Redwuld! Redwuld!"

Gavan had been right. Ironfist's son had ridden ahead and lain in wait for them.

Gavan had been right . . . and she had doomed them all. . . .

And then, as that thought burned in her mind, the darkness took her.

27

B RANWEN WAS BEING dragged along on her back. She opened her eyes to a whirl of dappled light that floated formlessly above her. There was a lot of unfocused pain in her body and head, and the light hurt. She closed her eyes, feeling the rough ground scraping away underneath her.

Then there was stillness for a moment. She wallowed in the pain, oblivious to everything else.

"Branwen!" A voice pierced the darkness. *"Branwen!"*

She felt a hard slap across her face. Her head was thundering, and there was lightning behind her eyelids.

Another slap.

She blindly raised her hand and caught the wrist. A slender wrist circled by a metal bracelet. She forced her eyes open again.

Asta was leaning over her, the long blond hair hanging, the face twisted with urgency.

"Are all others dead . . . ?" Branwen gasped, the sick pain condensing at the base of her skull.

"No! None yet! They were aiming at the horses. I think Redwuld wants to take us alive if he can—for sport back at the camp, like as not."

Branwen blundered to her feet. The pain in her head almost took her legs from under her. She leaned heavily on Asta. She could hear the sounds of conflict and see a blur of hectic movement through the trees.

"I dragged you away lest you be captured." Asta's voice was urgent. "Shield to arm and sword in hand, Branwen! You are needed in the fray!"

"Yes. Yes." Branwen screwed her eyes tight, fighting the pain and nausea and weakness. She drew her sword and slid her shield off her back, her fingers tightening on the grip. "Give me a moment!" She took in a deep breath, feeling discomfort as her ribs expanded. "Is Stalwyn dead?"

"I don't know. Dera and I were thrown when our horse was struck down by arrows. She rallied everyone—made a shield wall. I crawled away to find you."

"I was wrong," Branwen said. "Gavan knew the danger. . . ."

"Then make amends!" snapped Asta. "You're their leader! Save them!"

Branwen stared at the Viking maiden, surprised

286

by the forcefulness in her voice. But it was what she needed. It cleared her head. She took another breath and broke into a run, making for the sound of battle.

She saw Saxon horses tethered among the trees. There were bows and quivers of arrows, discarded by the Saxons after that opening volley; long-range weapons, they were of little use in close combat. The noise of battle grew. A dead horse lay close by, shot through by several arrows. Not Stalwyn—it was the horse that Aberfa and Banon had been riding. Anger began to rise in Branwen. Not anger at the butchering Saxons, but anger at herself for leading her people into this snare. She had known in her heart that Gavan was giving wise advice when he had said they should avoid this place.

She had ignored him out of stubbornness and vanity.

Now her followers were paying the price.

She came suddenly upon the dark heart of the melee. Saxons swarmed around a tight group. Swords rang. Shouts rent the air. Spears thudded into wooden shields. She saw a Saxon cut down and glimpsed Dera's face for a moment above her shield.

Farther away, she saw Gavan fighting, with Andras and Bryn at his side. Padrig was close by, sheltering Dillon behind his shield, stabbing with his spear, his back to a tree. There was no sign of Alwyn.

Branwen lifted her shield to her eyes, her sword

drawn back over her shoulder, speeding up as she ran headlong at the bunched warriors, ready to unleash all the mayhem of Annwn on her hated enemies.

She crashed into the Saxon rear like a battering ram. Two were dead before they even had time to turn. A third twisted, his pale eyes glowing with battle-fever under the rim of his iron helmet. He stabbed at her with his spear, but her shield turned the blow and her sword sank deep into his neck, almost severing his head from his body as the blood gushed.

A sword whirled at head height. She ducked, thrusting upward under a shield rim, finding an entry through the belly. She dug in her heels, bringing her shoulder into another man's abdomen, sending him staggering back. A blade came at her face, and she only just jerked her head aside in time to avoid certain death. Cold iron sliced her cheek. She swung her sword in a high arc, and her opponent's sword hand was cut from the wrist. The man fell back, bellowing in agony.

Another warrior came at her, his ax cutting down toward her head, his mouth snarling in the tangle of his beard. She lifted her shield to ward off the blow, expecting the sharp iron to sink into the rim. But the ax head glanced off the shield edge, and he stumbled forward onto her poised sword.

Now she was in the thick of things, surviving on instinct alone, swords and spears and axes coming at her from all sides as she buffeted blows away with her shield and sent the blood spraying high with the sharp edge of her sword. She heard female voices raised—her attack on the Saxon rear had put new heart into the warrior girls of Gwylan Canu. She heard Aberfa's stentorian voice rising above all others.

"Death to the Saxons! Glory to Brython!"

A huge warrior loomed toward Branwen, his pale hair flying under his helmet, his face bestial as he jabbed his broad-bladed spear at her. She fended off the blow with her shield; but such was the strength of the man that she was sent stumbling back, her feet slipping on earth turned to bloody mud. She fell and the man was above her, snarling.

She heard the whir of an arrow. The man stood astonished for a moment, a shaft jutting from his chest. Then he crumpled and fell forward so that Branwen had to roll aside to save being crushed under him. She glanced back along the flight of the arrow and was surprised to see Asta among the trees, fitting a second arrow to a bow and letting fly.

A Saxon roared, dropping his weapons as he clutched at his face. The arrow stood out from his eye.

A hand snatched at Branwen from behind, dragging her to her feet. It was Iwan, grinning fiercely, a shallow cut along his forehead spilling blood into his eyes.

The shield wall of her followers had pushed out into the attacking Saxons, and now she was drawn in behind it.

All were there behind the raised shields—all the girls of Gwylan Canu, back to back, fighting like furies. And Iwan was with them, and Rhodri, too, swinging a captured Saxon spear like a club. Blodwedd knelt behind him, still too weak to fight. Of the whole party, only Alwyn was unaccounted for. But Branwen had scant time to wonder where Gavan's daughter might have hidden herself.

"To Gavan ap Huw!" Branwen shouted. "Move together!"

Six shields formed a defensive ring around Branwen and the others as they pressed into the ranks of the Saxons, driving them steadily backward. And as the Saxons circled them, seeking to attack again from behind, they found themselves facing Dera and Aberfa, the first adder-quick and deadly with her sword, the second swinging Skur's battle-ax like a reaper in the wheat field at harvesttime, sending heads leaping from shoulders, separating limbs from torsos and souls from bodies. Gavan was surrounded by the dead, standing his ground like a mighty oak, beating back all who came at him. And Andras and Bryn fought well at his side, although Branwen saw blood on Andras's face and bloody rips in Bryn's clothes.

"To Branwen, my lads!" shouted Gavan, seeing the ring of Branwen's warriors approaching steadily through the tumbling ranks of the enemy.

And so the two groups came together; and with

Gavan on her left and Iwan on her right, Branwen turned defense to attack, driving the Saxons back into the trees, her feet sliding on the bloody fallen as they took the initiative.

Every now and then a Saxon would drop with an arrow in him, shot from behind by Asta as she tracked the slow progress of the battle.

Then, quite suddenly, the Saxons fell back, turning and running, leaving half of their number dead on the field. It seemed to Branwen that Redwuld Grammod had underestimated the prowess of her band—he had come here with too few warriors to gain victory over them.

"Don't let them get away!" shouted Dera, leaping corpses as she ran in hot pursuit. "Cut them down!" Aberfa and Linette raced after her, howling in triumph.

"No!" bellowed Gavan. "Do not be drawn into the woods! We must keep together!"

"Do as he says!" shouted Branwen. "Come back!"

Dera skidded to a halt and spun around, her eyes blazing. "Will you let them escape? We can destroy them to a man!"

"Or they you, child!" boomed Gavan. "You do not know their full numbers. The retreat may be a ruse to draw us to our destruction."

With grim faces, Dera and the others returned. Branwen turned to see Andras approaching, Dillon at his side, pale and trembling.

"They cried out Redwuld's name," said Iwan. "But I have not seen him."

"Like as not he stands off in the forest with more men, hoping to draw us into a trap!" said Gavan. "How many horses are alive still? Have we enough to quit this place?" His face paled. "Where is my daughter?"

"She ran into the trees when we were first attacked," said Aberfa. "I have seen nothing of her since."

"Then we must seek for her!" Gavan declared.

But Branwen was hardly listening to him. Four horses lay dead on the forest floor; of the others there was no sign. Scattered in terror into the forest, she guessed. A swift gallop from danger was not an option—not unless they could make a sortie to where the Saxon horses were tethered and take some of them from the enemy.

Stalwyn lay on the ground a little way off. Motionless. No breath in his stalwart body. A stain of blood around the arrow that stood out from his neck. He was dead. Branwen knew it. Because of her obstinacy and pride a great friend was dead. It was a sight to crush the heart.

But it was a sly movement from behind the body of the fallen animal that took Branwen's attention. The glint of a Saxon helmet, the hump of a scarlet cloak. Someone was on the ground, hiding behind the dead horse. She moved forward, sword and shield ready.

Gavan came leaping past her, springing over Stalwyn's body, his bloodstained sword in his gnarled fist.

"Get to your feet!" he shouted.

The man rose, Caradoc's casket half hidden in the folds of his cloak.

It was Redwuld Grammod, Ironfist's son. Not so handsome and haughty now as he stood trembling in front of Gavan, his head bowed, his eyes full of fear. He must have secreted himself there when his warriors fled, hoping to take possession of the casket and slip away among the trees without being seen.

"Do not kill me," said Redwuld, his eyes darting from Gavan to Branwen. "My father will pay great wergild for my safe return."

"Then he is a fool, and his money were better thrown in the midden!" Gavan's eyes narrowed in distaste. "I have heard tell of you, Redwuld Grammod," he spat. "A drunkard and a braggart, so they say. And must I now add coward to the list of your inadequacies?"

"My sword is broken," said Redwuld, his voice tight in his throat. "Would you strike down a weaponless man?"

Branwen walked around Stalwyn's pitiful body, trying not to look at the noble creature so cruelly slain. "I'd have that casket from you, son of Ironfist," she said.

He slid it from under his cloak. "Here, take it," he

whined. "But have mercy and spare my life; I can do you no hurt."

She lifted the casket out of his hands, disgusted by his cringing words. "Do you know what it contains?" she asked.

"It is a prized possession of my father," said Redwuld. "Some relic of victory from the distant past given to him by King Oswald as a token of good luck in the war. I have never seen it opened."

"Think yourself lucky you have not," said Branwen. "Your men have taken to their heels and deserted you, Redwuld Grammod. What treatment do you believe you deserve at our hands?"

Redwuld looked into her face, his lips quivering. "You are the one my father spoke of," he said, falling to his knees. "The *waelisc* shaman! Do not set demons upon me! Take me prisoner if you must, but do not slay me, I beg you."

Branwen turned away, sickened by his cowardice. "I would not soil my blade with such as you," she said.

"You will not be killed," said Gavan. "You will be bound and taken to King Cynon, and he will do justice on you, son of Ironfist, chicken-hearted child of a formidable father!"

"Thank you!" gasped Redwuld, falling onto his face at Gavan's feet. "A blessing on your mercy!"

A shrill voice sounded from among the trees. "Do not kill him!"

Branwen turned to see Alwyn rushing from some hiding place, her face distraught as she looked at her humbled lover.

Gavan turned to her, his eyes blazing with anger. "Do you see him?" he cried. "On his knees in the dirt, craven and broken although no hurt has been done to him? Is this the man you would wed, Alwyn? Is this the creature for whom you would forsake your homeland?"

"Ware!" shouted Rhodri. "Gavan—*beware!*"

Branwen spun around, alarmed by the panic in Rhodri's voice. Redwuld had risen to his feet at Gavan's back, his cloak thrown open, a seax glinting in his fist. His face vicious and exultant, he thrust the knife into Gavan's back, driving it in hard to the hilt, twisting it as the old warrior arched backward with a cry of agony.

"Treacherous dog!" Aberfa's voice rang out in horror. Her arm drew back, and she let a javelin fly. It skimmed Gavan's shoulder and sank into Redwuld's throat, the narrow iron tip emerging from the back of his neck in a cascade of blood.

In two bounds Branwen was at Gavan's side, her arms out to support him as he fell backward. But he was too heavy for her; and as he fell, she was dragged down to the ground with him, dimly aware of a thud as Redwuld struck the ground.

A piercing shriek rang out. "No!"

Shaking with dread and anguish, Branwen fought

to get to her knees, dragging Gavan's head into her lap, leaning close over him.

"Have no fear," she gasped, her voice choking in her throat. "All's well. Rhodri will save you!" She lifted her head, her eyes blinded by tears. "Rhodri! Quickly! He is badly hurt!"

Alwyn came to a stuttering halt, standing there for a moment among the carnage, swaying, her face white, her grieving eyes moving from Gavan to Redwuld. Then with a groan she fell to her knees at her father's side, her face wrung with agony, tears flooding her cheeks. "Father, no! Father—please . . ."

Through the veil of her tears, Branwen was aware of people surrounding her.

"The cur Redwuld is dead," she heard Dera exclaim. "A curse on us that we did not finish him ere he gave this dolorous blow!"

"Alwyn?" Gavan's voice was like the last flicker of a dying candle, thin but clear in Branwen's ears.

"Yes, Father. I am here." Alwyn's voice cracked as she caught up Gavan's trailing hand.

A pale smile lit the old warrior's face for a moment.

"Tell . . . Branwen ap . . . Griffith . . ." He coughed, and there was blood on his lips. "Tell her . . . to be true . . . to . . . her people. . . ." He paused, blood bubbling. "Tell her to go to . . . the . . . king. . . ." Another pause, and now his breathing was rapid and shallow.

"I am here, Gavan ap Huw!" Branwen said,

weeping. But he did not hear her.

"Tell her . . . if she honors me . . . she will do as I ask. . . . She will ally herself with King . . . Cynon. . . ." Gavan's gray eyes opened wide and he seemed to be looking into Branwen's eyes, but she knew that he did not see her.

"I come . . . ," he whispered, and there was a strange gladness and peace in his voice now. "You have waited long, my love . . . my wife . . . my dearest one . . . but your wait is . . . done. . . . I . . . am . . . coming. . . ."

And as those words trailed from his lips like the last wisps of a dying fire, Branwen saw the light go out of his eyes. There was a final soft breath and then a great aching stillness and the lifeless weight of his head on her knees.

A red storm came racing into Branwen's head. Lightning forked. Thunder growled and roared. The old warrior was dead.

An unquenchable pain swelling in her chest, Branwen lifted her head and howled her impotent anger to the sky.

28

"WE CANNOT LEAVE our master to lie among the Saxon carrion," exclaimed Bryn, his voice distraught as he shouted into Branwen's face. "Gavan ap Huw must be buried with all honor! You owe him that much—his death is on your hands!"

Branwen looked blankly at him. She felt numbed. Her heart was a stone in her chest. The grief and the guilt had been too much to bear; all that was human in her seemed to have fled her with Gavan ap Huw's last breath.

She was standing a little way from the old warrior's body although she had no clear memory of having moved from his side. Alwyn was kneeling over him still, holding his one hand in both of hers, her bowed face hidden behind hanging hair. Branwen could hear her sobbing. The others stood around in shock and disbelief, unspeaking, their eyes hollow, faces pale and drawn.

"We have no time for such niceties," said Dera, coming to Branwen's side. "There are Saxons still in the forest—and many more riding us down out of the east, if the falcon is to be believed. If we linger here now, our bones will lie in this place forever."

Branwen turned to her. The fierce warrior girl's emotions were etched deeply in her face, but the fire in her eyes did nothing to awaken Branwen's stupefied feelings. "We could build a pyre of fresh-cut logs," she murmured dully. "There is wood enough to hand. The old warrior could be laid on the top—as my brother, Geraint, was laid on the pyre below the hill of Garth Milain."

Dera stared at her, and now there was confusion and anxiety in her face. "What are you saying?" she asked. "We do not have the time to build a funeral pyre!"

Rhodri stepped forward. "We need horses if we're to reach the mountains before Ironfist catches up with us," he said. "Bryn? Dera? Can you organize a search for horses? Some of ours may still be close by—and there's a chance that the fleeing Saxons may have left some behind."

Bryn stared sourly at him. "Do you give orders now, Saxon lickspittle?" he growled.

"Watch your mouth, Bryn!" spat Iwan. "The runaway deserves better."

"And it is *half* Saxon lickspittle, by your leave," Rhodri replied mildly. "And no, I do not give orders. I simply make suggestions. But if you would rather stand here arguing till Ironfist arrives, then by all means do as you will."

"No," said Dera. "It is well thought, Rhodri. Horses indeed! I'll get to it. Bryn? Come, be of help—we have little time."

For a moment Bryn stood glowering at Rhodri as if wishing to dash his fist into the other's face. Then he turned and stomped away, calling to Andras and Padrig as he went.

"Well now, that is one thorn removed from your side," Rhodri said gently, gazing compassionately into Branwen's eyes. "I shan't ask how you are," he continued. "Such things do not need to be explained between true friends."

She returned his gaze but said nothing.

"You do know we cannot build a pyre, don't you?" he asked. "Or at least, if we tarry here to build one, then we should build it wide enough for all of us to lie on." He frowned. "That would be a way out for you, I suppose—to chop wood and heap it up and up until General Ironfist comes to put you out of your misery." He smiled bleakly. "But it will be hard on those of us who still wish to live, Branwen." He sighed. "I had hoped to die in bed at a great age, surrounded by doting grandchildren."

"Do you mock me, Rhodri?" she murmured.

"Yes, a little, perhaps," he said.

"Gavan ap Huw lies dead because of me," she said, her voice thick and graveled. "Stalwyn is food for crows." She thumped her fist against her heart. "Because of me, Rhodri! Because of my conceit and vanity. I deserve death!"

"Well, let's not debate who deserves what bad fate," Rhodri said. "We'll all hang from the gibbet if we take that path!" He rested his hand on her shoulder. "Do you know the difference between a wise man and a fool?"

She shook her head.

"A wise man learns from his mistakes; a fool is doomed forever to repeat them." He brought his head closer to hers, looking deeply into her eyes, his voice lowering to a compelling whisper. "Learn from your mistakes, Branwen. This is your greatest test; this is the moment when you learn who you truly are—what you are truly capable of. Would you die of shame and remorse, or would you make amends for past lapses of judgment and leadership?"

"Become who I am, you mean?" she breathed. "The Emerald Flame?" Her voice choked with bitterness. "The Bright Blade?"

"Indeed. All that and more."

She felt a painful thawing in her soul. "It's hard to carry on," she said heavily. "Easier to wait here for death, I think."

"Much easier, I'd say," agreed Rhodri. "But here's

the rub, Branwen—if you choose to stay here and die, Blodwedd will wish to face death at your side. And if Blodwedd stays, then so must I." He gave her a comically remorseful look. "Our futures are in your hands, no matter what you decide to do. Personally, I'd opt for life—but maybe that's just me."

"Hush, Rhodri," she said fondly, placing her hand on his and squeezing his fingers. "Your point is well made, and I thank you for it from the bottom of my heart." She shook her head. "But it's a hard taskmaster you are, Rhodri, descendent of the Druid lords of Ynis Môn! Like a wasp trapped in my hair you are to me"—she smiled—"and I love you for it, dearest of friends!"

"Then are you resolved?" Rhodri asked. "Shall we flee this place? Shall I be allowed to die ancient in years and in the comfort of my own bed?"

She laughed softly. "If it's in my power, then you shall," she said. She took a long, slow, cleansing breath. "Let's to it, then!" She gave his hand a final squeeze, then squared her shoulders and strode away from him.

Dera and Linette and Bryn and Padrig were gone into the woods, seeking horses. Andras stood with Dillon. Aberfa and Banon talked quietly together to one side while Asta sat under a tree, her legs drawn up and her face buried in her folded arms. Blodwedd was standing over Stalwyn, her head bowed in sorrow. Alwyn knelt still at her father's side; and Iwan was close by, his eyes thoughtful on Branwen.

"We have no time to bury our dead, nor to speed them to heaven with the purifying fire," Branwen called. "But let us do what honor we can to Gavan ap Huw! Strip all these Saxon dead of their weapons and pile them at his feet! Let any who come nigh this place know that he was a great hero!"

Iwan walked up to her. "Are you yourself again, Branwen?" he asked.

She looked candidly into his face. "I am."

"Thanks to . . ." He paused as if judging his words carefully. "Thanks to Rhodri?"

"Yes."

There was an odd silence between them.

"You have great affection for him, I think," Iwan said.

"I do. Of course I do."

"You know there are others of this company who would wish for . . ." He stopped, as if his glib tongue had for once forsaken him.

"Speak your mind, Iwan," Branwen said softly.

He reached out toward her. She held his eyes, not flinching as his fingers gently brushed her cheek. There was soreness—she had all but forgotten her injury. "You are wounded," he said. "Best have Rhodri tend it lest it fester."

She lifted her hand to where the blood was drying from the shallow cut on his forehead. There was strange delight in the feel of his skin under her fingertips. "You also," she said, her mouth suddenly dry. "Does it hurt?"

"A little," he said, his eyes huge and dark and dangerous. "Branwen . . . ?"

She felt as though the ground was shifting under her feet. "Yes?"

"Horses, ho!" shouted Aberfa. "We shall ride from this charnel pit after all!"

Branwen broke Iwan's gaze and turned to where Linette and Dera were emerging from the forest, leading a half dozen horses. Two of them were their own: Iwan's Gwennol Dhu and the great bay destrier of Skur Bloodax. The others she did not know—Saxon horses, she assumed, from the look of their saddles and bridles.

Six steeds and fourteen of them.

Branwen was still puzzling over how to accommodate so many on so few horses when there was a commotion from the other side of the forest, and Bryn and Padrig appeared, riding two more Saxon horses and leading another one by the reins.

"It seems we gave them such a beating that they did not even pause to gather up the horses of their dead comrades ere they fled!" shouted Bryn. "And the forest floor is scattered with fallen weapons!"

"Did you see any Saxons?" called Branwen.

"One or two wounded, left behind," said Bryn. "We helped them on their way to the next world!"

"But no sign of them rallying to attack again?"

304

"None," said Padrig. "Judging by the trail of discarded war-gear, I'd say they took flight eastward."

"Perhaps to join up with Ironfist's horsemen," said Iwan, his eyes glowing as he looked at Gwennol Dhu, alive when many others had died. "Let's be gone ere they arrive. We have horses enough now, and there's nothing more to be done here."

"There is one thing I'd do," said Dera. "Should we not make sure that Ironfist's son gives his father a fitting welcome when he rides into this place? Banon! Bring me a sturdy spear; I've a job of butchery to perform!"

"Be swift then," said Branwen, preferring not to ask what the grim warrior girl had in mind. "All others to horse! Take what provisions we may need, but waste no more time here. Asta! On your feet, now! You'll ride with me on Skur's destrier. Rhodri—you are with Blodwedd. Padrig, keep Dillon with you! And Linette—look to Alwyn! I do not fear she will try to escape, but I'd have you ride with her."

There was much activity now as people chose horses and attached what traveling gear they had to the saddles. Linette drew Alwyn away from her father's side. The once proud and contemptuous young woman seemed utterly crushed by Gavan's death, her shoulders shrunken, her face grimed with endless tears.

And she is not the only one! Not all of Rhodri's wise words will suffice to wash away the blood that stains my hands after this day's vile work! Gavan ap Huw died because of my misdeeds! I shall not forget that! But by the grace of the Three Saints, let me be not a fool! Let me learn from my mistakes and do better hereafter!

But a thought possibly even more daunting was also lodged in her mind, as deep and troublesome as a pricking thorn.

Gavan's dying wish had been for her to go to Pengwern. It was a grave thing to reject such a request—the last desire of a great hero of Powys. And yet, if she turned aside from her true path and went to the king as he had asked, what terrible consequences would ensue? No, if she was ever to take the southern road to Pengwern, it could not be until her duty to Merion of the Stones was fulfilled.

Asta climbed into the saddle at Branwen's back, her hands on Branwen's shoulders. "When leisure allows, I'd know where you learned to shoot a bow so well," Branwen asked the pale Viking maiden. "Your prowess did much to turn the tide in our favor."

"You'd know the truth?" Asta asked, her voice subdued. "I learned archery as a child from my father, but until this day it was no more than sport to me—shooting at wicker targets." Her hands tightened on Branwen's shoulders. Her voice shook. "Before today I had never killed a man, and the fondest wish of my heart is that I am never called upon to do so again!"

"Many a seasoned warrior would say the same," said Branwen. She rested her hand on the casket, tied securely to the front of her saddle. "But for what it's worth, you have my thanks. Your debt to me is repaid in full, Asta Aeslief, and I will do all that I can to see you safe home again!"

So saying, Branwen flicked the reins and led the others from the bloody scene of battle.

All that could be done had been done. Gavan ap Huw lay in peaceful repose with his hands upon his breast and with the shields and weapons of his enemies at his feet. Stalwyn and the other slain horses had been covered in leafy branches—some small token of esteem for their sacrifice.

Dera had also finished her grisly work.

At the eastern end of the battlefield, spiked upon a standing pole, the severed head of Redwuld Grammod stared sightlessly through the trees, awaiting the coming of his father.

29

THERE WAS NO exact moment when the riders
could have said they had left Mercia behind
them; there was just the gradual change from the
wide and undulating Mercian plain to the high
ridges and steep valleys, to the bluffs and gorges and
cliffs and gullies of the easternmost flanks of Cyffin
Tir—the uncompromising landscape of Branwen's
wild homeland.

The towering range of the Clwydian Mountains
seemed so close now that Branwen almost felt she
could have reached out a hand and grazed her fingers on the sharp, barren peaks that rose out of the
great green forests. The sun stood high above the
mountains, burnishing their lofty crowns and flanks
so that they had a sheen like old leather.

And hidden away among those bulwarks and

bastions of ancient rock lay the cave of Merion of the Stones—and journey's end!

Branwen reined her horse up on a raised knuckle of heathland, the powerful creature fetlock deep in the purple heather that Branwen knew so well. The others stopped, gathering around her.

"We have come now to the place where Gavan ap Huw would have parted ways with me and mine," she said, her eyes moving between Bryn and Andras and coming to rest on Padrig, with Dillon sitting astride the saddle in front of him. "The way to Pengwern lies southward." She made a wide gesture, stretching out her arm, her flat hand pointing. "If you travel south for half a day, you will come upon the Great South Way that leads from Gwylan Canu to the court of King Cynon. Another day's riding will take you to his citadel." She looked at Alwyn. "Go with them, daughter of Gavan ap Huw. I hope you find comfort there. It's certain that the child of a hero such as your father was will receive a generous welcome from the king."

"And what would you have us tell the king of Lord Gavan's daughter?" asked Padrig, glancing sideways at Alwyn, who was seated behind Linette with downcast eyes.

A good question.

Branwen frowned. "Tell him that Gavan ap Huw led you into the heartland of the great enemy, and that he plucked his beloved daughter from captivity," she said. "And say that on the road home, the great warrior fell in battle to defend his child and that she wept over his body."

"And what of Redwuld Grammod?" asked Padrig.

"Say that he is dead and that none lamented his passing, vile and treacherous dog that he was." Branwen held Padrig's gaze. "Tell that to the king, and he will know all that he needs to know."

Alwyn lifted her head and looked at Branwen; and among the harrowing grief and remorse in the stricken young woman's face, Branwen saw a glimmer of gratitude and hope.

"And what would you have us tell the king of *you*?" Padrig asked.

Branwen held back from answering. What, indeed!

Blodwedd's voice sounded in the charged silence, frail still but firm. "Tell this king of men that he is but a passing dream in the long story of this ancient land," she said. "Tell him that greater guardians than he have given thought to the future, and that their Chosen One walks the path of a high destiny."

Branwen smiled grimly. Doubts and conflicted loyalties had plagued her through this journey; but suddenly, at this parting of the ways, her mind became clear of doubt and uncertainty.

"And tell him that I will come to him shortly, when my present duty to the Shining Ones is done," she said. "And tell him that I will join with him, if he will have me, to help rid this land of enemies both without and within!" She could almost hear Gavan's deep voice as she echoed the words he had spoken to her under the arches of green willow in the dark time just before that day's dawn.

"I shall do that, if you wish it," said Padrig, a new respect dawning in his eyes. Andras also looked at her without disquiet for the first time, but Bryn's face showed nothing of what he was thinking. "But can you not come south with us now?" Padrig added. "It's the safer path, I think."

"We have an errand in the west first," said Iwan. "And safe or not, we cannot turn aside from it."

Branwen glanced at him, glad of his unhesitant support.

"Then give us the weapon of Skur Bloodax, and we will be gone," said Bryn, eyeing the great battle-ax that hung still from its leather harness on the saddle of the Viking's destrier. "It will be some token at least that we are telling the truth."

"By all means take it," said Branwen, reaching to loosen the straps. "Tell the king how you came by it! Tell him of the great champion of the Saxons that I slew."

"Is that wise, Branwen?" Asta asked. "Would it not be better for you to bring the battle-ax of Skur to the king yourself?"

Branwen turned in the saddle, looking into Asta's face. "How so?"

"The trophy belongs to *you*, Branwen—not to the king, nor to any other," Asta said. "You should keep it with you."

"There's sense in this," added Dera, looking doubtfully at Bryn and the other lads. "Why hand it into the keeping of others when you can ride into Pengwern with it and lay it yourself at the king's feet."

Branwen nodded, pulling the straps tight again. "Then I shall keep it," she said. She looked at Bryn. "Tell the lords of the king's court that Skur Bloodax is dead and that I will bring this token of my victory over him when I can."

Bryn's face became peevish at this, and Branwen got the impression that the big lad had been looking forward to riding into Pengwern with the dead Viking's battle-ax over his shoulder.

"Go with them, Alwyn ap Gavan," said Branwen. "I hope you live such a life from now on that all the past will be forgotten."

Alwyn climbed down from behind Linette. She walked to Branwen's horse and lifted her open hand to her. Branwen took it.

"Thank you," Alwyn said. "It was a bitter lesson that brought me from darkness into light, and I want you to know that I do not hold you to blame for my father's death."

Branwen nodded but didn't reply. Forgiven by Gavan's daughter, she would never be able to forgive herself.

Alwyn walked to Andras's horse, and he reached down to help her climb up behind him, a sad, penitent figure with eyes still brimming with tears.

"Good luck to you," said Padrig, turning to Branwen. "If such a thing as luck can play any part on the unhallowed path you tread, Branwen of the Old Ones." His eyes roved over the others of her band. "I'd advise you all to rethink your part in this and to take the road south with us," he said. "But I think you are all as fey as your leader, and doomed to suffer her fate."

"We are," Banon said with a laugh. "And we shall!"

"Gladly so!" added Rhodri.

Padrig shook his head and turned his horse to the south. Bryn and Andras followed him as he rode steadily away from the stationary riders.

Branwen sat watching them for a while as they shrank in the distance, thinking how doleful it was that Gavan ap Huw would never now come to the king—that he would never now lead the fight against the traitor Llew ap Gelert.

"Something comes," murmured Blodwedd from behind Rhodri. "On the east wind. A bird. I think it is Fain."

"Then thank the Three Saints for his safe return!" said Branwen, twisting in the saddle and staring back the way they had come. "I have been searching the skies for him since we left the forest!"

A dark speck came speeding from the fathomless

blue of the eastern sky, growing gradually and taking form.

Branwen lifted herself in the saddle, holding her arm up high as the falcon stooped and came swinging in to land on her wrist. No sooner were his wings folded than he began to give voice to loud, urgent cawings.

"What does he say?" Banon asked Blodwedd.

"He has news of Ironfist," said the owl-girl, listening carefully to the falcon's harsh cries. A sharp and merciless smile grew on her lips. "Fain tells that the great general met his son in the forest and was much affected by the encounter!" she said.

"As I hoped he would be!" said Dera. "Did his one good eye have enough tears in it to tell of his grief?"

"He wept copiously indeed," said Blodwedd. "He leaped from his horse and fell to his knees, cradling Grammod's head to his chest and lamenting in a loud voice. And amid his wailing he sent curses down on your head, Branwen—terrible curses! Oh, but he hates you now, with a raw hatred that has no surcease!"

Fain's scratchy voice sounded again.

"Ironfist has vowed never to sleep in a bed again nor to forsake arms and armor until he has hunted you down and slaughtered you, Branwen," said Blodwedd. "By the most terrible of oaths has he promised this! By Wotan and Thunaer and Tiw he has made his vow."

"And is he closer to us now?" asked Iwan, staring into the east. "I see no sign of horsemen out on the plain."

Again Fain cawed.

"He has stopped to perform the funeral rites for his son," Blodwedd translated. "We have gained ground on him. He is half a day and more behind us now."

"Then we will reach the mountains before him," said Branwen. "Let him hunt for us in Merion's domain if he dares! If all goes as I hope, he will by then have more than we few folk to contend with." She smiled grimly, her hand resting on the lid of the casket strapped to her saddlebow. "He will find him-self face-to-face with Caradoc of the North Wind!" she said. "And then we shall see how a god wreaks vengeance on his erstwhile jailer!"

30

A<small>S THEY RODE</small> on through the beautiful wilderness of Cyffin Tir, Branwen refused to let her thoughts dwell on how close they were passing to Garth Milain. It would do no *good* to think about hearth and home now. One day, if her destiny willed it so, when the raw wounds of these turbulent days had healed over and shriveled to nothing more than poignant white scars, she might sit at ease with her dear mother at the fireside of a new-built Great Hall talking over old agonies.

And maybe they would speak of Geraint and laugh again at the jokes he used to play, and of Prince Griffith ap Rhys, warrior-husband and revered father who died battling the enemies of their blood. Tales of triumph and loss, of joy and sadness.

One day . . .

. . . if her destiny allowed . . .

* * *

They were moving now through forested foothills, climbing slowly in a landscape as familiar to Branwen as her own arms and hands and fingers. She knew that if she traveled but a short way south through these green hills she would be able to look down on the solitary mound of Garth Milain.

Not that she felt up to that challenge—to see her home and to have to pass it by without running into her mother's arms. That was a thing that would test her beyond her limits. To be comforted by a mother's embrace, to be enfolded in a mother's love. She would never find the courage to leave again, and she knew it.

Fain guided them as they headed deeper into the rising forest. He would go soaring up through the roof of branches while they picked their earthbound way onward and return with news of what lay ahead, shepherding them away from dangerous places and keeping them always on the straight road to Merion's lofty cave.

Branwen became aware of something curious about the casket strapped in front of her. At first she thought it was her imagination; but as they delved deeper into the hills, she grew more certain that the casket would every now and then vibrate, as though something within was awakening and struggling to free itself. And although the afternoon was warm and the air was heavy and humid under the trees, the casket was always cold to the touch.

She thought that somehow the trapped god must know he was drawing close to his ancient sister of the stones and was eager to see the end of his long confinement. And as her thoughts turned to Merion, Branwen remembered again the horrors of that dark and dreadful cavern in the mountainside, and she shuddered.

"Are you cold, Branwen?" Asta asked, close enough to have felt the chill go through Branwen's body.

"No, not cold," Branwen said without looking around. "Anxious to be done with this, that's all. I'm not at ease, Asta, knowing what lies inside this casket. I'd be free of it."

"Yes," replied Asta, her voice strangely thoughtful. "It is a heavy burden to bear a god with you."

"It is indeed."

Up and up they climbed as the sun sank behind the mountains. The sky filled with vast gathering islands of billowing cloud, slate gray and threatening for the most part but tinted underneath with a pearly sheen and limned with silver.

The thick of the forest was behind them now, and they were zigzagging through heights where the trees grew ever more scant and where rock jutted more and more often through the thin earth.

The upper peaks were almost black against the clouded sky, although shafts of golden evening light would sometimes streak across a soaring precipice or stain some lowering palisade with a sudden brilliance that hurt the eyes.

No one spoke. The only sounds were the rattle and clack of stones under hooves, the puffing and snorting of the climbing horses, and the creak of leather harnesses. There was no birdsong. The air was oppressive and still. Fain led them upward, perching on rocks, sending them this way and that across the rumpled skirts of the mountain, until Branwen was sick of the sight of bare rock and so weary of this endless journey that she could almost have fallen asleep in the saddle.

The last time they had come to Merion's cave it had been from the north. Now they struggled up to it from the east—and Branwen could see nothing ahead that stirred any memory.

Dusk came creeping up out of the forests like a murky fog, swallowing the path behind them, drinking light and breathing out shadows. The east was a formless black ocean, the way ahead scarred and gouged and pocked with wounds that bled darkness.

Fain swept suddenly in front of Branwen's face, startling her. His cries were strangely loud in the gathering gloom.

"He has seen the cave," Blodwedd breathed. She and Rhodri were on the horse directly behind Branwen—the others trailing away in single file. "It is not far, but the path to it is steep and perilous."

Branwen let out a relieved breath. At last! Frightful

as the thought of confronting Merion a second time was, at least it would bring this ill-fated quest to an end. She reined the destrier to a halt.

"The rest of you will wait here," she said as the other horses came to a halt behind her. "I don't know what will happen when Caradoc is released, but I'd rather you were not close by."

"You can't go up there alone," said Iwan. "Let some few of us accompany you at least."

"I would be by your side," said Blodwedd. "Always by your side."

"I know you would," said Branwen. "And if you were not already weakened by the things you have done for me, I would gladly have you with me, because you at least are known to the Shining Ones. But as for the rest of you—Iwan and Dera—I see from your faces you would also go with me. What would you do in Merion's dark cave?" She looked from face to anxious face. "If Merion cannot save me from death when Caradoc is released, what hope do any of you have?" She rested her hand on the cold lid of the casket. "I do not believe that I go to my death, my friends, but my fate lies in hands other than my own. If I do not return, I want you to go to Pengwern and take up arms with the king. Fight on in memory of Branwen of the Shining Ones. . . ."

"We needn't make any such promise," said Rhodri. "You will come back to us; I know it in my heart."

Branwen smiled. "Then all is well!" she said. "So.

No more words of parting. Dismount and take what comfort you can. I shall ride a little farther, until the path becomes too sheer. Then it will be hands and feet to the cave." She looked to where her faithful falcon was perched on a spit of rock close by. "Fain, stay with them, please. Your work is done for now."

The bird bobbed his head as though in response.

"Asta, get down now and remain with the others."

"Would it not be better for me to ride with you until you have to quit the horse?" Asta asked. "I will hold him steady for your return. Who knows? You may wish for a speedy descent of the mountain once the god of the North Wind is let loose!"

Branwen looked into the gentle blue eyes of the Viking maiden.

"Very well," she said. "We'll ride together a little farther." She tapped her heels against the destrier's flanks, and it began to clop up the long slope.

"I shan't say good-bye," Branwen called back to the others. "We'll meet again soon."

She glanced back again after a little while. She could see the pale blots of faces turned toward her in the devouring gloom. Then the way ahead turned around a buttress of rock and she lost sight of them.

The horse snorted and nodded its head as it clambered laboriously up the rugged defile. Pebbles clattered away under its hooves.

"It's better like this," Branwen murmured to herself. "Better by far."

"Indeed it is," came Asta's soft voice, surprising Branwen a little. She had been feeling strangely alone, and she had almost forgotten that Asta was with her.

The horse stumbled. The way ahead was blocked with boulders and shale.

Branwen brought the animal to a halt. She untied the casket and slid down from the saddle, bringing the casket with her.

She looked up at Asta. The Viking maiden was the one bright thing on the mountain—a shaft of gold in the bleak evening.

"Wait here," Branwen said.

Asta nodded.

Holding the cold casket under her arm, Branwen began the difficult and dreadful climb to Merion's cave. She could feel her shield bouncing on her back as she scaled the final heights, hear her sword clinking on the stones as she pulled herself over broken rock and scrambled through the scree. It was tiring work, and the need to keep a firm grip on the casket made things no easier.

There were no more vibrations from the casket; but as she gripped it under her arm, Branwen was aware of the coldness seeping into her body. And as she ascended, she could hear a soft susurration, as though of a faint voice whispering in her ears.

. . . The key . . . take the key. . . .

She paused for a moment, listening hard. She shook her head. Imagination! She could not afford to let her own inner demons trick her; she must concentrate on the climb. A foot misplaced and . . .

. . . then she saw it. Above her. Black as Annwn. The mouth of Merion's cave.

She bit down on her lip, tasting blood.

The voice whispered to her again.

. . . *The key . . . do not fear me. . . . Take the key and open the lock. . . . No harm will come to you. . . . Set me free. . . .*

"You are wasting your words on me," she murmured. "Merion had warned me well of what you are capable! I am not the fool you take me for!"

"Are you *not*?"

Branwen spun round at the sound of that familiar voice at her back. Her foot slipped, and she came down heavily on one knee. She stifled a cry of pain, her face twisting in a grimace of discomfort and alarm.

Asta stood on a jutting slab of stone, her golden hair flaring like candle flame, her eyes filled with glittering sapphire light. In her two hands she bore Skur's battle-ax. On her sweet face was a smile as chilling as whetted iron under a winter moon.

"Asta . . . ?"

"I fear I have misled you, shaman girl of the *waelisc*," she said, and there was ridicule in her gentle voice. "My name is not Asta."

Branwen stared at her in confusion. "Then who are you?"

The cruel smile widened. "Can you not guess, child of petty southern gods?" Asta said, her voice ringing among the rocks. "Do you still not know me? Are you so much the fool that you cannot yet guess my name?"

The great double-headed battle-ax swung threateningly through the air. The sapphire eyes flashed. And suddenly Branwen knew. A moment before the Viking girl spoke her name, Branwen *knew* what Asta would say.

"I am Skur Bloodax!" the Viking maiden howled. "And knowing that, look now upon the face of death and drink deep of uttermost despair!"

31

THE CUCKOO IN the nest! The goraig's song of the beautiful bird filled with lies!

She never stops singing, till the mountain is near.

Not Alwyn—never *Alwyn*—but Asta all along!

Fool! Blind fool!

The great battle-ax whirled, and the deadly blade came scything down. Stunned as Branwen was, her thoughts moved quickly enough for her to twist aside and avoid the deadly blow.

The thundering ax split the rock on which she had been kneeling, sending splinters of stone flying about her ears, spitting and hissing. She scrambled to her feet, the casket falling from her hands. It tumbled away from her and came to rest among the rocks some way below the transformed Viking maiden.

Branwen fixed her eyes on her enemy, pulling

her shield off her back and drawing her sword. She leaped up onto higher ground, preparing herself for Skur's next attack.

The Viking maiden snarled as she wrenched the ax head out of the cleft stone. Although slender and slight, she wielded the ax with disturbing ease, swinging it around her head and lunging forward now to strike the rocks at Branwen's feet. Stone fragments filled the air as Branwen danced backward, glancing behind to ensure a safe footing on the rubbled mountainside.

She must be stronger than she looks! Rhodri had been all too prescient in that.

"Do not make this hard on yourself, Branwen," Skur cried out. "Accept the inevitable. You cannot survive Ragnar's ax; none can! It will cleave sword, shield, and bone as though they were cobwebs. Come—I will make your end as swift and painless as possible. I knew of you, and of your coming, before ever we saw each other. Ragnar told me of you and your destiny, and Mumir guided me to the place where we would meet. But I bear you no ill will, Branwen, witless servant as you are of small and trifling gods. Although it pained me that my good servant Arngrim had to die at your hand for Ragnar's desire to be fulfilled."

Branwen stared down at her. "What was the purpose of the deceit?" she shouted. "If your weapon is as great as you say, why hide your true self from us?

Why did you not slaughter us in the forest where we first met?"

"That would not have suited Ragnar's purpose," said Skur. "Do you not see, Branwen? Sweet as it will be to me, your death is not the reason why I had you bring me to this place."

Branwen moved slowly to one side, her shield up to her eyes, her sword arm bent back, muscles tense and straining, ready to strike the moment the opportunity presented itself.

If I throw myself down upon her, will I be able to sink my blade into her body before she strikes back? I do not know. It is risky. If I commit myself to such a course and fail, I will not be given a second chance.

"Then what is the reason?" Branwen called down. "Why would such a mighty warrior stoop to falsehoods and pretense?"

Skur's eyes burned like blue fire. "For a greater prize than the death of the shaman-child of the *waelisc*!" she spat, and Branwen could see that her taunts had angered her. "You are *nothing* to the great god Ragnar—you and your paltry godlings! You are morsels to be gobbled up!"

Branwen laughed. "Oh, but we'll stick in your craw, Skur Bloodax," she mocked. "Be sure we will! And if Ragnar has such contempt for the Shining Ones, why does he not present himself on this mountain? Why does he send the likes of you to mouth his idle threats?"

Now it was Skur's turn to laugh, and the sound of it was like claws scraping the inside of Branwen's skull. "You fool!" she crowed, leaning for a moment on her ax, as though so certain of her advantage over Branwen that she had no need to defend herself. "The ratcatcher must first be shown where the vermin lurk!" she said. "That was my purpose in having you bring me here—to reveal to my lord Ragnar the hiding place of the sniveling wretch that you call Merion of the Stones! It is done, and now it is the time for all masks and pretenses to be thrown aside!"

At last Branwen understood—and she cursed herself for being so gullible! Skur's deceptions had all along been driven by the specific purpose of tricking Branwen into guiding her to Merion's cave. Now that she knew its location she could return to whatever dark place Ragnar inhabited and lead him into the very home of the Shining Ones.

I should have listened to Dera! I should have driven a sword through Asta's heart at the first!

A sudden passion of anger and revenge flared in Branwen's mind. Skur must not be allowed to complete her deadly mission! Reckless of her safety, she flung herself down at the deceitful woman, her sword aimed for the heart, a red fury in her eyes.

But Skur was lizard-quick in her reactions. In a single liquid movement the huge ax rose and swung as Branwen came hurtling down. But Branwen was not entirely unmindful of her own defense. She turned her shield into the coming blow, and the arc of sharpened iron came smashing into the shield's white face like a hammer striking an anvil.

The power of Skur's attack was so great that Branwen was sent spinning through the air, her shield arm numbed from the buffet, her shoulder wracked with pain.

It was impossible to land well among the shifting rocks; and she came down heavily, the breath knocked out of her as she tumbled down in a flurry of loose scree.

Skur was upon her in an instant, legs spread, the ax clasped in both hands, poised high above her head.

And for that moment her body was unprotected. Dizzy among the stones, Branwen thrust upward with her sword. But she was too late. The ax spun as it came down.

Branwen let out a cry of pain as her sword was jarred from her fingers. She saw sparks fly as the blade was cut in two by Skur's ax. The huge weapon rose and fell a second time, but Branwen was able to bring up her shield in time.

Skur gave a howl of anger and frustration as the blade skidded off the face of the shield.

"So! There is power in that ancient device!" she snarled. "I guessed it was so when first I saw it! But Ragnar's strength will prove mightier yet!"

"Do your worst!" cried Branwen. "Your blade shall never draw my blood!" She scrambled to her feet. She needed a few moments to recover—the ax blow had shaken her to the very bones.

And yet as she went scrambling up the mountainside, she saw that her shield showed no sign of the impact of the great battle-ax. Not so much as a dent or a scratch disfigured its white face. Her sword might be broken and lost, but with such a shield, perhaps she could hold off Skur's attack for long enough to make her way up to the cave mouth.

She remembered what the mountain crone had told her after she had filled the six crystals with magic: *I have breathed part of my own powers into them. I am diminished by this loss, and I will not be whole again till you return from your mission and need them no more.*

Branwen would enter the cave—she would return the crystals to Merion—then let Skur come! Let her see what devastation the Shining Ones could bring down on her!

She turned and swarmed up toward the cave mouth, her shield arm twisted behind herself in case Skur came leaping after her.

But it was not from behind that the attack came. It came from above! First came the dry flutter of wings, then a dark shape dashed into Branwen's face, claws extended, a heavy black beak pecking at her eyes.

Mumir!

She flung up her arm, and the raven's claws scored

bloody grooves in her skin. Staggering and off balance, she brought her shield round and punched it hard against the attacking raven, her teeth gritted from the agony in her torn arm.

Mumir was driven off. But only for a moment. The bird rose in the air above Branwen's head, squawking his rage, his wings beating in a flurry, his black eyes glinting evil.

Again he flew at her, making always for her face—for her eyes. Again she hurled him back with her shield, all too well aware that while she battled the black terror, Skur was coming for her.

A claw raked the skin above her left eye. The beak stabbed deep into her hand, making her cry out as she snatched it away. Blood clouded her vision and she swung wildly with the shield, stumbling this way and that over the unstable rocks.

She saw Skur through a flood of red—her features distorted by a malicious grin, the ax already swinging at Branwen's face. Branwen ducked, feeling the wind of the ax head as it sliced the air a fraction above her head.

She launched herself forward, using her shield as a battering ram, crashing with all her weight into Skur's side as she spun off balance from her missed blow. Skur tottered for a moment, her mouth stretched, her eyes wide. Then she fell backward, the battle-ax slipping from her fingers as she clawed the air to save herself.

Branwen dug in her feet, halting the momentum that would have sent her plunging down with her enemy. She sprang erect, striking upward with the shield rim, catching the harrying raven with the sharp edge and sending him crashing to the ground in a whirl of black feathers.

Feeding off instinct more than thought, Branwen snatched up a heavy stone and hurled it with all her might at the fallen bird. There was a single cry—cut off. There were scattered feathers. There was blood.

Branwen turned to where Skur lay, weaponless and defenseless, a little way down the mountain. Wiping the blood out of her eyes, she picked her way down, her shield up and ready in case Skur was not entirely defeated.

There was blood at the Viking warrior's lips, and more in her hair. She had struck her head in her fall, and Branwen could see how the bone above her ear was dented in and showing white through the ruptured skin and the matted hair and the thick gore that crawled down over the gray stones.

Skur opened her glittering blue eyes as Branwen stood over her. The warrior's breath was loud, her chest rising and falling rapidly.

Branwen was too exhausted and heartsore to feel triumphant. One question drummed in her head as she looked down at her sprawling foe. *Is she dying of her injuries, or must I kill her where she lies?*

Skur smiled. There was pain in it, but there was

something else—something that sent a shiver down Branwen's spine. There was exultation—there was dark joy, as though Skur believed that even now, broken and bleeding on the mountainside, she had done what she had come here to do.

"Too little, too late," Skur breathed. "It is accomplished! This night . . . I shall sit in victory . . . in Valhalla . . . at Ragnar's right hand!"

"*What* have you accomplished?" Branwen asked. "Mumir lies crushed, and you are close to death. What have you accomplished?"

Skur swallowed, her forehead contracting—clearly the pain was growing in her ruined body. "Ragnar's will!" she mouthed. She lifted her right arm, and for a moment Branwen thought she was trying to claw at her with her curled fingers. But then she let out a snarl and brought her arm crashing down, the wrist striking rock and the dull bronze torque that circled her arm breaking in two.

For a moment nothing more happened. Then Branwen became aware of a sound, like the distant shouting and screaming of many voices; and as the sound grew louder, a thick black smoke began to pour from the broken ends of the torque.

Branwen staggered back as the plume of dense oily smoke curled and billowed all around her. Up from the shattered torque it gushed, filling the sky, shedding curtains of darkness. And as the brume of blackness grew, so the noise became louder, and it was no longer only the sound of voices; it was the clash of entire armies: the dreadful ring and clatter of iron on iron, the thud of arrows into flesh, the frantic neighing of horses, the screams of the dying, the howls of the conquerors—it was all the dreadful clamor and mayhem of war.

The black cloud rose high above her head; and in the heart of the expanding darkness, Branwen saw two red eyes.

And the eyes saw her and burst into livid flame.

"Well done, Skur, my worthy servant!" shouted a voice that shook the heavens. "Ragnar's will is fulfilled! And now let this land know of my power! Let the Shining Ones tremble—for I have come to devour them!"

32

THE BRONZE TORQUE! No wonder the Viking maiden had beaten Bryn unconscious when he had tried to take it from her. It contained the essence of a god. A god that was now released to bring annihilation to the land of Brython.

Branwen fell to her knees as the column of black smoke rose higher and higher into the sky. As it soared up, its shape changed, its colossal thunderhead bulging outward, its tail narrowing like a whiplash. It began to spin, whirling faster and faster, sucking in darkness, looming up over the mountain. And yet all the time the fireball eyes kept their position, glaring down balefully at her.

She felt as small as an insect, and smaller still as the dreadful Viking god roared up into the night and blotted out the entire world.

I did this! I brought this terrible thing here! The Shining Ones were fools to trust me! I've doomed them all!

The tail of the monstrous cloud went skidding across the ground, screaming like a thousand banshees. Rocks, stones, shingles, and boulders spewed out in its wake as it tore a deep furrow in the mountain's flesh.

Branwen threw up her shield to protect herself as the debris came raining down all around her. She felt sure she would be killed by the devastating rain of ruins, but although huge boulders and sharp spears of stone bounced and crashed all around her, she was untouched. The mystic shield was sheltering her from Ragnar's wrath.

The mind-shredding noise abated, and Branwen peered over the rim of her shield to see that the tail of the whirling cloud was now making its way up the side of the mountain toward Merion's cave, ripping open the mountainside in a spume of pulverized rock. Like a blind finger it probed the mountain, stabbing and searching until it found the black cave mouth.

Then, with a sound like a screaming hurricane, the black cloud began to feed into the cave mouth. Ragnar's burning eyes turned from Branwen, filled now with unholy triumph. And as Branwen knelt there in helpless horror, the whole sable mass of the Viking god drove deep into the mountain and was gone.

Too late to give Merion back the stones that would complete her. Too late.

Branwen staggered to her feet, her arms hanging at her sides.

The mountain trembled under her, and above her the peaks rocked and quivered and crumbled.

But above the low, resonant grind of the tormented mountain, Branwen heard a sharp voice calling.

. . . The key . . . you still have the key. . . . Set me free, you fool! Set me free or he will destroy her!

Branwen spun around, her hand coming to her waist, her fingers gripping the small golden key.

Yes! There was still Caradoc!

But where was the casket? She had seen where it had fallen, but the entire mountainside had been overturned since then. Even Skur had been swallowed up in the chaos.

. . . Here! I am here, Warrior Child! Do you not see me . . . ?

"No! Where?" Branwen shouted, stumbling over the cracked rocks. "Where are you?"

. . . Here, child! Under your very hand!

She dropped to her knees and scrabbled wildly in the rubble, heedless of torn nails and bleeding fingers.

Where? *Where?*

The mountain was shaking now, shedding entire cliffs in its agonies, sending bastions and pinnacles thundering down in clouds of streaming smoke and ash.

Branwen's fingernails scratched against something that was not stone. She leaned into the hole she had delved, tossing rocks aside.

The casket was there—unharmed and whole, humming and vibrating as though Caradoc was straining to break free.

She dragged it out, the vibrations thrilling up her arms. She turned it right way up, one hand unlacing the key from her waistband.

"Will you kill me?" she gasped as she fought to insert the key into the quivering lock.

. . . I may. . . . Who is to say what I will do when I am unleashed . . . ?

She stabbed the key into the lock and turned it. "I don't care!" she howled. "Kill me if you must! But destroy Ragnar first, I beg you!"

She felt the lock come loose.

Farewell, Rhodri! Farewell, Iwan and Blodwedd! Farewell, my beloved mother! Farewell to all!

She wrenched open the lid. The casket was full of seething white mist.

She picked up the casket in both hands and offered it to the sky.

The white mist went surging upward, filled with laughter and madness and anger and power and joy and retribution.

"Free! Free at last!"

Branwen stared up in reverence and awe as the white cloud cavorted and gamboled in the air, sending out loops and trailers of itself, turning somersaults, dancing its acrobatic triumph across the skies.

But then the gleeful display halted; and although Caradoc had no form or face or structure, Branwen felt quite certain that his attention had become focused on the trembling mountain within which Ragnar was doing battle with Merion of the Stones.

The nebulous mass of white cloud imploded, condensing and writhing and shape-shifting, re-forming itself until the chaos found structure and the god of the North Wind hung in the air above Branwen in human form. She gazed up at him, overwhelmed and breathless. Caradoc had taken on the shape of a slim boy, beautiful and tempestuous, limber and strong, alluring but remote, wreathed in veils of shining mist. Golden eyes gazed down at her, and pearly teeth showed in a smile. The lithe arms reached up and the boy soared into the sky, trailing a comet's tail of cloud.

Higher and higher the boy-god rose, bursting through the lowering clouds, sending them scudding away. And then when Branwen thought his hectic climb would never end, he turned suddenly upon himself like a diver and came plummeting down, trailing white fire, booming with thunder, hemmed by lightning, making for the black mouth of Merion's cave.

Caradoc struck the mountain with a force that blasted Branwen off her feet again and sent her whirling like a leaf across the erupting face of the world.

I shall die! I shall surely die!

But even as she was sent careering down the mountain, she was aware that she still had her shield on her arm, and that a silvery cocoon of light had blossomed out from it—and that she was protected within its glittering shell.

Unhurt, she came crashing to the ground. She got dizzily to her feet, amazed to be alive. As the smoke and fume of Caradoc's impact filtered away, Branwen saw that where the cave mouth had been, a great hole had been blasted in the mountainside—a huge dark chasm in which white lightning darted and stabbed at a moiling black whirlwind.

There was a noise like no noise she had ever heard: a ferocious roaring and screaming and howling that did not come from human throats.

Then she heard a voice crying out; and she knew the voice, although it was a thousand times louder than she had heard it before.

It was Merion's voice, shaking the mountain.

"Begone, formless horror of the frozen north! You have no power here! The Shining Ones outmatch you! Brother Wind and Sister Stone banish you back to the pit where you were spawned!"

The mountain shuddered to its foundations, the noise dinning in Branwen's head so that she felt as if her skull might crack open. She was only just able to keep her balance as rocks and boulders came hurtling down toward her, striking off the mystical shield, buffeting her from side to side.

And then when Branwen felt she could endure the noise and the chaos no more, the black whirlwind seemed to diminish and to cringe under the forks and darts of the lightning. It burst out of the mountain, shedding black threads as it went, racing away over Branwen's head, drawing such a wind in its wake that it was all Branwen could do to stay on her feet as it fled over the forest and wilderness of Cyffin Tir and went wailing into the east until the dark evening swallowed it.

An uncanny silence came down over the land. A silence more profound than any Branwen had ever known. A silence that was like the yawning nothingness at the uttermost end of the world.

The gaping chasm was like a wound in the mountain, bleeding pulverized rock. But from the darkness two shapes emerged. A glorious boy made of silvery cloud and an ancient crone leaning on a gnarled stick.

Branwen heard a noise behind her. She knew that it must be her friends and followers approaching her, but she did not turn—her eyes were riveted on the two Shining Ones.

"It is done," said Blodwedd, her voice astounded. "And we are alive to see it!"

"Branwen?" Rhodri's voice. "What happened? Where is Asta?"

"Dead," Branwen said. "She was our enemy. She brought Ragnar, but he is defeated and fled."

"I see there is a great tale to tell here when time allows!" Dera declared.

"Wait for me," Branwen said. "I shall not be long." She began to make her way up the mountain to where the two gods were waiting.

Iwan called after her. "Branwen, don't go up there! Remember what you were told about Caradoc!"

She turned and looked down at them. All of her companions were gathered there, looking up at her, anxious and bewildered and amazed.

She smiled. "They will not harm me. I must speak with them. Prepare the horses; we will be leaving very soon."

It seemed a long climb up the mountain, but Branwen felt a renewed strength flowing through her veins as she clambered up toward the two gods. Strength and resolution and an unbreakable determination to hold to the course she had decided.

At last she was on a level with them: the blazing boy and the withered crone.

"You have done well, Warrior Child," croaked Merion, striking her stick on the ground. "You have taken another step along the great path of your destiny."

"I am set free by your faithfulness and devotion," said Caradoc, and his voice was as gentle and sweet as his smiling face. "But now we have a new task for you, Warrior Child."

"It must wait," Branwen interrupted. "There is something I must do first."

"It cannot wait, child!" growled Merion, her eyes darkening in her wrinkled face. "Your life belongs to the Shining Ones; our will is your only purpose."

Branwen looked into Merion's dreadful yellow eyes. "A friend is dead," she said. "And I must honor his dying wish."

Caradoc's voice became suddenly harsher. "Do not seek to thwart our will, Warrior Child. It will go ill with you."

Branwen looked at him, her heart steadfast. "Then you must act as you see fit," she said. "Neither by coercion nor threats will you deflect me from the duty I have set myself. I will go to the court of Pengwern, and I will offer my services to the king of Powys." Her voice became firmer. "And know this, Ancient Gods of Brython: if you seek to turn me from this course, I will only fight the harder to have my way." She looked from one to the other. "To stop me, you will need to kill me."

And so saying, she turned on her heel and made her way back down the mountain to where her companions were waiting.

Merion's harsh voice followed her. "Know this, Warrior Child," Merion called, grinding like an earthquake. "Try as you might, you cannot hide from your destiny!" The voice rose. "Go now, if headstrong fervor drives you, but you will return to us. You will not be able to help yourself! Remember the words of Rhiannon, Warrior Child: *You will run in a circle, Branwen ap Griffith, and I will be there!*"

Heedless of Merion's words, Branwen mounted the great bay destrier.

She is right. In time I will surely return to them, but not until my duty to Gavan is fulfilled. I will go to Pengwern. They will not stop me from having my will in this. I killed Skur and freed Caradoc from his prison. Weighed on the scales, they are deep in my debt. I shall walk the path of my destiny—but I shall do it in my own way; and any who try to stop me will know what it is to cross swords with Branwen ap Griffith, the Emerald Flame of Brython.

Branwen turned away from the mountain; and with her friends and companions about her, and with Fain flying above her head, she rode down through the forests and out into the wild lands of Cyffin Tir.